THE BERRYBENDER NARRATIVES,
BOOK 4

LARRY McMURTRY

FOLLY AND GLORY

A NOVEL

DOUBLEDAY LARGE PRINT HOME LIBRARY EDITION

SIMON & SCHUSTER

NEW YORK   LONDON   TORONTO   SYDNEY

This Large Print Edition, prepared especially for Doubleday Large Print Home Library, contains the complete, unabridged text of the original Publisher's Edition.

SIMON & SCHUSTER
Rockefeller Center
1230 Avenue of the Americas
New York, NY 10020

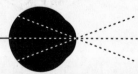

This Large Print Book carries the Seal of Approval of N.A.V.H.

The Berrybender Narratives *are dedicated to the secondhand booksellers of the Western world, who have done so much, over a fifty-year stretch, to help me to an education.*

BOOK 4

At the end of *By Sorrow's River*, Book 3 of *The Berrybender Narratives*, Pomp Charbonneau is killed by a vengeful Mexican captain. The Berrybenders are removed to Santa Fe and put under luxurious house arrest. Jim Snow, the Sin Killer, was guiding a wagon train east when the arrest occurred.

CONTENTS

Contents

Contents

CHARACTERS

BERRYBENDER PARTY

Tasmin
Jim Snow (The Sin Killer)
Bess (Buffum)
High Shoulders
Mary
Piet Van Wely
Kate
Monty, *child*
Talley, *child*
Lord Berrybender
Vicky Berrybender
Little Onion
Petal, *child*
Petey, *child*
Randy, *child*
Elf, *child*
Juppy, *half brother*
Father Geoffrin
George Catlin
Cook
Eliza
Amboise d'Avigdor
Signor Claricia
Mopsy, *puppy*

MEXICANS

Governor
Doña Margareta, *the Governor's wife*
Julietta Olivaries
Doña Eleanora, *Julietta's aunt*
Tomas, *footman*
Joaquin, *blacksmith*
Major Leon
Corporal Juan Dominguin
Rosa
Emilio

MOUNTAIN MEN AND TRADERS

Kit Carson
Josefina Carson, *Kit's wife*
Tom Fitzpatrick (The Broken Hand)
Old Bill Williams
Charles Bent
Willy Bent
Lonesome Dick

Characters xvii

INDIANS

The Ear Taker
Cibecue, *Apache*
Ojo, *Apache*
Erzmin, *Apache*
Flat Nose, *Comanche*
Na-a-me, *Kiowa*
Greasy Lake, *prophet*
Oriabe

SLAVERS

Malgres
Ramon
Draga
Blue Foot
Tay-ha
Bent Finger
Snaggle
Chino

TEXANS

Stephen F. Austin
Jim Bowie
Davy Crockett
William Travis
Sam Houston

Characters

MISCELLANEOUS

William Clark
Harriet Clark
Toussaint Charbonneau
Joe Compton
Elliott Edgechurch
Inspector Bailey

FOLLY AND GLORY

I can only regret being myself.
I suppose all regret comes to
that. . . .

I. COMPTON-BURNETT,
Darkness and Day

. . . Petal was prepared for ruthless attack . . .

Petey, the sensitive twin, aged one year and a half, began to sneeze and couldn't stop, giving Petal her chance: she at once seized a stuffed blue rooster the two had been fighting over and slipped behind her mother, waiting to see what her twin would do when he stopped sneezing and discovered the theft.

Petey did finally stop sneezing, discovered that his rooster was gone, and looked at his mother in stunned dismay. Petal's crimes never failed to shock him.

"The girl is smarter than the boy—quicker-fingered too," Mary Berrybender observed.

Tasmin looked around the nursery, a large, airy room in the spacious adobe house on the Plaza in Santa Fe—the house in which the Berrybenders were spending a lengthy but largely comfortable house arrest. Besides her Monty and Vicky's Talley, there were four new arrivals—her twins; Vicky's new boy, Randall; and Buffum's charming Elf (short for Elphinstone). There were five boys in all, Petal the only girl, and yet Petal casually had her way with the nursery, snatching toys left unattended and hiding them until they could be put to her own use. Some challenges she met with defiance, others with guile. Now that she had the much-coveted blue rooster, she meant to keep it. Tasmin could feel her daughter's soft breath on her neck—Petal was peeping through her mother's hair, waiting to see if Petey was going to make a fight of it. Petey seldom rose to much belligerence but if he should, Petal was prepared for ruthless attack.

"She's not merely smarter than her twin, she's smarter than all five of these little males put together," Tasmin remarked.

The toy rooster had been a gift from the Governor's wife, Doña Margareta, a bored young woman who spent as much time as possible with the Berrybenders. Margareta had been raised in a great ducal household in the City of Mexico—she found provincial society all but intolerable and was often at tea at the Berrybenders', the only company available that she considered worthy of her. It had sometimes occurred to Tasmin that the reason they were still detained in Santa Fe was because Doña Margareta didn't want to lose their entertaining company.

"Give your brother his rooster. It's his, not yours," Tasmin ordered. She did not turn to look at Petal.

Petal didn't answer—in the face of such an absurd claim, silence was surely called for.

"I fear you are raising up a very defiant brat," Mary said.

"Give your brother his rooster," Tasmin repeated, in slightly sterner tones.

"I lost it," Petal said. "It's a bird. It flew away."

"What bosh," Kate Berrybender said. "Stuffed roosters don't fly, as she well knows, the little thief."

At the sound of Kate's voice Petal instantly hid the rooster under her mother's skirts. Kate Berrybender could rarely be bluffed. She often gave Petal vigorous shakings, and was not averse to pulling her hair.

"The rooster left the room," Petal amended.

No one cared to credit this remark, so Petal tried again.

"Mopsy ate it up," she declared. Mopsy was a tiny short-haired mongrel the family had adopted. All the little boys adored Mopsy, but Petal dealt sternly with the dog, occasionally even hoisting Mopsy up by his tail, an effort that was likely to leave Petal red in the face.

Tasmin turned quickly and grabbed her daughter, who had reclaimed the rooster and was about to slip away with it.

"It's my rooster!" she claimed boldly, when her mother looked her in the eye.

"What I'd say is that you have the devil in you—I wonder who could have put it there?" Tasmin inquired.

"You!" Petal cried—from the amused look in her mother's eye she judged she was going to get to keep the rooster.

"You!" she repeated, more loudly.

No one in the room bothered to disagree. Vicky and Buffum, mothers of mere boys, both smiled. Queen bee of the nursery, Petal swept all before her. Little Onion was particularly susceptible to Petal's manipulations, though often aghast at her daring.

"Wasn't it you, Tasmin, who once said that only small children are sincere?" Vicky remembered.

"I did say that, but this child has taught me better," Tasmin admitted.

Petal, confident now that none of the older boys—or her twin brother either—were going to challenge her possession of the stuffed rooster, strolled casually toward the five small males.

"I got the rooster. I like him because he's blue," she said. "He'll always be my rooster."

Petal liked to rub it in.

Above all, she didn't want to think . . .

In the dark months following Pomp Charbonneau's death, Tasmin had wished she
could be a bear or some other burrowing
animal, capable of hibernation, of a cessa-
tion of thought. Above all, she didn't want to
think, because when she did think, it was
only of Pomp, and every memory brought
pain. When the wagon rolled into Santa Fe
with the five dead men in it, the Governor of
Nuevo México was the person most horrified. The last thing he would have wanted
was to harm any of the English party—he
had only meant to keep them under lucra-
tive house arrest for several months before
allowing them to go home. Captain Reyes's
job had been to escort them over the pass.
No one should have been chained, much
less executed. How was the Governor to

know that Captain Reyes was vengeance-crazed, insane? At once profuse apologies were offered. The best house on the Plaza was made over to them. Servants were provided, every consideration shown. The fugitives, High Shoulders and Tom Fitzpatrick, were allowed to return without penalty. It had all been a mistake, a dreadful, tragic mistake. A very high official was sent off to make apologies to the Bents—after all, had the Bents not been most considerate of the Governor and his suite when they came to Bent's Fort for the weddings?

Once settled into their handsome house, the Berrybenders were frequently invited to the Palace. Doña Margareta loved music—Vicky was often asked to play her cello, and she did play. Lord Berrybender was even provided with a guard when he went out shooting. The Indians were not to be trusted. The Governor wanted no more English dead.

All this had meant nothing to Tasmin, in her sad hibernation. She rarely left her room. From a large window she could see the cold sky, the mountains draped with snow. She stared for hours, as the children in her belly grew. The only visitors she welcomed were Kit and Geoff, the former because he had been there when Pomp was arrested; he had observed the mad Captain Reyes. With Kit she could go over the tragedy, try to understand it. She wanted Kit to talk her out of the notion that somehow Pomp Charbonneau had wanted to die. He had not fled; he had not fought; the firing squad had fired and missed him and still he had not moved. Tasmin feared it had something to do with her. Why had Pomp just stood there passively, as the mad captain advanced with his musket leveled? Why had she herself not attacked the captain? She could not stop her mind from reenacting the scene. Pomp had shown no fright—when she rushed out and spoke to him for the last time he seemed at ease, content. But why? It was a mystery that she feared would always haunt her. Talking to Kit, a true friend of Pomp's and her true friend, helped a little.

Kit had been as shocked as anyone when he heard that the silly little captain with the plume in his hat had shot and killed Pomp Charbonneau. Of course, the captain had been mad. He shot his own officer—then he shot himself. It was madness, and madness could seldom be predicted. Pomp had no reason to expect execution. The arrest was a formality that had long been expected; Pomp's mistake had been a failure to recognize how crazed the little captain really was.

"I'm sure Pomp thought it was a bluff, otherwise he would have fought," Kit assured Tasmin. "Reyes was just a captain. He had no business ordering up firing squads."

"I should have seized a gun," Tasmin said. "I should have but I didn't, and now it's too late."

Kit was almost as shocked by Tasmin's appearance as he had been by the news of Pomp's death. Tasmin's cheeks were sunken, her eyes dull, her hair a tangle. She only wanted to talk of Pomp. When Kit told her that her husband was expected back at Bent's Fort soon she showed little interest. Kit, happily married now to his Josie and living in a little house in Taos, soon exhausted his opinions. He had followed the wagon with the prisoners in it—Pomp, High Shoulders, Tom Fitzpatrick—expecting them to escape as soon as it was dark. The Mexican soldiers were just boys, too cold and scared

to stop anyone who really wanted to escape. In the chill reaches of the night, with
the snow blowing, they would have been
unlikely to stop experienced men bent on
flight. Kit, using the blizzard as a shield, had
stayed close by, leading three horses; at
midnight, just as he had expected, High
Shoulders appeared, and then Tom Fitzpatrick. When Kit asked old Tom where
Pomp was, he merely shrugged. "Wouldn't
come. Too fond of Jimmy's wife, I expect,"
Tom said. Kit thought it was a poor reason:
when you were caught, the first order of
business was to get away—then there
would be plenty of time to be fond of
Tasmin.

Facing Tasmin in the big cool room in
Santa Fe, seeing her hollow cheeks and list-
less movements, he waited while she cried
a little—but mostly Tasmin seemed beyond
tears; blank, empty. The woman whose
spirit had meant so much to Kit for so long
had lost her spirit, and all because Pomp
Charbonneau had been too big a fool to run
away from a troop of Mexican soldiers
whose captain was crazy as a bat.

"Pomp, he was always different," Kit remarked—and yet, when Tasmin pressed

him to expand on his statement, he was at a loss. Pomp could do all the things the other mountain men did—and he could do some things the mountain men couldn't do, such as read a book or speak in foreign languages—and yet he wasn't like the other men. He was friendly to a fault, and could read the country as well as Kit could, but in times of danger, when it was necessary to be quick, he often lingered, as if to inspect the danger and understand it. At the fort, the day of the arrest, he could have hidden himself in the woolshed, as Kit had. It might have worked, only Pomp didn't try. He probably thought he could slide by the crazy captain and explain things to the Governor; he waited and watched when he should have hidden or run.

Tasmin was very large with child. Kit thought that might be one reason she looked so bad. But large or not, on a cold, snowy day, she made him walk with her to the graveyard near the church, where Pomp was buried. Kit felt awkward. Why visit the dead? Yet Tasmin insisted on standing there, cold and sad, for almost an hour.

Tasmin knew that Kit didn't share her grief—no one did, nor could she expect them to. Eliza, the kitchen girl, to whom Pomp had often been kind, came closest to feeling what Tasmin felt; and yet Eliza had merely responded to Pomp's kindness— she hadn't been in love with him. Mary Berrybender had an inkling as to how deeply attached Tasmin was to Pomp; she made no effort to reason with her. "There is no reasoning with grief," Piet told Mary. "It wears away slowly, like the face on a coin."

"Mine would never wear away, if you died," Mary said. They went out often to chip at fossils in the pale, snowy hills; they were happy.

Jim Snow came, as he had promised, a few days before Tasmin was delivered of the twins. Buffum had had her Elf the week before; Vicky's Randy arrived two weeks later. Tasmin wept when Jim appeared; the eager way Monty ran to his father touched her. And yet when Jim tried to kiss her she turned her mouth away.

"There'll be a wait, Jimmy," she told him flatly.

Jim, like Kit, was shocked by Tasmin's appearance; but Monty was healthy, at least—he babbled about Mopsy, the little mongrel dog.

"We won't eat Mopsy, not ever!" Monty insisted. He had not forgotten that Hugh Glass had eaten the bear cub Abby. He wanted to make sure nobody would ever eat Mopsy.

"I expect we can find better things to eat than a skinny pup," Jim said, wary of absolute promises. Lord Berrybender was talking of going on to Texas—there were said to be fine plantation lands near the Gulf. But even Lord B. recognized the impracticality of setting off with so many infants and decided to wait in Santa Fe for some new guns he had ordered while in Bent's Fort. The order had to go to England—he only trusted English guns—and come back, a wait of perhaps a year and a half, by which time the infants ought to be safely mobile.

Tasmin didn't take her husband to Pomp's grave—she had no wish to share it with him.

A week after the twins were born Jim asked Tasmin what she wanted him to do. Commerce on the prairies was rapidly increasing; the Bent brothers were fearful of losing ground to rivals. Jim Snow and Willy Bent had made a perfect haul to the east—

now Charles Bent was pressing Jim to go again. There was no employment for him in Santa Fe, and there were three children to think of now.

"Go," Tasmin said. "Perhaps when you come back I'll like you again."

At the moment she felt empty—what did she have to say to this man, her husband? They now had a brood of children, and yet she felt little connection to Jim. Better that he go.

Jim hesitated. He didn't understand his wife, but he knew that the Mexican authorities had behaved capriciously once, as a result of which Pomp was dead. What if war broke out between Mexico and America? What would happen to his family? And yet Tasmin, indifferent to his presence at first, began to be hostile. She clearly didn't want him around.

Cook, seeing that Mr. Snow was confused, took it upon herself to explain matters to him. Cook liked Mr. Snow. In her opinion it was only his abilities that had brought them safely thus far. She had studied maps. It was clear that Northamptonshire was still very far away. There might be more savages to contend with, more parching distances to cross—in her opinion doom would overtake them if they lost Mr. Snow.

"It's only that Lady Tasmin was such a good friend of Mr. Pomp's," Cook explained, as Jim listened, grateful for any clue that might help explain Tasmin's hostility.

Much as Cook liked Jim Snow, she had no intention of telling him all she knew about Lady Tasmin and Pomp Charbonneau. She was far from the opinion that delivering the whole truth was a good thing. Much harm could come with truth, in her opinion.

"When my husband died, God bless his soul, I hated any woman who still had a husband. If I couldn't have my old John, who gave me eleven bairns, then I didn't see why other women should get to have their men. That's not Christian, I know, but that's how womenfolk are. And maybe not just womenfolk."

Jim looked surprised. Was Cook telling him that Tasmin disliked him at present just because he was alive and Pomp dead? Weren't people always dying? He missed Pomp himself—they had enjoyed many fine scouts together—but it didn't make him hate Kit Carson or the Broken Hand.

Jim felt reluctant to leave the kitchen, with its good smells. Cook said no more—in her view explanation was mostly wasted on men. Though her opinion of the scrawny Mexican chickens was low, she had managed to catch a fairly plump hen, just browning over the roasting pan. She had meant it as a small treat for her suitor, Mr. Fitzpatrick, who had left off suggesting indecencies and was on the whole behaving well. But seeing Jim Snow's despondency, she changed her mind, slid the hen on a plate, and sat it in front of him. "You'll be needing your strength, if you have to climb back over that pass," Cook told him.

They had crossed the pass with five dead men in the wagon. Tasmin, inconsolable, had sat by Pomp's body all the way. Cook remembered the sound of ice crackling under the wagon wheels as they rose higher into mist and cloud. The pass was so high it seemed they were rising to heaven, although, under the circumstances, with five men dead and all of them half frozen, it was more like entering a cold hell.

"I want some!" Monty cried, seeing the

chicken. Talley crowded around too. Jim gave each boy a drumstick. Traveling as he did, eating whatever he shot, singeing it, sprinkling on a little salt if he had any, with only now and then the treat of a buffalo liver, he could not but wonder at Cook's skill. She made the best meals he had ever eaten. The plump hen was delicious. He thought he might just have a slice or two, but before he knew it, the hen was eaten and he and the two little boys were licking the greasy bones.

3

Snowflakes swirled around him . . .

All the way to Taos, Jim kept remembering how desperately Monty cried when he real- ized his father was leaving. Little Onion couldn't shush him—he kept stretching out his plump arms to Jim, who had not ex- pected such a display. He did his best to assure the little boy that he would be back, but Monty's sobs increased until finally Tas- min stepped out of her room.

"Go," she said. "You're just making it worse. Ever since I've known you, you've been an expert at leaving. One looks around to find you gone. Perhaps it's the right way. Babies don't cry for the vanished, just for those about to vanish."

"I had no idea he'd carry on this way," Jim said.

"Nor did he, but I assure you he'll live," she said. "Just *go! Vamos!* Scat!"

Jim went, but he couldn't free his mind of the image of Monty's distress. He had never supposed himself missed. Men had tasks that took them away, sometimes far away. From the heights of Taos the plains beyond looked as if they stretched on forever, yet Jim had just crossed them twice and was about to cross them again. Jim didn't like the bustle and noise of Saint Louis—he was always glad to get back to the quiet spaces; and yet, when he considered the future, he wondered if Saint Louis might be the right place to lodge his family. Tasmin would have some society. Captain Clark admired her and would see to that. There'd be someone to see to the children's lessons. The tiny twins were just mites yet, but Monty had been just a mite not long ago, and now he was a boy possessed of a good appetite.

Coming down toward the Kaw on his recent trip, he had seen a curve and a thicket of reeds that looked familiar, but he couldn't think why until they were well past it and dusk had fallen. It was on that curve that he had first seen Tasmin, stripped off, preparing to bathe in the cool dawn. He had been stepping into the river for the same purpose; he too was naked. He could remember his startlement vividly. He had taken in nothing of Tasmin's beauty, so profound was his own embarrassment. All he had wanted to do was hide. A little later he had killed a deer and fed her its liver.

That had not been very long ago, and yet, in that modest interval, the two of them had married, gone up the Missouri, crossed to the Yellowstone, and then gone all the way back south to Santa Fe. They had three children—it was Little Onion's opinion that it had been the big meteor shower on the plains that had caused the twins. Whatever caused them, they were born, healthy, and in Cook's opinion, likely to live. For the moment they were well provided for, but that might change. Jim had nothing to sell except his skill as a plainsman—he supposed there would always be a need for reliable guides, more and more need as the Americans filtered into the West; but guiding kept him far from his family, and his son's outburst had shown him that absences didn't suit everybody. They had once irked Tasmin as much as they now irked Monty. What the twins might want, as they got older, he couldn't guess. As he approached the little house Kit Carson and Josie had taken he didn't feel at ease in his spirit, as he usually did when he traveled alone.

The small house Kit and Josie lived in was little more than a hut—fortunately, both were short people. Jim thought he might stop in for a night as he headed east. Snowflakes swirled around him as he rode up. It was chilly weather. Kit was behind the house, chopping firewood, a fact that rather surprised Jim. Two walls of the house were already banked high with chopped firewood, and yet Kit was going at it as if he and Josie were down to their last stick. How much wood could they burn anyway, in one small fireplace?

Cold as it was, Kit was soaked with sweat from his vigorous work with the axe.

"If you don't slow up on the firewood there won't be a tree left standing," Jim said. "You got enough chopped to heat a fort, and you don't live in a fort."

Kit stuck his axe in a log and left it. He stared at the towering stacks of firewood as if noticing them for the first time.

"I hate running out of firewood," he said.

Then he sighed.

"There's nothing wrong with having plenty of firewood, is there?" he asked. To Jim he seemed distracted, even rather gloomy.

"I don't know what else to do when Josie's mad at me," Kit admitted. "It's too cold to just sit around. So I chop firewood."

This was the first hint Jim had had that the newly married Carsons were experiencing marital unease—though, once he thought about it, it was not surprising that Josie got mad at Kit. Jim himself was frequently mad at Kit—at least he was if he had to be in his company for a day or so. Josefina had been mightily taken with Kit before the marriage, but now that she actually had to live with him it was no wonder that she found him irritating.

Jim was about to ask what Josie was mad about when the girl herself popped out the door. She looked as friendly and cheerful as could be.

"Come in, Jimmy—we got posole," she said.

Then she looked at her husband.

"What about you, woodchopper?" she

asked. "Don't you ever get tired of chopping wood?"

Kit was perplexed. Twenty minutes earlier Josie had been seething like a kettle, so angry with him that she spluttered when she tried to talk. But now she was his old, cheerful Josie again, a twinkle in her eye as she stood beneath the high piles of stacked firewood towering above her head.

"If this wood falls on the house it will be the end of us," she said.

In fact she *had* been furious with Kit, earlier—she had given him a long list of supplies to bring back from the trading post, but he had let the list blow away and had forgotten half the things on it, including the most important item of all, a swatch of soft flannel which she had ordered specially from Saint Louis and had been waiting for for a year. She wanted to make the flannel into a warm nightgown to wear on cold nights, when the north wind howled through Taos. Kit had promised her faithfully that he would bring the flannel, but then he had carelessly lost her list and had returned with some scratchy wool cloth instead. When she blew up at him he just looked puzzled. For a man as finicky as Kit was about his

moccasins and his buckskins, it was absurd
to think that he couldn't tell the difference
between wool and flannel. Every time she
entrusted him with an order from the trading
post he forgot half her requests and mud-
dled the rest. Kit was famous among the
mountain men for his exceptional eyesight,
and yet, in a store, he couldn't tell the difference between two cloths.

Of course it was vexing to have a husband who constantly forgot what he was
sent to fetch; Josie had given him a fiery
dressing-down, but then she cooled off. It
was over. She would get someone with an
errand that required going to the trading
post to bring her her flannel. Now it was
time to forget it—time for supper and bed.

Kit was so relieved when he realized his
wife was no longer angry with him that he
became giddy for a moment. Josie's tem-
pers, when they flared, were so violent that
Kit always concluded that he had ruined his
marriage beyond repair. Her angers seemed
to signal the end of everything. Then, when
they abated and domestic life went on, Kit
felt so happy that he usually hit the bottle, if
there was a bottle to hit, as there happened
to be on this occasion, even though he

knew the abstemious Jim Snow didn't much approve of drinking. He poured himself a cup of whiskey, Josie watching him merrily all the while. Josie had a tendency to become amorous after one of her fits—she would certainly be amorous if she sat there and got drunk.

"He forgot all the things I told him to bring—that's why I chased him out," Josie said. She saw no need to be reticent with Jim Snow, who had traveled with Kit and must often have suffered from his forgetfulness.

"I hope all that firewood don't fall on the house," she said, a second time.

"It won't fall on the house—don't you think I even know how to stack firewood?" Kit asked, flaring a little himself. Jim and Josie looked at him as if he were a rank incompetent.

Jim polished off two large bowls of posole and sat staring into the fire. The fact that Kit had made peace with Josie reminded him uneasily that he hadn't made peace with Tasmin, and would have no opportunity to do so for many months—not unless he refused to lead the wagon train that the Bents were even then loading. He *could* refuse; but he didn't think Tasmin would welcome him back to Santa Fe, just then. Tasmin, like Josie, sometimes seethed and settled down; but Jim felt her present mood was different. Probably Cook's explanation was the right one. Tasmin was grieving for Pomp—no doubt it would wear off someday, but not necessarily soon. He might as well go on to Saint Louis while she was struggling with it—or so it seemed.

"I'll have some whiskey, if you care to share it," Jim said, startling Kit so greatly that he almost dropped the jug.

"Have it all, I'm drunk enough—Josie will get me down and beat me if I get any drunker," Kit declared.

Josie smiled. She meant to get her forgetful husband down all right, but beating him wasn't what she had in mind.

The whiskey jug Kit handed Jim was more than half full—yet in the space of an hour, to Kit's shock and Josie's surprise, Jim Snow drank it all. He became a little flushed, but otherwise merely sat, staring into the fire. Kit started to remind Jim that whiskey cost money, but thought better of it. It didn't cost enough to risk making Jim Snow mad.

For Jim to drink like that suggested to Kit that there was trouble somewhere—probably at home. Tasmin had never been an easy wife. Kit, curious, decided that the best policy was to ask no questions.

When the whiskey jug was empty Jim thanked both the Carsons for their hospitality and stood up to leave. Kit was startled: it was after midnight, cold and blowy, whereas their house was snug, warmed by some of the sweet-burning firewood he had stacked up. "You're welcome to sleep here," he said. "It's freezing out and you're drunk. Surely you ain't fool enough to ride off this hill tonight."

"I'm not drunk, but I reckon I could ride down a hill even if I was drunk," Jim said. "You're wife's a sight drunker than me."

With a nod, he disappeared into the darkness and the wind.

Josie was glad Jim left. She liked having Kit to herself, in their little house. There'd be nobody but her husband to hear her, if she got loud.

"He drank half a jug of whiskey—that ain't like Jim," Kit said. "I bet he and Tasmin had a fight."

"Don't think about him, think about me,"

Josie demanded, wobbling a little from the whiskey she had imbibed. She began to pull Kit into the bedroom; they had a good corn shucks mattress on their low bed. Kit was still staring at the door, worried about his friend. Josie began to feel impatient.

"Come on, get your prick out—make it hard!" Josie instructed. "Get in bed and make it hard."

His wife's directness sometimes shocked Kit—she spoke coarsely when she was excited, and she was usually excited when they drank whiskey.

"I guess I've been married long enough to know what to do," Kit said, a little annoyed. A few hours earlier she had been screaming at him for forgetting her flannel—now she had her hand down in his pants, in a hurry for his prick to stiffen up.

With Josie rushing him, Kit did as instructed, but for a moment, he couldn't get Jim Snow out of his mind. Jim had looked lonely—Kit could not remember seeing that look on his friend's face before. If he was lonely, why hadn't he at least stayed the night? Why go riding off in the dark when there was plenty of firewood—he wouldn't have had to be cold.

4

*In the sad months before the twins
were born . . .*

In the sad months before the twins were
born, and afterward too, for many dark
weeks, Father Geoffrin had been the only
companion Tasmin would consistently
admit. Kit Carson had come once, but
Tasmin's condition had troubled him so
that he hadn't come again—it was Kit's
view that Tasmin no longer wanted to live;
and if she didn't want to, very likely she
wouldn't. Here was a trouble Kit couldn't
bear to face.

Father Geoffrin faced it. He came into
Tasmin's room day after day, and sat with
her, as silent as she was. Tasmin stared at
the hills, Father Geoffrin merely sat. Sometimes Tasmin allowed him to hold her
hand—other times she pushed his hand
away. Once he tried to read her a bit of

Racine, thinking the beautiful French lines
might reach her, but Tasmin shook her head
and he put the book away. Tasmin's room
was at the top of the house. The sounds of
the Plaza—donkeys braying, people quarreling, the blacksmith pounding—hardly
reached her. Monty was talking now, but
Tasmin only occasionally responded to his
babble. She scarcely ate. Vicky Berrybender told her husband that she feared Tasmin
would die.

"No, no—she mustn't—can't spare
Tassie," Lord Berrybender said. "Need her
to help me run my plantation, once we get
to Texas. Excellent soil for cotton in Texas,
I'm told. Cotton's sure to be the coming
crop."

Fear lay over the household—fear of losing Tasmin, their most able crisis manager.
Even Lord Berrybender fell into a funk,
hunted less and less, rarely put his hand on
his wife. Gloom seeped like fog through the
company. Even though Tasmin was far
above them, everyone spoke in whispers or
subdued tones. The fact that Jim had come
and gone, effecting no change, was not en-
couraging. They all trusted in Jim's ability.
But Tasmin's heavy sadness, her evident

resignation, defeated them. Jim left, promising to come back.

Only Father Geoffrin took the optimistic view.

"She's not dying," he insisted. "She's just sad."

"But she only eats chicken soup," Cook insisted. "Just chicken soup."

"That's quite enough," Father Geoff assured her. "Keep making soup. This will pass."

When he said the same words to Tasmin she looked at him scornfully.

"How would you know what will pass and what won't?" she asked. "Watch what you're saying, or I'll put you out."

"Don't put me out," Geoff said, smiling. "The priests here are filthy and mean. The natives hate them. They'd like nothing better than to burn a few at the stake."

"No doubt you deserve it, you heretic," Tasmin said, beginning to cry, a change Geoff thought for the good. It was her blank days that worried him most. Hours passed, even days, without Tasmin saying a word. Little Onion was profoundly disturbed. Many times she crept to the door of Tasmin's room and peeped through the keyhole, only to see her mistress still in bed, staring, silent.

When Tasmin did cry it was no short tear burst. She went from being dry to being in flood. Father Geoffrin waited. He put his arm around her; she shrugged it off; he tried again; she let it stay. Finally she leaned her head against his shoulder.

"I can tolerate you because you're like me—you have no one," she said.

"That's the stupidest thing I ever heard you say," Geoff told her. "You have a father, sisters, a child, a husband, and devoted servants and friends."

"I meant I had no lover—you know perfectly well what I meant," she chided. "Every time I leave this room I'm faced with the fact that my younger sisters have better judgment than I do, when it comes to men. Buffum is very happy with High Shoulders, and Mary, if anything, is even happier with Piet. I can hardly bear to see them, they're so happy. I know that's shameful, but it's how I am. Why did I have to fall in love with a man who let himself be killed?"

Father Geoffrin sighed. Her mind would not be denied its torment, and it seemed easily to beat the body down. Tasmin, once full-bodied, was now thin and half starved because of the punishment her mind gave out.

"You may recall that I saw you in your first flush of happiness, when you married Jimmy," he told her. "You were creatures of astonishing beauty. Jimmy seemed to be everything you wanted—yet you fell in love with Pomp, the one person you could never really have—but that's merely the way of the world.

"I'm capable of doing exactly the same thing," he admitted. "But folly doesn't last forever. You're a healthy woman—you're young. And you still have Jimmy."

"Don't mention him. I don't want him at all—even his beard irritated me," Tasmin protested.

"Did you confess anything—to Jimmy I mean?" he asked.

"I don't know why I didn't," she said, shaking her head. "It was on the tip of my tongue. Jim should have figured it out. He should have beaten me . . . if he had . . ."

She stopped, shrugged, shook her head, cried, now helplessly confused. Jim Snow had slapped her for trivial slips of language. If he'd known she had been an adulteress, what would he have done? Killed her? And yet the fact was she'd mainly been a *failed* adulteress—for all her shameless chasing she had only managed to catch Pomp twice. She was far less of a sinner than she had hoped to be. Could she explain that to Jim? Why *should* she explain it to Jim? After all, he had been the one who had entrusted her to Pomp. He was half to blame—but would he understand that, if she confessed?

"Pomp's dead, Jim's not—don't you dare confess," Father Geoff advised.

"I know I make an exceedingly difficult friend," Tasmin admitted. "I've been even ruder to you than I was to George Catlin, and I was damned rude to George. Why do you bother with me, Mr. Priest?"

"Curiosity," Father Geoff said, at once. Tasmin's eyes, for a moment, had shone with their old sparkle. It confirmed his optimism. Tasmin would recover—it would just take time.

"Curiosity about what?" she asked.

"About how you'll look in ten years," he said. "Despite all that's happened you're a young woman yet. I hope I'm alive to know you when you're about forty. That's when the real mischief begins."

Tasmin, at the time only a week from delivery, suddenly pulled up her gown and exposed her great belly.

"If I keep letting Jim pour babies into me I won't look like much at forty," Tasmin said. "I'll look like an old sow with many litters."

"It's rather extraordinary, how very large women do get," he said, looking at Tasmin's belly, a sight more gross than he had expected to be shown.

Later, when the priest was gone, Tasmin remembered that she had first thought Pomp, not Jim, had got her with child. Probably that had merely been a romantic conviction.

When her labor began Tasmin insisted on having Father Geoffrin in the room. Cook was shocked, but Tasmin prevailed: Father Geoffrin sat at her head, holding her hand. Cook learned it meant that Tasmin expected to die in labor. Petal came out first and was being lavishly admired when, to everyone's surprise, Petey followed. Jim was out walking around the Plaza. When he came in he was told he was the father of twins. From the moment that Petal uttered her first indignant cry it was evident that a new and formidable force had appeared among the Berrybenders.

5

And yet, in this unsettled place . . .

"It will be at least a year before Papa's new guns come—and his new wooden leg," Buffum pointed out, in troubled tones.

"Yes—or longer. Why?" Mary asked.

Buffum was loath to put her fear into words: the fear that High Shoulders, already restive, would leave and insist that she and Elf go with him.

"His dislike of the Mexicans is extreme," Buffum reminded them. "The fact that they chained him is an insult he cannot forget."

They were having the discussion in the nursery. The four newborn infants were all in cradle boards, all asleep except Petal, who surveyed the company with unblinking and not wholly friendly blue eyes. Monty and Talley were galloping around on stick horses that the kindly Signor Claricia had made them. The clatter was considerable. Tasmin wandered in for a moment. She pointed in a menacing fashion at the two stick-horse caballeros, whose fear of her was considerable. Both dismounted at once.

"He killed two Mexican soldiers as he was escaping," Tasmin reminded her sister. "You'd think he'd be satisfied with that."

"He isn't," Buffum declared. "I fear that he might snap. They are very rude to Indians, you must admit. It all makes me very uneasy.

"He doesn't really like this country, anyway," she went on. "Thinks it's too dusty." She stammered a little, from apprehension.

"I guess her handsome Ute wants to go home," Vicky said. "Men do want to go home, eventually. I live in hope of a day when Albany wants to."

"Well, he only wants to go to Texas—too bad for you, Vic," Tasmin said. "I fear you're destined to be the mistress of a cotton plantation. It's Papa's new ambition."

She judged Buffum's problem to be the more serious. High Shoulders was deeply devoted to Buffum and Elf—he would expect them to go where he went—and it *was* dangerous for him in Santa Fe. Nor would

Buffum consider being apart from him. She seemed in good health, but how long would she stand up to the rigors of aboriginal life? When circumstances permitted, Buffum still demanded a poached egg in the morning, and Cook, when provided with an adequate kitchen, still poached her eggs to perfection. But there would be no Cook in the Valley of the Chickens—and no eggs, either. Besides that, there was little Elphinstone. What if Buffum's milk gave out? What would little Elf eat?

"I will not be parted from my husband," Buffum vowed. "If he goes, I go."

"It will not be easy," Mary told her.

"No, but it's better than waiting for High Shoulders to be shot down by some Mexican, as Pomp was," Buffum said. "I believe I would be less fearful in the wilderness than I am here.

"I'm sorry, Tassie," she added. "I should not have mentioned Pomp. I know how you grieve."

Tasmin shrugged. "You merely said what's true," she replied. "It's not a crime to mention Pomp. In fact it's better that he's mentioned."

"I've a thought," Mary said. "Piet could

start a school. Perhaps High Shoulders could go to it, and Little Onion. For that matter, our own sister Kate is of an age to need tutoring."

"Surely you will remember that I know mathematics," Kate avowed. "I believe I shall soon master prime numbers with no help from Piet."

"So?" Mary retorted. "Have you Latin? Have you Greek? Have you chemistry? I think it's abundantly clear that you could profit from Piet's instruction."

Tasmin had no objection to Piet holding some sort of school. The Berrybenders were more or less settled; there was time to be filled. Little Onion had picked up a few English words, but was too shy to try them in public, though she eagerly tried them when alone with Tasmin. Whether the volatile High Shoulders would sit still for these studies Tasmin doubted. Lately he had been going on hunting trips with much success—perhaps if the hunting held up he would not take Buffum and their child and leave. Certainly his attentions had wrought a good change in Buffum. From being pale and spotty, wavery and quavery, she had blossomed into an appealing, robust young woman. She was no longer frail, no longer pompous. Her health improved, and her complexion. Tasmin had finally come to like her sister—to like Mary also, even though the latter still occasionally exhibited traces of the diabolical. With Tasmin sunk in gloom, it was Buffum who instructed the servants—what few were left—and ordered the nursery. Even in the last weeks of her pregnancy she had remained active and competent. Her confidence in her husband was total—High Shoulders, for his part, was gentle with Bess, rarely churlish. He had only a half dozen words of English, and Buffum scarcely more Ute, and yet the two seemed to communicate serenely. They obviously made more sense to one another than Tasmin had ever been able to make with Jim Snow. It was obvious that High Shoulders was unlikely to be wholly comfortable in Santa Fe. He stood out in the Plaza crowds because of his height; he towered over the small Indians of the pueblos and scarcely bothered to conceal his contempt for the Mexican soldiery. Buffum's fears were clearly justified. Still, since Tasmin had finally come to enjoy her younger sisters, she wanted to keep Buffum there, if possible.

In her unhappy state, Tasmin scarcely slept. She dozed—rarely did she sleep deeply. She thought that might improve once she was relieved of the discomforts of late pregnancy, but she was wrong. Once the twins were born it became even harder to slip into sleep. Confused dreams pursued her: dreams of Jim and Pomp, of buffalo, of the bear cubs, ships, England. Sometimes, in the clear mornings, she woke furious at her father for having taken them so far from what they knew—even from what they were, English gentle people, not wilderness trekkers. He had brought them into a situation for which they had no training. All the graces that, as young ladies, they had been encouraged to develop were useless to them in the American West, where there was little opportunity for them to display their comeliness and fine deportment to eligible gentlemen who might want them as wives.

That night Tasmin watched the moon move from one side of her window to the other, as it cast its pale light on the hills. What Buffum contemplated, leaving with her husband, seemed the wildest folly, and yet she didn't have to cast back in memory very far to recall that she had been prepared to do exactly the same thing when she had fallen in love with Jim Snow. She had been fully determined to fling off Englishness and follow Jim into the wilderness—and *had* done it even, for several weeks. She had tried to learn to shoot a bow and arrow; she had even, accidentally, skewered a skunk. She had made love in nakedness while, nearby, hundreds of buffalo bulls were roaring in *their* rut. She would have chanced anything with Jim; but if the recent trek had taught them much, it was that such daring was only romantic folly. The plains, the hills, the West were far stronger than any strength they had to set against it. It had already crushed two of her brothers: Bobbety and the mysterious Seven. It had killed most of their servants: Fraulein Pfretz-skaner, Gladwyn, Señor Yanez, Milly, Tim, Master Jeremy Thaw, and good George Aitken, the steamship captain. And of course it had taken Pomp, a man adept in its ways.

But Tasmin had been willing to chance it, as Buffum was now, mainly on the basis of attraction to a certain man. Attraction could shift and slip; she knew that now. And yet, in this unsettled place, where there were no manners, no society, no pattern, what, except feelings, was there to trust? She who would once have followed Jim Snow anywhere was now not even sure she liked him. Would the attraction she had once gambled on ever return? Would Buffum, if she left, survive the wilderness?

Tasmin didn't know, but she was extremely sulky with her father, whose selfishness had landed them in their predicament. She passed him in the halls without a word or a look.

Lord Berrybender eventually became disquieted by his daughter's icy attitude. What was the matter with Tasmin? They were housed in a good house, provided with ample comforts. Old pleasures—cards, music, claret—could be resumed. Why couldn't there be harmony in the household? Why did Tasmin look at him as if she wished he were dead?

"Tassie's very short with me," he told his wife. "Extremely short, one might say. Can't think why."

He began to fumble under her gown.

Vicky, half asleep, offered no opposition. She rarely did, when her husband was in a mood of disquiet. Better to accept him, let the the old boy squirt off, as he would in a few moments, usually. Otherwise he'd toss and turn, grumble and groan, half the night.

. . . the river, flowing quietly, quietly flowing . . .

Captain William Clark was at table with Toussaint Charbonneau when the river man Joe Compton brought the sad news. Everyone who worked the river, if they knew what was good for them, hurried to William Clark's offices when they arrived in Saint Louis. Nobody was hungrier for news of the West than Captain Clark—after all it was he, with his long-dead partner, Captain Lewis, who had opened it. One wall of his office was covered with a huge map of the trans-Mississippi regions; the Captain loved nothing more than augmenting his map, adding a stream here or a pass there, whenever he was brought information that he considered reliable.

Of course, the Captain's great trek had occurred some thirty years ago. Hundreds of men—trappers, miners, adventurers, hunters, scientists, soldiers—had gone up the river since then. There had been substantial expeditions. Fewer and fewer areas of doubt remained, where the geography was concerned—those few gaps persisted because certain tribes, the Blackfeet principally, were still too strong to trifle with. The Captain was not satisfied that the course of certain rivers—the Green, for example—was understood sufficiently. The explorer Jedediah Smith, a man possessed of keen geographical intelligence and sufficient curiosity, had meant to pursue the matter of the Green, but had run afoul of some hostile Kiowas on the Cimarron and had been killed some three years back. Progress was certain, but progress was slow.

The news Joe Compton brought—that Pomp Charbonneau had been executed by a deranged Mexican captain while on the road to Santa Fe—was such as to drive all thought of geography out of the Captain's mind. Compton, a skinny fellow the ends of whose long mustache curled down toward his shoulders, was startled to see the famous Captain Clark flush and begin to cry.

"Not Pomp! Surely you're wrong, man!"

he cried. "Why would anyone shoot our fine, friendly Pomp? Why couldn't someone stop it?"

"As to that, I couldn't say," Joe Compton replied. He had heard that the Captain had been good friends with young Charbonneau—he thought it his duty to report the lad's demise. But the sight of two men weeping—for old Sharbo, the boy's father, was soon sobbing too—was more than he bargained for.

"Just thought you'd like to know, Captain," he said, and left. He had been a long time on the river and was anxious to get to a tavern and perhaps find a whore. The sight of grown men crying unnerved him considerably. The last time he himself had shed a tear was when an impetuous dentist had pulled three of his teeth at one time—two more, in Compton's opinion, than had been strictly necessary.

"I feared it! I feared it!" Toussaint Charbonneau told his old friend. He wiped his dripping eyes on a sleeve that was none too clean.

"I always feared that Pomp would go before me—and now it's happened," he said.

Captain Clark made no immediate attempt at consolation, though he did pour the old man a strong brandy, and another for himself. He thought of his own seven children, all of whom he loved dearly—and yet Pomp's death stung him as deeply as would that of any child of his own loins. All the long way west, from the Mandan villages to the great Pacific and then back again to the Mandans, the lively little Pomp—delivered by Sacagawea not long before the expedition proceeded upriver in the spring of 1805—had been his chief delight. All the men liked Pomp. As soon as he was old enough to walk, his principal aim had been to escape control—principally his mother's control. Sacagawea was always losing Pomp and having to hunt him—her reprimands were severe, and yet nothing could suppress the little boy's good spirits for long. William Clark could not but love the child—and had come close to loving the mother as well. He liked to think that Janey, as he called Sacagawea, had a kind of fondness for him too. Why else had she presented him with a dozen weasel tails; they hung in his office still, by his great map. His own clear delight in their little dancing Pomp had won Janey's trust—won it so thoroughly that, as soon as the little boy was weaned, she brought him to Saint Louis and left him for the Captain to educate. That had been the last time Bill Clark saw his Janey—she died of a putrid fever, in one of Manuel Lisa's forts, a few years later. The Captain himself had had two good wives—his Julia and now his Harriet—and yet his lively Janey sometimes still appeared in his dreams, chattering at her shambling husband or else chasing her errant child. With Janey gone, and now Pomp also, he felt it could not be long before his own life waned.

"I named a big tower of rock after your boy, Sharbo," he said. "It was when we were crossing to the Yellowstone, on our way back. There was a kind of pillar, as I recall—mostly that reddish rock. So I named it Pompey's Tower and carved my name and put the date. I expect it's still there—it was the only sign I felt like making, on the whole trip. It was the sight of that pillar that gave me the notion."

Toussaint Charbonneau put his head in his hands. He felt that never in his whole life had he done anything right. It seemed to him that this tragedy was the result of his own inconstancy. If only he had not taken a notion to leave the Berrybenders, his boy might still be alive. He himself had been to Santa Fe—he knew how to cozy along the hot-tempered Mexicans. But Pomp was making his first trip—he must somehow have angered whoever was in charge. Compton suggested that the captain had been crazy, killing himself and a soldier, besides Pomp. He felt sure he could have found a way to soothe the infuriated captain, if only he had been there. Now, of course, it was too late.

"I feared he'd go before me—I always feared it," he said, several times, until, the brandy bottle empty and his step very unsteady, he stumbled back to the little room where the Charbonneaus stayed when with Captain Clark. His little Hidatsa wife, Coal, kept it neat; their little boy, Rabbit, bright-eyed and quick to smile, was also a delight to Captain Clark. He was much like Pomp, and yet he wasn't Pomp.

Not wanting to sleep, heavy in his heart, Captain Clark said a word to his wife and left the house, another bottle of brandy tucked into his coat pocket. He walked a mile or more through the misty night to a place where he could see the river, flowing quietly, quietly flowing, as it passed on south toward the distant sea. A patriot, an American, a soldier, a farmer, the Captain had lived through great times and seen great things. He had seen the plains completely covered with buffalo. He had seen the remains of a great whale, on the beach in Oregon. With his friend and partner, Captain Lewis, he had just managed to bluff the furious Teton Sioux, who might well have made, at the outset, an end to all of them, had a misstep occurred.

Glory had been theirs, when they returned to the excited young nation—of all Americans only Mr. Jefferson was then more famous. And yet glory had not lasted. Within three years his moody friend Captain Lewis had killed himself in a filthy tavern on the Natchez Trace. The great sweep of land to the west that he and Captain Lewis had crossed and recrossed, measured and studied with all the scientific rigor they could muster had seemed, when they inched across it, so vast that it could never be filled. And yet it would be filled. He and Captain Lewis had not been stopped—no more would other Americans be stopped.

The Mexicans would soon enough be swept aside. Pomp had merely been the first to fall, in the war that would surely come. He himself had seen the whole country, from the Palisades of the Hudson to the Columbia River Gorge; in his youth he had been one of the few who could claim such a comprehensive view; but now many could claim it. Immigrants were steadily filtering into the land across the river. And yet only thirty years had passed. What was thirty years? Another thirty and westward-tending Americans would fill all the habitable places, and render some habitable that had not seemed so before.

Bill Clark was a busy man—he had the myriad needs and activities of the Indians to administer. He was happy in his work, proud that the Indians respected him. And yet, beneath his pride was the sure knowledge that the glory of the native peoples, as he had seen it in its fullness, would soon pass away—much, thanks to smallpox and cholera, had already passed. Little Indian boys no older than Rabbit would live to see the end. The Teton Sioux that might have killed him would be tamed or broken.

The Captain walked a half mile closer to

the Mississippi, close enough that he could hear a fish jump and plop back. He heard the slap of water against a not-too-distant wharf. Far away, somewhere on the Missouri shore, a steamboat tested its horn. It was cloudy—only a weak moon shone through. The Captain took a seat on a stump and pulled out his other bottle of brandy. He considered himself a healthy man. He loved his Harriet. He loved their children. And yet the child who had touched him most, his little dancing Pomp, was now dead in New Mexico. Janey long dead, Pomp just dead—it seemed to Bill Clark that the happiest parts of his life had been with that young mother and that spirited child—neither of them his exactly; they were the family of an old drunk man now sleeping off his grief in a little back room.

Had it been glory, or had it been folly, the unrelenting American push? Were town and farm better than red men and buffalo? Bill Clark didn't know, but he could not but feel bittersweet about the changes he himself had helped bring. He was happy, though, to live near the Mississippi—nothing wore away grief but time, and yet the sound and sight of moving water helped. Perhaps old men could not help questioning the life they had lived, as their life approached its end. He would never deny, nor could he forget, the great march—the land, the vast and various land, was so beautiful that there was a kind of glory in it.

When dawn came William Clark was still sitting on his stump, the brandy bottle empty. He would always miss Pomp Charbonneau. Below him the sunlit river rolled on.

⁔ 7 ⁔

Petal, her interview ruined . . .

From her earliest age Petal recognized that her mother was the most important person in their world, and their world, for almost two years, was the large household in Santa Fe, where her mother reigned and where she meant to reign herself as soon as she mastered the ways of adults sufficiently to be able to outwit them.

Petey, her twin, she tolerated—sometimes she was good to Petey and sometimes she was bad, but if he tried to climb into their mother's lap at a time when Petal wanted sole possession of it, she had no qualms about shoving him off the bed. Her mother was hers: no one else—not Petey and not Monty—was allowed to make a claim, unless, of course, they made it when Petal had other things to do.

Tasmin, for her part—and indeed, the whole household—had soon to recognize that an unusually strong-willed child had come among them. And not merely strong-willed, either. As Mary Berrybender had once been able to sniff out tubers and edible roots, Petal seemed able to detect the nature of feelings—even feelings that the adults themselves had thought were buried deep.

When Tasmin was carrying the twins—before she knew they *were* twins—she had suspected that she might be with child by Pomp Charbonneau. Yet before the twins were six months old it was evident to the whole household that they were Jim's. Their fingers were Jim's, and their hands, and the way they moved. Petal's startlingly direct look was identical to Jim's. The realization that she had not, after all, borne Pomp's children added, for a few days, a new weight of melancholy to Tasmin's sadness. And yet it was not, finally, a heavy weight, nor long held. Tasmin knew she had to let the memory of Pomp go, if she were not to become insane. She had several times wished herself dead, but she could not wish herself insane. Seeing Pomp in the twins would have been too much; besides, in her steadier moments, Tasmin acknowledged that it was better that the children have a living father such as Jim—a competent man on whom their lives might yet depend.

When the twins were brought in to nurse, Tasmin sometimes let the babies loll on her bed for an hour. She cuddled and coddled the boy, Petey, who seemed to need much hugging. Petal sometimes spent her whole visit quietly staring at her mother. There was something a little disquieting about Petal's capacity for inspection.

Not long after the neat theft of the blue rooster, Petal one day planted herself in front of Tasmin and looked her mother dead in the eye.

"Are you happy?" she asked.

The question was so unexpected that Tasmin flinched—what sort of child was this little girl with the raven curls? No adult in the household would have dared ask Tasmin that question. None would have needed to. They all knew much too clearly that Tasmin was not happy.

"You tell me," Petal insisted. "Tell me right now. Are you happy?"

"I can sometimes be a little bit happy

when I'm with you and Petey and Monty," Tasmin confessed.

Petal's stare turned icy. Why bring up Petey and Monty, minor players in this drama of affection?

"I want you to be happy when *I'm* here," Petal insisted. "When *I'm* here."

Tasmin was amused—she felt as pure a moment of amusement as had been hers since Pomp's death.

"Petey and Monty," Tasmin repeated, or tried to repeat, for at once a small and not very clean hand was clapped over her mouth, muffling her efforts at repetition.

"When *I'm* here!" Petal repeated.

"All right, when you're here, if you insist on strict accuracy," Tasmin said. "Get your dirty paw off my mouth."

"Speak right!" Petal warmed, and then started to drift away. Tasmin caught her.

"You do want your mother to be happy, don't you?" Tasmin asked. "You surely don't wish me unhappier than I am."

Petal thought her position had been made perfectly clear.

"Just be happy when I'm here," she once more repeated.

"But you aren't always here, my love,"

Tasmin told her. "If I'm only allowed to be happy when you're here, then I shall have to languish in unhappiness a good bit of the time."

Petal ignored the comment—she had something else on her mind.

"I don't know how you die," she told her mother. She had heard her aunts Buffum and Mary talking about death, the business that followed dying. Already an accomplished eavesdropper, Petal had got the sense that her mother was unhappy because somebody had died. But death was not an easy thing to puzzle out. It seemed to be rather like a long nap, and yet different in nature from a nap. It was obviously an important state, and yet the adults never made its nature very clear. Petal was very curious about death. She once asked Monty about it—Monty was older. Though often rude, Monty could be amusing. He didn't like it when Petal held the dog Mopsy up by his tail; but when she wasn't pestering the dog, Monty could be agreeable.

"When you're dead you don't breathe," Monty told her. "They put you in a hole and cover you with dirt."

"But I *want* to breathe," Petal insisted.

"Well, you can breathe if you go to heaven," Monty concluded.

"Is heaven over there?" she asked, pointing across the Plaza.

Monty concluded that his sister was a very ignorant child.

"Heaven is in the sky—it's so high you can't see it," he told her.

After that Petal kept a close watch on the sky, but except for an occasional bird, she saw nothing but clouds. Unable to gain a clear notion about death from her brother, she took the matter up with her mother.

"I don't know how to die," she repeated.

"Well, and a good thing too," Tasmin told her. "You've certainly no business dying for at least the next eighty years."

"Monty says you don't breathe when you die—but I like to breathe," Petal confided.

"It's the accepted thing to do," Tasmin allowed.

Kate Berrybender came in at that time. Petal, never happy to be interrupted, did her best to ignore Kate—but Kate had little respect for the wishes of children, Petal particularly.

"Cook is wondering about dinner—must it be goat again?" Kate asked.

"Why not a pig? There are plenty of swine running around this town. Have Papa buy one," Tasmin suggested.

"I was talking about how you die," Petal reminded her mother.

"It's too late to cook a pig today—I fear it will have to be goat," Kate remarked. Petal was glaring at her.

"My, such a dark look," Tasmin said.

Petal, her interview ruined, turned and marched out of the room. How one became deaded—the term she preferred—was still annoyingly obscure.

"There's going to be trouble with that child," Kate observed.

"There's trouble with all children, as you'll discover someday," Tasmin told her. "But I agree. There's likely to be rather more trouble than usual with that one."

. . . a quick soldier caught his foot . . .

The Ear Taker, the small dark man who had first been known to his people as Takes Bones, knew it was folly to return to Santa Fe. On his way back from the north the jack rabbits began to stare at him again, as they had before he left to explore the northern lands. That was certainly a bad sign. Then, in the space of three days he saw three owls, which was a worse sign. It was foolish to ignore such obvious signs, but the Ear Taker came back to the southwest anyway. He had not enjoyed the north. There were no Mexicans, only a scattering of whites, and Indian tribes which were so wary he could not approach them. Their camps were full of dogs, quick to pick up unfamiliar sounds or scents.

Old Prickly Pear Woman had told the Ear

Taker that if he walked north far enough he would come to the edge of the world and perhaps be able to catch a glimpse of the great snowy void where spirits were said to go; but that had turned out to be just an old woman's lie. The Ear Taker walked north for many weeks, but instead of coming to the edge of the world he just came to a place that was extremely cold. If he had not been able to find a snug den that had once been used by a bear, he might have frozen. The bear's smell was still strong in the den. He thought the bear might return and want his home, but no bear came. In his whole time in the north he had only taken two ears, one from a young white boy who had been traveling with some men who could fly in a basket and the other from an old trapper who was extremely drunk. He hated to give up on a place he had walked so far to see, so he stayed through another winter and learned to snare animals that made their lives in the snow. Food was never a problem—the northern ponds were covered with ducks and geese. Now and then he came across an old man or an old woman who had become too old to move with the tribe and so had been left to die. He liked to sit

with such old ones, even though he didn't
know their tongue. Once he even ran into an
old shaman who made his home in the bole
of a big tree. Old Prickly Pear Woman had
told the Ear Taker that there were shamans
who could teach people to move in and out
of time, so they could visit their ancestors,
but the old man in the tree, though he mumbled constantly, didn't know how to move in
and out of time.

The first thing the Ear Taker did, when he
came back to the country of his people, was
to pay a visit to old Prickly Pear Woman. He
intended to point out to her that she had
misled him badly in the matter of the edge
of the world, which was not in the north, as
she had insisted it was. But when he came
to the vast field of prickly pears with the
narrow tunnel underneath, the hole where
she had lived showed no signs of recent
habitation. Several rattlesnakes were using
the hole as a den; they were irritable when
the Ear Taker showed up. He killed one fat
snake and ate it, but left the others alone.
He remembered that the old woman had
a hiding place nearby, under a flat rock;
she kept the equipment she used in
her spells there: dried-up toads, scorpions,

dead mice. The Ear Taker found the large rock easily enough but the only thing there in the hole was some of the bitter cactus buds that the old woman sometimes chewed when she was seeking a vision. The buds he took for himself—now and then he would chew one and feel as if he were flying.

Soon the Ear Taker began to take ears again, slicing ears off drunken drovers, just as he had before. His skills had eroded somewhat; several times he made bad cuts, once by accident even cutting a drover's throat. Once again he became fired with his mission, which was to humiliate whites as the whites had humiliated the People they took captive after the big pueblo revolt many grandfathers back.

The irritating thing, though, was that the jackrabbits continued to stare at him in an unnatural way; also, he kept seeing owls. Once one flew directly over his head, a sure sign that his death was near. He was glad to be back in the country of red canyons and piñon trees, but the owls worried him. Before he could make up his mind to go farther off the now busy trails to Santa Fe, the thing that had been coming happened: a quick soldier caught his foot. He had the soldier's ear in his hand, having just sliced it off, but for some reason he hesitated a moment before springing away. He did not think any soldier could be as quick as this soldier was. The quick soldier hung on to his foot; the soldier yelled out and very soon the famous Ear Taker was caught and firmly tied with rawhide cords. Before they tied him he quickly crammed all the remaining cactus buds into his mouth and chewed them, hoping they would poison him and allow his spirit to float away before the torturers got busy; but he vomited up the buds while the excited soldiers were beating him and kicking him. From time to time, in the days of pain that followed, it seemed that his spirit might fly away, but the feeling didn't free him from the pain entirely. The Mexicans were convinced that he had special powers—to make sure that he didn't escape them, his feet were chopped off and the stumps seared with hot irons. Then they hung him on a gibbet in the center of the Plaza, where all who wished could observe his pain. At first he was hoisted off the ground with hooks through his ears, a fitting punishment for an Ear Taker, it was felt. But the weight of his body soon pulled the hooks through and he fell. Many soldiers, convinced that he was a devil, wanted him garroted right away, but the Governor refused to hurry. Any man who was missing an ear was allowed to come and give the Ear Taker twenty lashes: fourteen men took advantage of the offer. The Ear Taker was by then close to death, but he was not dead. Screws were driven into his skull through what remained of his ears; the screws would hold his weight whereas his ears wouldn't. Thin rawhide cords were attached to the screws, and the Ear Taker, naked and bleeding, hung several feet off the ground, his facial muscles horribly distorted by the weight of his hanging body. Through it all the Ear Taker scarcely cried out. He sighed great sighs—but his sighs grew fainter as he weakened. The native people shuffled about the Plaza, doing their little bits of business. They kept well away from the gibbet. They did not need to see what was happening to this small man. Their memories were full of terrible stories about things the Spanish had done to the People.

But the Mexicans watched: laborers, soldiers, women. The Governor's wife, Doña Margareta, spent hours at her window, staring at the dying man whose practice had been to take ears. Watching the blood drip from his numerous wounds gave her an unexpected satisfaction. When two more one-eared men turned up and claimed their right to lash the Ear Taker, Doña Margareta watched every stroke. She even sent a manservant to search about the city and see if one or two more earless men could be found. When none turned up she persuaded her husband to allow some of his victims who had already lashed him to lash him again. What were lashes compared to the loss of an ear?

While the Ear Taker was dying, a process that took four days, the Berrybenders all stayed away from the windows that looked out on the Plaza. Amboise d'Avigdor, who had lost an ear, declined to claim a turn with the lash. Lord Berrybender, leaving the Plaza on his hunts, turned his face from the spectacle.

"Excessively cruel, I sometimes think, the Spanish race," he said. The sight of the hanging man rather upset his digestion—once he even called off a hunt without firing a shot.

It was Amboise who happened to notice

the stranger, a thin bald man sitting well back in the shade, with a drawing board on his lap. The man was watching the Ear Taker's suffering with an almost scientific interest—he looked down from time to time, sketching what he saw.

"Why, where'd that fellow come from—I'd swear he's English," Lord Berrybender announced, when Amboise called his attention to the stranger.

Then he looked more closely and drew back with a start.

"My God, it's Edgechurch," he said. "Elliott Edgechurch. Met him in England more than once."

"Is he an artist, then?" Amboise asked. "He's drawing this poor hanging man."

"I suppose he can draw but he's not precisely an artist," Lord Berrybender replied. "In London he's called the Torture Man."

. . . soup would be spilled and wineglasses knocked over.

"That man's too scabby!" Petal announced, in what was, unfortunately, her most carrying voice—the remark embarrassed everyone at the table except the mild gentleman it described, Dr. Elliott Edgechurch, who peered at the little girl in a kindly way.

"Oh damn, she's escaped again," Tasmin declared, setting down her fork. Before she could jump up and seize her impolitic child, Petal had darted under the table, amid a thicket of adult legs. She knew from experience that if she could just get right under the center of the wide table nobody would be able to reach her, though as various diners made the attempt, soup would be spilled and wineglasses knocked over. Sometimes, if pressed, Petal might seek sanctuary in her grandfather's lap. Lord

Berrybender—though, to Vicky's annoyance, quite indifferent to his own two young sons—could seldom resist Petal, even when she had just delivered an embarrassingly accurate description of their distinguished guest, a man who had been physician royal to several majesties and was generally thought to be England's most eminent surgeon.

"She won't stay in the nursery—finds the dining room more exciting," Tasmin explained. "If I had a dungeon I'd fling the brat into it, but I have no dungeon."

"Oh, it's no matter, I *am* scabby at present," Dr. Edgechurch admitted. "It's the harsh American waters. I am from Wiltshire, where the waters are far softer. Even in London I am sometimes troubled with eczema. I generally carry various emollients and a very delicate soap that can only be obtained from France—not cheap, my soap, I assure you. But a vital piece of my kit bounced out of the wagon and the muleteers absolutely refused to go back and look for it, so here I am, entirely at the mercy of American waters. The young lady was being no more than truthful, as the young so often are. I *am* too scabby."

Petal remained under the table, just out of reach of various grabbing hands. She didn't really object to the scabby man— what she objected to was being left in the nursery with the five boys while, downstairs, the adults were eating exciting meals. Sometimes Kate would mind the nursery, but usually that chore was left to Little Onion, the more easily eluded of the two. All that was necessary was to pinch a little boy hard enough for the boy to raise a howl. While Little Onion soothed the injured male Petal could often sneak out and slip down the big staircase; by the time Little Onion realized that a miscreant was missing, Petal could be under the table or in her grandfather's lap. It was an exciting game, one Petal didn't always win. Sometimes Little Onion ran her down before she could reach the stairway.

"Leave her be, the brat," Tasmin said. The tall doctor with the scabby skin seemed kindly, on the whole. He also seemed to know everyone in Europe, including the French doctor who had taught Father Geoffrin anatomy. When he discovered that Amboise d'Avigdor had lost an ear to the Ear

Taker he examined Amboise's head carefully and took some arcane measurements.

"The fellow was a specialist, and a sound one," he announced. "He knew how remove an ear, but I doubt he knows much else. The appendix would stump him, I imagine, or even a joint."

Lord Berrybender was uneasy. Somehow he couldn't quite like this kindly surgeon, though he was certainly vigorous in pursuit of his goals. He had arrived in Santa Fe from California, where he landed after making a long and thorough examination of the elaborate tortures practiced in China and Japan. All the way to China just for torture? It seemed to Lord Berrybender that there was something slightly unwholesome about it, but the Governor's wife, Doña Margareta, found Dr. Edgechurch fascinating—she couldn't get enough of hearing about the many severe cruelties the famous doctor had witnessed. It annoyed her that the little Berrybender girl had distracted Dr. Edgechurch from an elaborate description of how the Ottoman sultans punished women who failed to please them: by tying them up in sacks with wildcats and flinging them off a cliff, or else crushing their breasts with viselike instruments designed solely for that purpose. Doña Margareta meant to encourage her husband to try to keep Dr. Edgechurch in Santa Fe—then she could draw the man out at length. Santa Fe was filled with criminals—it was her opinion that better tortures needed to be devised, in order to subdue this element.

"How much longer do you think that little Ear Taker will hold out?" Lord Berrybender inquired. "Rather puts us off our feed, having him hanging there. My cook is even reluctant to go to market. The sight of him preys on the mind, you know."

"Two more days will finish him," Dr. Edgechurch assured them. "He has no very serious injuries, but it's a strain on the heart, having the muscles pulled out of shape as they are. It's the mistake most torturers make: they don't understand that the nerves grow fatigued. Pain exhausts before it destroys. The Japanese understand this well. They allow their victims regular respites."

Tasmin found that she disliked Doña Margareta intensely. About the English doctor she wasn't sure. He was a surgeon; he cut people for their own good. Torture, of an approved sort, must be all in a day's work for him. While recognizing that humans must sometimes be cut open to remove diseased organs, Tasmin still felt that it must take a curious sort of human being to choose cutting as a profession.

"What drew your attention to torture, Doctor?" Piet Van Wely asked. He saw in Doctor Edgechurch a fellow scientist. But to his dismay, the question drew a frown from the great man.

"I am *not* drawn to torture—as a humanist I strictly oppose it," he replied. "If a criminal must be put to death I advocate doing it humanely, with a bullet or a noose."

He took a long swallow of wine.

"What draws me to the torture chambers—and I've inspected more than one hundred, most of them quite bloodily active—is not torture but nerves," Dr. Edgechurch said. "The human nervous system is as yet poorly understood. I am even now attempting a comprehensive atlas of nerves, but my atlas is far from complete. Nerves are not easily traced. They mainly reveal themselves under extreme conditions— such as torture. There's more to be learned about nerves in torture chambers than in anatomy classes."

"Excuse me, I believe it's time for my devotions," Father Geoffrin said. He had grown pale, he felt queasy; he did not want to hear of any more horrors.

"So tell me, Dr. Edgechurch," Tasmin said, determined to tough this curious diner out, "which nations produce the best torturers? Or do I mean the worst?"

"Oh, that's easy, the Japanese," the doctor said at once. "There's something aesthetical about it. They're very good with cords, for example. Very good with cords."

Doctor Edgechurch paused to reflect on his long experience.

"Of course great specialists do pop up here and there—you might almost call them artists," he said. "There's a Viennese called Schoensiegel. Extraordinary fellow. Confined himself entirely to feet, and yet he broke the strongest men. Plenty of nerves in the foot, I can tell you that."

Tasmin found the situation curious in the extreme. All the Berrybenders, even the usually unshockable Mary, were looking discomfited. Petal had crawled up in Lord Berrybender's lap and was rapidly polishing off his *cabrito.* Buffum and Vicky looked distinctly peaked. And yet Dr. Edgechurch had said nothing improper or suggestive. He was a famous physician, determined to understand the workings of the human nervous system. Accordingly, as he had politely explained, he went to places where nerves were stretched to the limit: that is, torture chambers. It made sense, and the doctor had been modest and matter-of-fact in explaining it. And yet Geoff, turning green, had to flee. Buffum excused herself, Vicky remained expressionless, and Lord Berrybender was too distracted even to play with his granddaughter. Mary Berrybender, who could talk about the most recondite sexual practices without turning a hair, was now twisting her hair into curls, a nervous habit she was thought to have outgrown. With the exception of Doña Margareta, whose eyes shone more brightly every time a torture was mentioned, the whole table had been quelled.

The odd effect he was having on his hosts did not escape Elliott Edgechurch. He drained his wineglass, stood up, thanked Lord Berrybender, and bowed to them all, in his face a touch of sadness.

"There! I've done it again—spoiled a perfectly good dinner party," he said.

"Now, now," Lord Berrybender said, but the doctor ignored him.

"Healthy people don't want to hear about tortures—and why should they?" he asked. "It's the same with operations. Healthy people don't like to watch them. In both instances there is always the possibility that such agonies will in time be theirs.

"Thus," he added, "my investigations will of necessity have to be of a lonely nature."

"But one day you'll have your atlas," Tasmin told him. "No doubt it will win you great fame."

"I hope not—that too would be a form of torture," Dr. Edgechurch said; then he left the room.

"Too scabby!" Petal said again. In this instance no one disagreed.

. . . a snug stall, well provided with straw . . .

Amboise d'Avigdor had a stall in the stables, a snug stall, well provided with straw; yet he did not even try to sleep. From his stable door he could see the Ear Taker, hanging from his cords. At first the man's deep sighs could be heard across the Plaza, but now there were no sighs. The two soldiers who were supposed to guard the dying man—lest he dematerialize and slip away—were asleep, wrapped in their heavy coats.

Amboise walked over and stood looking at the small hanging man. The Ear Taker's eyes were closed, but he was not dead. Amboise could hear the rasp of his breath. Amboise wished the man would open his eyes—he wanted the Ear Taker to look at him once more, to realize that he came as a friend. He wanted the man to know that the loss of his own ear meant little. Amboise supposed that the taking of his ear, and all the others, was an act of vengeance. He had seen how the Mexicans treated the Indians and could well imagine that any Indian might want vengeance. Taking ears was a novel vengeance, but Amboise wanted the little man to know that, for his part, all was forgiven. He liked to think that if he and the Ear Taker met in a time of peace they could be friends.

Amboise waited a long time beneath the gibbet. It was cold. Finally his teeth began to chatter and he stumbled away to his stall, deeply disappointed. The moment of recognition that he wanted had not come.

In the morning the Ear Taker was found to be dead, his eyes frosted shut by the bitter chill. The Governor didn't allow the body to be cut down. The Ear Taker hung in the Plaza until his body fell apart, a warning for all transgressors and food for the carrion birds.

11

The Governor was vexed—he couldn't find his wife.

The Governor was vexed—he couldn't find his wife. There were thirty servants in the Palace and yet none of them seemed to know where Doña Margareta had got to. Even the majordomo, a thin, severe fellow who, as part of his job, attempted to keep track of all the rumors floating around the intrigue-ridden city of Santa Fe, merely shrugged when the Governor asked if he had seen Doña Margareta. The Governor went to the kitchen, but no one was helpful there either; he went to the carriage house, thinking his wife might be taking a drive, but all the buggies and carriages were correctly lined up. No one in the stables had seen Doña Margareta. It was most annoying. Normally the Governor's heavy responsibilities permitted him little freedom. He was the

Governor—the paperwork seemed endless. He employed two secretaries and several scribes, but still, all day, he had scarcely a chance to lift his head, to sit and think, to smoke a cigar—or to visit his wife.

Today, though, the paperwork had been unaccountably light. It was only a little past noon, yet his desk was clear. Even a governor was human—it was a rare day when he could escape in the afternoon. He stood at the window for a moment, watching some soldiers drill, and then his thoughts turned to Doña Margareta, the wealthy beauty he had captured in the City of Mexico. He enjoyed his cigar—why not take advantage of the fact that his desk was clear and go enjoy his wife? He was a heavy man and Doña Margareta a petite, small-boned woman. Sometimes he wondered whether Doña Margareta really liked him. With a wife it was sometimes hard to say. She didn't refuse him, but it could not be said that she performed her conjugal duties with much enthusiasm. The Governor suspected she found him gross, a sweaty bulk to be tolerated. After their lovemaking Margareta would sit and fastidiously pick his chest hairs off her breasts and belly. It embarrassed the Governor slightly. He tried to be considerate in their lovemaking but he was a hairy fellow and somehow the hairs kept coming off on Margareta. She never said a word but it was clear she didn't like it that she rose from their bed sweaty and covered with hairs.

Still, a wife had her duties. It was not to be expected that she would enjoy every one of them. He was home unexpectedly and hoped to have a little fiesta and then a little siesta, and yet the first impediment was that his wife seemed to have disappeared. None of the thirty servants would even venture an opinion as to where she might be. Of course, Margareta was not a favorite with the servants. She had been brought up to take a firm line with servants and she *did* take a stern line. She had once even cuffed one of her own ladies-in-waiting in public, at the beginning of a state dinner. The girl had failed to complete some small chore and was given a ringing slap, an action that drew much negative comment. The lady-in-waiting had been of good family herself; that this haughty woman from the City of Mexico had so forgotten decorum as to slap her was an action the old families of Santa

Fe would never forgive. Doña Margareta
had made little effort to conceal her contempt for local standards—no, it did not
make the Governor's job easier; but then
wives had to be lived with and there was no
denying that Margareta was a great beauty.

But where, the Governor asked, had
this great beauty gone? Probably she was
out visiting, but about the only family she
still visited regularly was the Berrybenders,
where she had dined only the night before.
The Governor, his mind on a fiesta, was
about to settle for a siesta when he happened to pass a storeroom where a lot of
heavy furniture had been stored while one
or two of the bedrooms were getting a
fresh coat of white paint. The Governor was
strolling down the hall when he heard what
sounded like a grunt from inside the storeroom. A moment later he heard another
grunt, followed by a swishing sound. His
first thought was that two servants were
probably fornicating in the storeroom; servants could not be particular when an opportunity to fornicate came. The Governor
was a tolerant man; he did not expect servants to behave like saints. He himself, as a
young captain of cavalry, had fornicated in

some pretty unlikely places: on saddle blankets, in corn cribs, wherever he could go with a willing girl. He was about to pass on, but then he heard a third grunt and stopped, confused. The grunt sounded like Margareta. Hadn't she grunted like that in the early days of their marriage, when he still managed to excite her? He couldn't remember. Lately she had ceased even to pretend that his caresses excited her. It struck the Governor—as it should have sooner—that the reason Margareta had no interest in him was because she had a lover. *Of course* she had a lover. In the City of Mexico it was no doubt the expected thing, for a woman of her class. Immediately the Governor wished that he had had the good sense not to go looking for his wife. Why hadn't he been content with a nice long siesta? As the grunts continued the Governor had less and less doubt that his wife was behind the door, in the storeroom, copulating with—whom? A soldier? One of his generals? A trader? A servant, even? The Governor began to feel angry—then he became furious. But even his fury was mixed with doubt. Part of him knew that the wise thing would be to walk on—after all, many women grunted in their passion. It might just be two servants. If it was merely a servant girl, then nothing need change. But if he opened the door and found his wife in the arms of, say, General Juan Diego, then everything must change. He might have to kill the lover, banish the wife. If he discovered his wife with another man he would certainly have to take strong action or else become a figure of ridicule. There would be disorder in the Palace for a long time to come.

For a moment, as the grunting and swishing continued, the Governor struggled with himself. He was by nature prudent, deliberate in his actions. He had been made Governor of Nuevo México precisely because he was not impetuous. He took his time. He studied each question carefully; he wasted neither money nor men. His superiors in the City of Mexico trusted his judgment, his discretion. Was he willing to risk throwing it all away for a faithless wife?

A moment later the male won the struggle with the administrator in the Governor's breast. He kicked open the door.

. . . she was whipping Tomas . . .

The first shock the Governor received was that his beautiful, fastidious wife, noted at every assembly for her cool elegance, was drenched in sweat. It ran down her cheeks, pooled at the base of her neck, stained her armpits as she wielded the heavy whip— the same whip that had been used to lash the Ear Taker. But Doña Margaret wasn't whipping the Ear Taker, she was whipping Tomas, the Governor's most effective young footman, the one who rode on the running board of the Governor's carriage.

Tomas had been stripped to the waist and tied at the wrists to a bedpost. Doña Margareta grunted when she struck, so intent on her task—her fine features distorted, her eyes shining—that for a moment she failed to notice her husband standing in the

doorway, as shocked by what he was wit-
nessing as if he had seen a dead man rise.
Though the whip was heavy, Margareta was
small and inexpert. Though Tomas had a
few red marks on his back she was not
really hurting the boy—what was hurt was
his pride, the pride of a young gentleman of
good family who had risen to the post of
first footman to the Governor of New Mexico. It was plain that Tomas was terribly embarrassed. When Doña Margareta called for
him he was rather surprised. Tomas was the
Governor's footman—Doña Margareta's
was a vain young man named Jesus, whom
the Governor would not have put up with for
a minute. But Tomas had gone obediently to
Doña Margareta's chamber, only to be
marched, without a word of explanation,
down a hall and into a dusty storeroom,
where he was told to remove his shirt.
Tomas found himself trapped in a nightmare. Why was he in this storeroom full of
dusty beds and tables? Why must he remove his shirt? Why was Doña Margareta
carrying a whip with dried blood still on it?

"Get your shirt off at once or I'll tell my
husband you raped me," Doña Margareta
demanded. Tomas felt the nightmare close

around him. If Doña Margareta made good her threat, then his life was over. Unhappily, Tomas removed his shirt and allowed Doña Margareta to tie him to an old bedpost. She didn't tie him well—he could easily have freed himself, but then what? If someone saw him half unclothed with the Governor's wife they might jump to the wrong conclusions. What seemed clear was that Doña Margareta had become a madwoman. Her breathing was harsh, her bosom heaved, her hands became so sweaty that she could hardly hold the whip. At first she struck him on the shoulders, but then her blows were directed lower. At one point she came close, squeezing him and mauling him before stepping back to strike again. The whipping didn't hurt, but where would it end? What if Doña Margareta took his pants down? The prospect horrified him.

When the Governor opened the door and stood there with a shocked expression on his face, Tomas felt greatly relieved. Now surely it wouldn't become anything worse than it had already been. The Governor was too stunned to speak, but at least he could see that his wife, and not his trusted footman, had brought the strange proceedings about. She held the whip, he was tied; as the Governor's footman he should not have been subjected to such indignities. It was a craziness of some kind; there was no explaining it.

The Governor, stunned for a moment, was trying to find an explanation that made sense. Tomas was not one of Doña Margareta's servants. Could the boy have somehow committed some mild offense that set Margareta off? It was hard to imagine what the boy could have done that would cause Margareta to march him off to the storeroom and whip him. Usually she just slapped servants where they stood, if they displeased her.

"What has Tomas done?" the Governor managed to inquire.

Caught in her frenzy, Doña Margareta had scarcely noticed her husband's entrance, but when she did notice she whirled on him. There he stood, gross and fat, the man whose sweaty belly she was often beneath, pressed into the mattress, ugly hairs plastered to her body, feeling nothing but distaste. Why had *he,* of all people, followed her to the storeroom? What could this big-bellied ox possibly want?

"Go away!" she hissed, her look so furious that the Governor retreated a step. For a moment, it seemed his wife might turn the bloody whip on him.

"But what did he do? Why are you whipping Tomas?" the Governor asked. "He's my footman. Why have you brought him here?"

"Go away!" Doña Margareta screamed—her scream echoed down the empty halls. Old Constancia, folding linen, heard it all the way across the building.

"But he's such a good footman, I only want to know what he did," the Governor said meekly. He very much wished he had not opened the door. It was not pleasing to see one's wife, soaking in her own sweat, vicious with anger.

"He was insolent!" Doña Margareta insisted. She didn't want to make any broader accusation—that might result in the slim, handsome Tomas being removed from the household entirely.

"I told you to go away!" Doña Margareta screamed a third time.

The Governor, looking at Tomas, realized the boy was too embarrassed even to meet his eye. Tomas had always been shy and polite—the last thing he could be accused of was insolence. The Governor wondered if his wife's screams could be heard outside the Palace. He didn't know what to do, how to help the trembling boy, what to say to his sweat-soaked wife.

"Don't be too long," he said finally. "Remember, we are having guests." He who had fought savage Indians, neither giving nor expecting any mercy, quailed before the anger in his wife's eyes.

The minute he stepped back Doña Margareta kicked the door shut. Before the Governor turned away he heard the grunt again and knew that his wife was already applying the lash. It made him feel a fool. He was, after all, the Governor of Nuevo México. He should have struck her down, the vicious woman who was whipping one of his finest young footmen.

And if he had struck her down, would that have changed anything? Men, after all, were supposed to rule women. He should have taken the whip from her and lashed her a few times himself. He should have dragged her to their bedroom and had his way with her, sweat or not, hairs or not. He should have paid the woman back in her own coin.

But he hadn't. He had been cowardly. Besides, shut up in an old storeroom with a handsome boy, who could know what else she might do?

The two secretaries and the scribe were shocked and disappointed when the Governor walked back into his office. They thought they had the afternoon off. They were playing cards. On a normal day the Governor would not have tolerated the cards or the idleness. He sat down at his empty desk, in his big chair. He stared out the window. He did not move until the shadows began to fall.

. . . extremely fine features and a long, graceful neck.

"Take a lover if you need a lover—there are several handsome young officers here," Tasmin pointed out to Vicky, who looked sad and downcast. Her labor with her second son, Randy, had been long and difficult—she could not seem to reclaim her energies. It was always a struggle to be a good wife to Albany Berrybender, and the struggle had recently been made even more difficult by Lord Berrybender's infatuation with Julietta Olivaries, wild, a beauty, and of the very highest nobility—Spanish, not Mexican. Married at fourteen to an elderly French banker, Julietta had run away with a conscript; captured and put in a convent, she had escaped. Exiled to Mexico City to cool off, she seduced so many young men that she was exiled all the way to the end of the road, which was Santa Fe, where she had an aunt.

Neither Tasmin nor Vicky was used to being overshadowed in the looks department, but the dazzling Julietta made them both feel old, dowdy, child-ridden, heavy, past their prime.

"I don't know that I want a lover," Vicky said, finally. "I haven't the energy. I just resent being displaced by a sixteen-year-old."

"Well, that's a very natural resentment—you should just kill the old bastard," Tasmin suggested. "You did once threaten to tear his throat out, I believe."

They were on a balcony, watching Lord Berrybender hold hands with his new love. He and she were in a buggy, about to set off for a jaunt—they merely waited for Signor Claricia, their driver, who had been poorly lately.

Julietta Olivaries had extremely fine features and a long, graceful neck. Both Tasmin and Vicky remembered being—or at least remembered *feeling*—that beautiful once. But they were no longer sixteen, at which age Tasmin had been seduced in a horse stall by Master Tobias Stiles, her father's head groom. For more than a year they copulated frequently in that stall, a liaison that only ended when Master Stiles was killed at a jump.

"I so want to go back to England," Vicky said, coloring—she looked tearful. "I miss it so. I think if I were in England I could accommodate myself to whatever regime Albany wants. I could have in my musical friends. There could be a proper nursery, with proper nannies. I know Little Onion does her best, but she doesn't really speak the language and I can't help feeling that that's important.

"Do you miss it, Tassie?" Vicky asked, drying her eyes.

Tasmin's thoughts were elsewhere. She was watching Little Onion help the ailing Signor Claricia into the buggy. Of late, thanks to the dust in the high capital, Signor Claricia had had difficult breathing, especially at night. Little Onion had gone round the stalls of old Indian women, seeking herbs to ease her friend's respiration. In defense of Signor Claricia, Little Onion flinched at nothing. She even tried to persuade the startled Lord Berrybender that his old carriage maker was too sick to be going on jaunts.

"No should go!" she insisted, and Lord B. seemed inclined to agree, but Signor Claricia wouldn't have it. Angrily, a male defending his prerogatives, he shook off all opposition, took the reins, and issued a command. Soon the buggy clattered out of the Plaza.

Little Onion stood watching, obviously worried.

"When Jim Snow shows up again I intend to insist that he divorce that girl," Tasmin vowed. "She loves that old Italian. They may make an odd couple, but then I'm half of an odd couple myself. Why shouldn't she have a bit of happiness? Without her our children would be wild as beasts."

"Your daughter is wild as a beast anyway," Vicky pointed out. "She's cowed all the boys—it's not a good sign."

No sooner had Tasmin mentioned Jim than she realized that she missed him. Almost two years had passed since Pomp Charbonneau's death. Her pain was still keen at times, but it was no longer constant. On Jim's last visit she had been stiff; she wanted no husband yet. If told that life must go on, she would have disagreed. And yet, despite her, it *had* gone on. Pomp's memory had clung to her; he was a ghost that could not be quickly shaken off. But time had begun to wear away memory. Tasmin had become a little impatient. Where was Jim Snow? She was anxious for him to come.

"That girl's fifty years younger than Albany—did you see them holding hands?" Vicky asked.

"Oh well, Spain—read the histories," Tasmin told her. "In the high nobility the prettier little girls are made to marry when they are about ten. Dynastic reasons, of course. In that society our Julietta would be considered almost elderly."

"I don't care—I still don't like them holding hands," Vicky said.

~ **14** ~

*He fanned his mouth with one hand,
but the fanning did no good.*

Cook had her doubts, and the Mexican girls
who worked in the kitchen began to smile in
an amused way when they saw the green
chilis that Little Onion had procured in the
market. Yanquis might sometimes consume
red chilis with pleasure if the red chilis were
well mixed with meat or corn; but for a Yan-
qui to consume green chilis, however dis-
guised, was a thing unheard of in Santa Fe.
But Little Onion was insistent. Signor Claricia was become more and more congested
in his chest. He ate less and less. Little
Onion pressed her two fingers alongside her
nose, to show Cook where the problem
was. She didn't know the words, but she
knew she needed to help her friend, before
he weakened even more.

The old woman in the Plaza who sold her

the green chilis seemed to understand when Little Onion pointed to her breathing passages; the old woman insisted that green chilis would help her friend breathe better.

When Cook cautiously cut one of the chilis the juice made her skin prickle and her eyes sting. She put a speck of the juice on the tip of her tongue and her tongue at once became numb. Cook's suspicions of the green chilis was so deep that Little Onion took over the cooking of the chili stew herself, chopping the chilis fine, dicing the pork, adding corn and a few dry beans, and stirring and stirring until the stew was ready.

She was much relieved when she heard the buggy returning. Soon Signor Claricia came into the big kitchen. It had been a dusty ride. He rolled up his sleeves and washed his hands and face in a basin one of the servant girls provided. Then Little Onion poured him a good glass of wine and set the steaming green chili stew before him, along with some tortillas.

Since steam rose from the stew Aldo Claricia judged it too hot just yet to eat. He sipped his wine. He was hungry; he blew on the stew to make it cool more quickly. It smelled delicious. After a short wait, during which Little Onion stood by anxiously, he picked up his spoon and took three large spoonfuls before stopping. He took a fourth spoonful and stopped. He put down the spoon—the heat of the green chilis had hit him; suddenly fire seemed to fill his head. It was as if he had eaten flame. He dropped spoon and gulped down the rest of his wine, indicating, by a desperate gesture, that he needed more. Little Onion poured him some but Aldo Claricia promptly spilled it. He fanned his mouth with one hand, but the fanning did no good. His forehead was flushed; he began to sweat copiously—it seemed to Little Onion that even his eyeballs were sweating. Signor Claricia jumped up, grabbed the big water pitcher, and began to pour water down his throat. Soon his shirtfront was drenched.

"I am set afire!" he cried, just as Lord Berrybender entered the kitchen, hungry, as he always was, after a brisk ride.

"Hoping for a bit of something—a hen perhaps—something to last me till dinnertime," he said.

Then he noticed Signor Claricia, his carriage master, very red, his shirtfront drenched—yet still the man was pouring water down his throat.

"Why, what's made the man so thirsty?" he asked.

Cook pointed to the bowl of stew.

"The stew's a-burning him, I fear, my lord," she said. "It's made with the local peppers—too strong for civilized people."

"Oh fiddle, not likely," Lord Berrybender said. "I like peppers myself. It's the reason English food is dull. Not enough peppers."

He picked up Signor Claricia's abandoned stew and sniffed it. Then he sniffed again, approvingly.

"Got any more?" he asked.

Little Onion was horrified; Cook no less so. Catastrophe loomed.

Cook rarely lied, but she thought she must lie this time.

"Just a bit for the local girls," she said.

Signor Claricia noticed Lord Berrybender looking hungrily at his stew.

"No, no!" he said. "You'll be scalded."

"To each his own," Lord B. remarked. "Smells good to me. If it's too peppery for Aldo I don't see why I shouldn't eat his. Do you suppose I can have a fresh spoon?"

Cook was about to protest that all the

spoons were dirty, but before she could, Eliza, who had failed to note Signor Claricia's agony, handed Lord Berrybender a soupspoon.

"Thanks, my girl," he said, and dug into the stew.

Little Onion wondered if she ought to flee. She had only hoped to improve her friend's health a little, and now Lord Berrybender was about to have his mouth set on fire.

But to everyone's astonishment, particularly Aldo Claricia's, Lord Berrybender ate the stew as he would any other dish. In a moment the bowl was empty.

"Very tasty," he said. "Best stew I ever had, in fact. Why not give the hen to the local girls—that way I can have a bit more of this good peppery stew."

Signor Claricia could hardly believe what he was seeing.

"But isn't it hot?" he inquired.

Lord Berrybender accepted a second large bowl from Cook, sniffing it as if it were a rare wine.

"Of course it's hot—it's supposed to be hot, signor," he said. "That's the whole point of the chilis."

He ate the second bowl with relish.

"Hope you'll see that we always have a good supply of those tasty little chilis—the green ones," he said, when he finished. "The red ones I find rather bland."

Cook contemplated the stew, of which there was still plenty. She knew she had better learn to cook it. When His Lordship liked a dish he would soon be calling for it again.

When Aldo Claricia found out that Little Onion had provided the stew in hopes of improving his health he flew into a fine Mediterranean rage, which Little Onion weathered patiently. Later in the evening she had her reward. Signor Claricia, once asleep, was breathing normally. The chilis had cleared his head. The next morning he was feeling so good that he did something he had always wanted to do. He pinched Little Onion's bottom and tried to give her a hearty kiss.

Little Onion was profoundly shocked. What was Mr. Aldo thinking? She fled to the nursery, trembling and confused. Buffum, Vicky, and Mary were all there, helping Tasmin watch the babies. When the women understood that all that had happened was a pinch and a kiss, they were much amused.

"That's just how men are," Mary assured her.

"Particularly, it's how Italians are," Buffum added.

"Shut up, for her it's important!" Tasmin insisted. "It's one of those moments when life changes. I'm myself good friends with Kit Carson and George Catlin and Father Geoff. Doesn't mean I want them kissing me, of a sudden."

"Then they can kiss me!" Petal exclaimed, though she had not been following the conversation.

"But perhaps his intentions are serious," Buffum suggested. "Perhaps he wants to marry our Onion. I do believe she loves him. What then?"

"Each of us has followed our hearts," she added. "Why shouldn't Little Onion have some happiness? Jim hardly needs two wives."

"Mr. James Snow can have as many wives as he wants," Kate Berrybender said.

Mopsy began to whine, as he often did at stressful moments.

"Be quiet, you puppy!" Petal ordered.

"I will take this up with Jim when he comes back," Tasmin promised. "Though I *will* say that being allowed to follow one's heart is no guarantee of earthly bliss."

Petal began to drag the dog around the room by the tail, which irritated Monty. He came over and tackled his sister. Mopsy escaped. Petal bumped her head on the tile floor.

"Bumped," she cried, hoping for a broad show of sympathy. But her mother and her aunts remained unimpressed by her injury, so she flung herself into Little Onion's arms.

"Shameless child," Mary remarked. "I fear our Onion is too softhearted."

"Go away, Mary," Petal said.

. . . very staid, very severe.

Doña Eleanora knew that lecturing her young niece on the scandalous impropriety of her liaison with Lord Berrybender was bound to be wasted breath. Julietta Olivaries, reckless to a fault, vain from birth, secure in her high position, would not listen. Yet the Governor's wife herself had come especially to try and persuade Doña Eleanora to make some attempt to curb this wild girl, whose excesses were so blatant that they seemed to threaten civic order. Santa Fe was not Paris—it was a small place, and its handful of respectable families were very staid, very severe. The behavior of young señoritas was strictly chaperoned. Girls married whom they were expected to marry. The young officers might priss and preen a bit, flirting with their superiors' wives and daughters; it was a way of livening up balls. Doña Eleanora, herself a renowned beauty in her youth, had had suggestions whispered in her ear by some of the bolder young officers. A few had even attempted to bestow kisses on her fine plump shoulders, but in Santa Fe, by and large, courtship was a game with strict rules. Doña Eleanora had made a good match— her husband ran the Treasury. With any luck he would be governor someday himself, besides which he was handsome, lively, and the best dancer in Santa Fe. He knew the rules and codes as well as she did. Once a charming young officer had been seated by Doña Eleanora at dinner. He let a hand rest on her knee, a gesture she tolerated. But when the hand attempted to move up, Doña Eleanora took it in both of hers and pushed it away. "Someday, perhaps," she said. "Not now." After all, why close off possibilities? Her handsome husband might die. Besides, just across the table, her husband was paying witty attentions to the Governor's young niece. Life, after all, was to be lived. Her husband would soon have to make his biannual visit to the City of Mexico—a long and hazardous trip. The "someday" might come for the young officer, if it appeared that he was capable of playing by the rules.

Rules, however, meant nothing to Julietta Olivaries, a young woman bitterly discontent in her exile and determined to do exactly as she pleased. When her aunt suggested that she might be a little more discreet in her liaison with Lord Berrybender, Julietta arched her lovely neck and practically spat with fury.

"Some peasants saw you naked in a buggy, doing something ugly with that old Englishman," Doña Eleanora told her. "You'll bring disgrace on us. At least you could go inside, if you want to do these nasty things.

"Besides, it must be awkward," she added—she tried to picture herself doing the nasty things in a buggy and concluded that it wouldn't work. But Julietta, of course, was young and lithe. Acrobatic love would come easier for her.

"I like doing things in a buggy," Julietta told her aunt. "I don't care if the peasants see me."

"But he's so old!" Doña Eleanora remarked, trying to think of some argument that would register with this defiant little bitch.

Julietta gave her an icy smile. "You forget my history," she said. "That old French banker they married me to was nearly eighty. He even had a wart on his prick. Then they put me in a convent and the nuns beat me. When I ran away they caught me and sent me to Mexico, where I was expected to marry an old hidalgo, whose bad sons raped me. I bit one of them, so they sent me here, to the end of the world. I can behave any way I want. There are no more places they can send me, unless they give me to a wild Indian or something. Lord Berrybender is a great noble. He does as he pleases. If we want to play games in a buggy no one can stop us!"

"His wife is a fine musician," Doña Eleanora remarked.

"She was only a servant," Julietta replied, with a look of scorn. "She bores him and I don't."

Doña Eleanora gave up. No one could control this girl—there was no one in either the New or the Old World who could make her behave. She took her pleasures where she found them. The Olivarieses had always been that way.

Later, when Julietta flounced out, Doña

Eleanora tried again to picture what had
gone on in the buggy. Would she, a woman
of mature dimensions, be able to do it? She
had to admit that it was an exciting thought.

⊰ **16** ⊱

*A troublemaker, that one—a great
beauty . . .*

The Governor didn't quite know how to
begin. All Santa Fe was talking about Lord
Berrybender and the Olivaries girl. A troublemaker, that one—a great beauty with an
absolute absence of morals. The old families who supported his governorship were
outraged. Some of them wanted the English
people sent away. Pressure was mounting
on the Governor to do something. And yet,
in financial respects, the old lord had been
liberality itself. His wife and daughters spent
lavishly in the Plaza, on jewelry mostly. His
cook bought pigs and sheep and goats for
the table. Lord Berrybender even had no
objection to ransoming himself, when the
time came to leave. He was a genial, agreeable man of the world who much enlivened
Santa Fe's staid society. If the Olivaries girl

hadn't shown up, there would have been no trouble—perhaps a wife or two would have been seduced, but wives were always being seduced, if not by Lord Berrybender, then by someone else. It was this wild highborn girl who upset everything.

So the Governor had invited Lord Berrybender to the Palace, to talk about the situation, and Lord Berrybender, as genial as ever, had come.

Still, the Governor didn't know quite how to begin.

"Julietta is very beautiful, yes?" he offered.

"She certainly is," Lord Berrybender agreed. "I met her father at Salamanca—he was on the other side, of course. The whole family's beautiful. Julietta's a top-grade beauty. She's got that long Olivaries neck."

"And your lovely wife?" the Governor inquired. He felt in a heavy quandary. Who was he to tell this English lord what to do? He might be the Governor of Nuevo México, and yet, facing Lord Berrybender, he felt like a provincial clerk.

"Haven't seen much of Vicky lately," Lord Berrybender admitted. "Got my hands full with Julietta—vexing little wench she can be. No inclination to stint, when it comes to fornication."

"There was something about a buggy," the Governor said, awkwardly. "The people are talking, a bit."

Lord Berrybender looked puzzled. Something about a buggy. *What* about a buggy?

Then he remembered—it had been Julietta's idea. She was always looking for ways to spice up the tupping—had little interest in just the common old grind. It had been touch and go, he had to admit. Of course, Julietta was nimble as a cat. No problem for her to skip around. A little harder for himself, of course, but the occasion had been on the whole a success. Julietta got quite stirred up. But how the devil had the Governor learned about it?

"Some people saw you—some peasants," the Governor told him.

"Doesn't surprise *me*—I told Julietta there were bound to be people around," Lord Berrybender replied. "Annoyed her that I bothered to mention it. Called me provincial. Me! High and mighty folk, the Olivarieses. Of course I didn't want to look a prude. Suspected there might be a peasant or two, peeking at us. But there's no restraining a girl like Julietta, not when she's bent on her pleasure."

"A man in your position, a great nobleman, should be careful," the Governor mumbled.

"Now, now, Governor, you've got it backward," Lord B. said pleasantly. "It's the peasant folk who have to be careful. A man in my position doesn't have to be careful. That's the whole point of being a man in my position—you can do as you damn please, and the devil take the hindmost."

The Governor made no answer. He looked unhappy.

Lord Berrybender felt a little bored. What the devil did the man want? To chide him over a little tupping? Julietta would be much amused, once he reported.

"How's *your* wife?" he asked. "Didn't see her at the dance last night. Missed her, in fact. I always enjoy a dance or two with Margareta. Crippled as I am, I still like to hobble around with the pretty ladies."

Since discovering his wife in the storeroom, whipping Tomas, the Governor had become a silent man. His secretaries and scribes didn't know what to make of it. Sometimes he sat silently at his desk most of the day, staring out the window. He was the *Governor,* a man who wielded great power, and yet now he felt powerless. It seemed to him that the peasants, even the barefoot Indians, were luckier than he. He could not get the thought of his sweaty wife out of his mind. He didn't like even to walk past that storeroom. There were other handsome boys in his employ; lately several of them had looked down in embarrassment when he approached them. Perhaps they too had been led to the storeroom, stripped, and whipped. A governor could not stop work. Already more than one hundred documents awaited his signature. And yet he sat; he looked. At home Margareta ignored him. When she did look at him it was with defiance.

Lord Berrybender saw that the Governor seemed to be preoccupied—at mention of his wife he had seemed to flinch. Mildly curious, Lord Berrybender tried again.

"Doña Margareta *is* well, isn't she? No trouble, I hope."

"She likes to whip boys," the Governor blurted out.

"What's that?" Lord B. thought he must have misheard.

"She whips boys," the Governor said,

tonelessly, ashamed of speaking and yet unable to stop.

Lord Berrybender supposed that to be a small matter. Servants often needed disciplining.

"Good for her," he said. "Doesn't do to be soft with servants. I've had plenty whipped myself."

But the Governor, now that he had launched into his revelation, wanted the matter made clear.

"They are good boys, all of them," he said. "She whips them because it gives her pleasure."

Lord Berrybender, about to take his leave, sat back down in his chair.

"Oh, I see—*that* kind of whipping," he said. "Do the boys enjoy it?"

It occurred to him that he had been rather attracted to Doña Margareta when he first got to town. There was scorn in her look— he found that rather interesting. A man only needed to know how to put such feelings to good use.

"The boys are ashamed," the Governor assured him. "Some of them may even leave the service."

"Oh now, that's surely unnecessary,"

Lord Berrybender replied. "Women *will* play their games—no wilder I suppose than what Julietta and I did in the buggy—though if it's only a one-way game that's rather different.

"Wouldn't have supposed it to be a Latin flourish," he added. "Far more of an English thing—or German—or Dutch. My daughter Mary used to flagellate her little botanist, you know, and he's as Dutch as they come."

Lord Berrybender felt rather wistful—he wished he had made a point to get to know Doña Margareta better.

"You might try taking her to England, Governor," he said. "There's a different attitude toward rustication there. Doña Margareta could easily find plenty of English lads who'd let her whip them. Some have even been known to pay for it."

The Governor was nonplussed. "Pay to be whipped?" he asked.

"Why not?" Lord B. said. "I suppose it reminds them of school. Canings and such. *I* never liked it particularly, but it's surely no reason to leave the service. All part of the great sport of love. Julietta bouncing up and down in a buggy, while Doña Margareta would rather be whipping a boy. Whatever it takes, I say. Whatever it takes."

17

Below them in the Plaza, the grandees of Santa Fe . . .

"Julietta's worse than I ever was," Tasmin remarked to Father Geoff.

Below them in the Plaza, the grandees of Santa Fe were enjoying their evening promenade. Old widows, dressed in black, strolled hand in hand. Vicky stood watching too, with angry eyes. Her husband, Lord Berrybender, was hobbling along with his young mistress, whose beauty was evident even in the dusk.

"Oh, you weren't so bad—you've only had one affair, unless I missed something. Perhaps a rather limited one at that."

"*Very* limited—it hardly counts," Tasmin said. "I was prepared to be faithful to Pomp forever, and yet now I can hardly remember him."

"When I married Albany I supposed I'd be

happy," Vicky said. "I supposed I'd have someone to promenade with, in the evenings."

"Now, now . . . no self-pity," Tasmin told her. "We've all made our beds. There's no reason to suppose they'd be easy beds."

"And also no reason to think a little slut from Spain would show up and steal Albany," Vicky said. She could barely control her bitterness.

Lately Tasmin had had a talk or two with Julietta Olivaries and had to admit that she rather liked her. She was determined to escape the inevitable arrangements that were made for highborn girls in the old country. Tasmin had begun to suspect that she and Julietta were a good deal alike. Of course, the girl was willful—but so had she been.

"If you married Papa expecting fidelity, then you were a very great fool," Tasmin told Vicky.

But Vicky, larger now, was staring at Lord B. and his slim mistress. Hatred kept her rooted.

"I must seem a cow beside her," she remarked. Then she burst into tears and left the balcony.

"Julietta won't be slim either, if she lets Papa start giving her babies," Tasmin said.

Father Geoff did not seem interested.

"I suppose life is inevitably coarsening," Tasmin declared, poking him with her elbow to see if he might stir. "One's choice is to be coarse or be dead. I'll take coarse, myself."

"I miss Bobbety," Father Geoff admitted suddenly. "It's all very well to read poetry and novels, but it doesn't compare to having a true friend."

"Ain't I a true friend?" Tasmin asked.

"Yes, but you're strong—Bobbety wasn't," Geoff told her. "I was the person he turned to when he was sad. I admit I liked that."

Tasmin heard a squeal from the nursery— the squeal was coming from Petey, the softer of her twins. What if Petey, like Bobbety, grew up to be sad? The likelihood of Petey beating Petal at much of anything was remote—it made Tasmin love him the more. She went in to discover Petey in tears and Petal, the picture of innocence, playing with some blocks.

"Did you hurt your brother?" Tasmin asked.

"Petey had the blocks first and she knocked him down," Monty reported. Petal looked at him sullenly—Monty never took her side.

"Petey doesn't know how to stack," Petal said coolly. "He was going to make the blocks all fall down."

"That's hardly a reason to knock *him* down," Tasmin said. "Sharing is a virtue, you know."

"She never shares, and besides that she steals," Monty said. "She stole my big marble."

Petal had in fact hidden the marble in one of her mother's pouches—for good measure she shoved the pouch under her mother's bed, where it would never be found.

"Your father's coming soon," Tasmin told her. "We'll see what he makes of this behavior."

With a sweep of her hand Petal knocked down the tower of blocks. This was not welcome news—Petal was not sure she liked her father.

"His beard's too scratchy," Petal said. "I don't want him to come."

"Then he'll merely have that much more

time with Monty and Petey, which I'm sure he'll enjoy," her mother told her.

Petal, kicking out wildly, scattered the blocks all over the room.

18

. . . the bearded stranger was first brought into the nursery . . .

The twins had been almost eight months old when Jim came to Santa Fe a second time. He had meant to be back sooner, but the trip east with the goods train was a trip where everything went wrong. The Bents had insisted that he use mules—faster than oxen—but the party had been repeatedly harassed by Indians and some of the mules were stolen. It was unusually wet; several more mules got foot rot. A drover was killed in an ambush. Jim was forced to go east and secure replacement mules before he could bring the goods to the river. Once delivery was complete, he hurried back as quickly as he could.

On *that* visit, when the bearded stranger was first brought into the nursery, Petal, not yet speaking, set out to charm him, only to

discover that he seemed to be more interested in Monty, who was ecstatic to see his
father; Monty clung so tight that Petal had
few openings. Also, it was on that visit that
the really bad thing happened: her father
and mother went into the bedroom together
and the door was firmly locked. Petal's efforts to push it open only made it rattle.
When she cried out in protest, Little Onion,
not her mother, came and carried her away
to a place where she could not interfere with
what was going on behind the door.

Petey soon forgot the episode of the
closed door, but Petal didn't. The first rule of
her life was that she must always come first
with her mother. That a stranger with a
beard should preempt this right was intolerable. Every time she found her mother's
door locked she kicked it and screeched
with anger until Little Onion came and carried her away. For the rest of that visit Petal
ignored her father completely. She wanted
him to go away, so that things could be as
before. But he didn't go quickly—her
mother's door continued to be locked, a
source of deep bitterness to Petal.

In her months of grief Tasmin had feared
that she might never want any man again,

but this time, when Jim kissed her she did not put him off. She was soon a wife again. On the day before his next departure the bedroom door stayed locked all day. Petal, wiser, did not rattle it; but she listened: she heard scufflings, little cries. In time Tasmin developed suspicions. Holding a shawl in front of her, she got up and suddenly opened the door. Petal crawled away as fast as she could go. Tasmin, naked behind her shawl, did not pursue. She got back in bed and put her hand on her husband—she liked it that she could still make him hard with a touch. She had now borne three children—she felt that she must be aging rapidly, but Jim seemed not to want her less, which was reassuring. Yet their lovemaking didn't lessen the complexity of life. The Berrybenders had been in Santa Fe for a year; Tasmin was for staying another year, for the sake of the babies—but Jim didn't like the town, or any town. What would he do?

"Guide for the Bents, I guess," Jim said. "They never get enough. Now they're wanting me and Kit to lay out a route to California. They think it's the coming place."

"What does that mean—how many

months?" Tasmin asked. As always, when she actually *had* Jim, she was reluctant to relinquish him to the prairies, even though she knew he would never tolerate city life for long.

"Half a year, maybe more," Jim said. "I'm not anxious to take Kit. He can't travel ten yards without complaining."

"I wish I could go with you, but I'd be afraid for Petey—he's not strong," she said. "How quickly children alter the way of things."

Jim was a little surprised that Tasmin wanted to come—but then she had never shied from adventure. But he judged the situation too uncertain, the water scarce, the Indians most likely hostile. With three young children it made no sense to take her.

Then his eye caught a movement—the little girl had crept back to the doorway. As soon as she saw that her father had seen her, she scuttled away again. After that she ceased to have anything to do with Jim. He was a serious interloper. A man that caused her mother to lock her out was bad.

One day Kit showed up—were they going to California, or not? To Kit's shock Tasmin flew into him as violently as she had the day

he descended into camp in the hot-air bal-
loon.

"Don't you rush us, Kit Carson!" she
raged. "If the Bents are in such a hurry, let
them go themselves."

Kit wondered why, in Tasmin's eyes, he
could never do anything right. All he was
asking was that Jim make up his mind.

That night Tasmin and Jim visited the
nursery—all the children were asleep. Seeing them sleeping, the two little boys and
the little girl, Jim had an odd feeling, half
proud, half sad. Tasmin clung to his arm—
she felt distressed.

"It's no more dangerous to try for California than it is on the Santa Fe Trail," Jim reminded her.

"Jimmy, just don't talk about danger anymore," Tasmin pled. "I was there when the
Utes came, and the Pawnees. I drank that
awful froth from the horse's belly. I can
imagine the dangers all too well.

"Just come back," she added, grimly.
"Just see that you come back."

Jim felt so much tension that night that
he got up and began to get his few things
together. Thinking about going was too mis-

erable. Better just to go. But Tasmin wouldn't have it.

"I'll just have you one more night, thank you," she said. But tension even overrode passion. Neither could sleep. Both lay awake, staring. Tasmin contented herself with a few timid kisses.

"This is awful, you're right, go," she finally said, just before dawn.

When Petal woke up she immediately crawled to her mother's room—to her delight the door was wide open and the bearded stranger gone. The old order was restored. Petal went back to the nursery and began to hide some of Petey's toys.

. . . there he was again, kissing her mother . . .

Petal had almost forgotten the bearded stranger when she came round the corner and there he was again, kissing her mother, who clung to him happily. It shocked Petal so that she walked into the nursery and pressed her face into a corner—her new way of showing extreme displeasure. When people refused to do what she wanted them to she hid her face in a corner until Monty or some big person pulled her out and offered compromise. The only person who didn't seem to care when Petal removed herself to her corner was her mother, who proposed no compromises.

"You can stand there a week, if you want to be stubborn," Tasmin said. "Why should one care?"

Jim thought Petal the very image of Tasmin, with high similarity of disposition too. She looked daggers at him when he tried to play with her a little: it was the same look Tasmin gave him, when she was angry. He not only had a forceful wife, he now had a forceful daughter too.

After enduring another day in which her mother's door was firmly locked, much of which she spent with her face pressed bitterly in a corner, Petal decided to take her concerns directly to the intruder—the man had gained a power over her mother that was not acceptable.

The next day, catching her father alone, she made a blunt demand.

"You go away from here," she said. "And you go quick."

Jim was amused. The child's tone of voice was exactly like Tasmin's, if she happened to be giving Kit Carson an order.

"I been gone so long you nearly got grown on me," Jim told her. "Why do I have to go away?"

"You bother my mother too much," Petal said. "That's why."

"What if your mother likes for me to bother her?" Jim suggested. "Suppose she'd *rather* I bother her."

Petal didn't like this equivocation. Why wouldn't the tall man just go?

"When you go away I can take my nap with Mommy," Petal explained.

"Well, you're welcome to take your nap with both of us, I guess," Jim said. "You and Petey too, and Monty."

The last thing Petal was prepared to tolerate was having her brothers around at nap time. Nap time meant her and her mother— no strangers.

"You bother my mother too much, that's why you have to go away," Petal insisted, returning to her original charge.

A few hours later, clutching the blue rooster, Petal wandered into her mother's bedroom, only to find the tall stranger there beside her mother.

"I told him to go away, he bothers you too much," Petal insisted.

"In fact he doesn't bother me at all, little girl," Tasmin said. "He bothers *you!*"

Exasperated that her mother would take such a tack, Petal went immediately to a corner and pressed her face into it. Her mother and the tall man took no notice. If she threw a tantrum Little Onion would come and carry her away. After a bit she left the corner and approached the bed. She gave the tall man a bit of a smile.

"Lift me up," she said—and he did.

"Now she's going to pile on the charm," Tasmin warned.

Petal tried to put her hand over her mother's bad mouth.

"I have a blue rooster," she remarked, holding it up so Jim could inspect it.

"Here comes the charm," Tasmin said.

Petal ignored her mother. "His name is Cockadoodle," she said.

"I eat roosters," Jim said, deadpan.

Petal was taken aback. She studied her opponent.

"Blue roosters make mighty good eating," Jim said.

Petal put the rooster behind her.

"It was Petey's rooster but he gave it to me," she said.

"What an outrageous lie!" Tasmin said. "You stole that rooster."

"It followed me home," Petal said, keeping a close eye on the stranger.

"She'll argue for hours, you won't wear her down," Tasmin warned.

"I may be hungry when I wake up from

my nap," Jim said. "I may want to eat a rooster. I hope I can find a blue one."

He then shut his eyes—in a minute he emitted a faint snore.

"I hope he goes away," Petal remarked.

"It won't help you—next time he goes away we're going with him," Tasmin informed her.

Petal studied the sleeping man. Then she slipped off the bed and hid the blue rooster amid Little Onion's kit. It was going to be necessary to watch this sleeping man.

. . . when it came to deciding on a route the two could not agree.

Though they had been absent from Santa Fe for almost a year, Jim and Kit had not attempted California; when it came to deciding on a route, the two could not agree. Kit insisted that the better route lay south, along the Gila River. Jim, who wanted to strike due west, was taken aback.

"The Gila River?" he said. "We'll starve before we get anywhere near the Gila River."

"That's the way I'm going, you can do as you please," said Kit.

A moment later, though, he revealed more conflicted feelings.

"Josie don't want me to go at all," he admitted. "If the dern Bents like California so much, let them go. Josie don't think it's right for a husband to take off and be gone that long."

"I expect most wives would take that line," Jim told him.

While they were grappling with these issues the matter was settled for them by the surprising arrival of a counterorder from the Bents, delivered by the taciturn old hunter Lonesome Dick, who seemed put out that he had had to ride so hard on their behalf.

"I've sweated my horse," the old man said, leaving no doubt that he considered it their fault.

"It don't hurt a horse to sweat," Kit pointed out. "What do they want now?"

"They want you to go to New Orleans," Lonesome Dick informed them. "I'm going to Californy. If they'd sent me in the first place I'd already be halfway there."

"Dick's never been friendly," Kit said, as they watched the old man ride off.

Two months later the two of them were on the under deck of a Mississippi River steamer, watching the low buildings of Saint Louis fade out of sight to the stern. It seemed that a large shipment of goods off an English ship that had encountered foul weather had been put off at New Orleans, rather than Baltimore, as had been planned. It was said to contain Lord Berrybender's new guns, as well as a large quantity of cloth and other tradable items.

Kit, who couldn't imagine an easier way to travel than by steamboat, was in high spirits.

"I bet there's a passel of fish in this river," he claimed. "They say catfish get as big as horses."

"If there's fish that big I'd hope to stay out of their way," Jim observed. "A whale swallowed down Jonah, I recall."

He was glad to be out of Saint Louis—its jostle and stench were not to his liking—but he at once took to steamboat travel. He found that he could sit and watch the widening waters for hours, letting his thoughts drift to no purpose. Clouds formed; rainstorms blew in and blew out. Jim preferred the spacious, grassy plains to the thick forests that now covered the shores, but the river itself he liked. Kit felt the same.

"It'd be easy, being a waterman," he said. "You just float along—no tramping."

"We'll get plenty of tramping on the way back," Jim reminded him. Charles Bent, ever hopeful of new territory, wanted them to pack the goods overland much of the way back, crossing a long stretch of dangerous country. It was Charles Bent's opinion that there would soon be a steady stream of immigrants along the southern route, and he meant to have a trading post somewhere along it, preferably near the Canadian River. Scouting possible locations was Jim and Kit's real mission.

"Time waits for no man," Charles Bent declared. "If we don't get us a post down that way you can bet somebody else will."

Neither Jim nor Kit felt any eagerness to see what the southern tribes felt about this—they agreed in advance to avoid these tribes, particularly the Comanches, and concentrate on getting the goods safely back to the big post on the Arkansas. If Charles Bent wanted to persuade the Comanches to lay down their lances and scalping knives, let him do it himself.

As the steamer proceeded south, the gradual widening of the river filled Jim with amazement. He had never expected to be riding safely down such a vastness of water. The constant traffic in all manner of boats, as they approached the port, was in itself a delight to watch.

The gradual spread of the great plain of water had a sobering effect on Kit.

"A river this big could swallow this boat like a pill," he observed. "I could never swim a river this wide. I'd be drownt."

"Or swallowed by one of them big catfish," Jim reminded him. On several occasions the boatmen, using ropes for lines, had hooked catfish that were not much smaller than horses; the fish were so large that they had to be cut up before their flesh could be brought on deck.

"The more I think about all this water the less I like it," Kit remarked.

"We'll be there tomorrow—go away if you're going to complain," Jim protested. "I'd like to enjoy the sights, if you don't mind."

Jim sat on deck all night, watching the starlight on the water, listening to unfamiliar bird cries, wondering why the movement of water was so soothing.

The turmoil on the docks was more intense even than what they had encountered in Saint Louis.

"I am certainly surprised to know there

are so many black people in the world," Kit said.

Jim was surprised on that score too—although the shades of color on the New Orleans waterfront were more various than he had seen anywhere. There were very black people, and lightly black people; there were yellow people and people the color of coffee; Spanish people, Choctaw Indians, French sailors, English sailors, large whores and small whores; drunks lying in the mud; wagons being loaded and boats being unloaded; fishermen hawking their catch: such a bustle of people that Jim wished immediately to be back on the broad, calm river. Besides the jostle, he felt closed in by the heavy vegetation. The humid air left them both sweating profusely. Flies and mosquitoes were persistent. They passed a pen full of dusty cattle, and another pen full of silent, apathetic slaves.

All the waterfront was a boil of activity, heaps of goods piled here and there; and yet no one seemed to be in charge. Neither Jim nor Kit had any clear idea of how to locate the goods they were supposed to secure. While they were considering the problem two small men fell to cursing one another in a tongue neither Jim nor Kit could recognize. The men had blue bandannas on their heads. They quickly fell to fighting with knives—a crowd gathered, drawn by the possibility of violence: the crowd was not disappointed. Neither sailor was killed, but both were cut—the dusty ground beneath them was soon bloody. Finally the two combatants stopped and walked away together.

Jim eventually managed to locate a wizened little man with long chin whiskers who seemed to be an inspector of some kind. When Jim mentioned the English boat that had supposedly unloaded, the little man nodded.

"It's about time somebody got here," he said. "It's six months now we've been putting up with that cannibal."

"Where's a cannibal?" Kit asked, not pleased.

The small inspector, whose name was Bailey, led them quickly through an alley where two pigs were quarreling over a fat brownish snake. When they came out of the alley Inspector Bailey pointed to a grassy spot under some huge trees draped with trailing whiskers of Spanish moss. The boxes and bales piled up were being guarded by an enormous black man, who sat comfortably on one of the bales, fanning himself with a hat.

"That's the cannibal—calls himself Juppy," Inspector Bailey told them. "Take him with you, if you don't mind."

Jim and Kit were startled by the size of the man, who was light brown rather than black. They had both seen tall men before, but none as tall as this man—and in most cases the tall men were skinny. But this man was thick in the trunk; his arms and legs were massive, as were his thighs.

"Why do you think he's a cannibal?" Jim asked.

"People don't get that big by eating regular food," Inspector Bailey declared. "There's a witch up the street that's been trying to poison him, but the poison don't take. That's a sure sign of a cannibal.

"Come by my shack and sign the bill of lading when you're loaded," the inspector told them.

"Loaded? Loaded how?" Jim inquired. "We don't have a wagon yet."

"Juppy's got a wagon, and the mules to

pull it," the inspector informed them, before departing.

The big black man was walking toward them now, seeming to cover the yards in only a step or two.

"Would you be the gentlemen from Messieurs Bent, St. Vrain and Company, by any chance?" the large man asked, smiling agreeably. "I hope so because I'm ready to travel—too many little old black witches in this town. I'm Juppy."

He extended a very large hand—somewhat at a loss, Jim and Kit shook it.

"I hope you're not a cannibal," Kit told him. He had begun to feel some anxiety on that score and felt it best to be frank.

Juppy laughed an easy laugh.

"See any tasty-looking people around here?" he asked. "All I see are some ugly sailors and a few old skinny witches. Nobody plump enough to eat."

Then Juppy laughed.

"Just joking," he said. "If you're from the Bents I guess we better get loaded so we can be on our way."

Jim and Kit felt uneasy. Charles Bent had said nothing about a black giant named Juppy.

"Nobody told us about you," Jim admitted. The giant seemed perfectly friendly, but he certainly was a giant. On a practical level, bringing him with them posed problems. Could they expect to find a horse big enough to carry such a heavy man?

"Don't be worryin'," Juppy said. "I've made all the arrangements, and I've got my mule, Jupiter—he's been my mount since I was thirteen. My instructions from Father were to give you every assistance, but not to let his expensive new guns out of my sight, and they haven't been out of my sight since I picked them up in London. As you'll see I've not wasted my wait—I've got a good bunch of pack animals and a wagon we can use as long as the terrain permits wagon travel. The upriver steamer leaves at six. We better start loading, don't you think?"

Jim and Kit were deeply puzzled. Juppy was efficient, as well as friendly. He had got things ready. The pack mules looked healthy. And yet he referred to his father's instructions. Who could his father be?

"Why, Lord Berrybender, who else?" Juppy informed then. "I assumed you knew."

Jim and Kit could only shake their heads. Of course both of them had heard that Lord Berrybender had fathered a great many bastards, but no one had informed them that one of his bastards was a brown giant.

"He probably didn't mention me because he wants to surprise the girls—my half sisters," Juppy speculated. "Papa met my mother in a circus—she was the giantess."

Jim and Kit were still startled, but Juppy produced the wagon and the pack animals and loaded most of the bundles and bales. By six they were on an upriver steamer. There had been some awkwardness at the customs shed. Jim and Kit were forced to admit that neither of them could write their name. The bills of lading were incomprehensible to them. Inspector Bailey handed the papers to Juppy, who inspected them closely and signed them "Jupiter."

"Jupiter, same name as my mule," Juppy said, with a smile.

Soon they were aboard the boat, watching the great river pour on toward the sea.

. . . knocking over a bowl of pudding . . .

When Petal looked up and saw the brown giant in the doorway of the nursery she screamed as loud as she could and raced for Little Onion, who was rather surprised herself. Jim Snow, just returned, had already been in for a visit with Tasmin, but he had said nothing about the brown giant. Juppy wanted to be a surprise.

Only that morning Petal had caused trouble in the kitchen, knocking over a bowl of pudding in her eagerness to lick the spoon; she compounded her disgrace by allowing Mopsy to eat most of her porridge. Efforts to make her behave were met with the usual defiance, exasperating Cook so that she told Petal that a big black giant would soon arrive to carry her off.

Petal was used to such threats from

Cook—indeed, used to threats from everybody. Very few of them were ever carried
out; Petal merrily went on doing as she
pleased, which was why the sight of the big
brown giant was such a tremendous shock.
She had never thought a *real* giant would
appear—and yet there one stood. Worse
yet, he was blocking the doorway. There
was no way she could flee the room.

Tasmin was bending over Petey, tending
a rash he had broken out with, when Petal
screamed. Petal was hoping her mother
might know a way to kill the giant, but instead her mother forgot Petey and, with a
big smile of happiness, jumped into the
giant's arms, kissing him warmly.

"Oh, Juppy!" she cried. "Mary, Buffum—
Juppy's come!"

Soon, to Petal's astonishment, her two
aunts had run into the room and were hugging the brown giant. Then her grandfather
came—he began to weep at the sight of the
giant.

"Why, Juppy boy—here you are at last,"
Lord Berrybender exclaimed. "Did you bring
my leg and my guns?"

"Got the leg, got the guns—looks like I

should have brought you a few fingers, while I was at it," Juppy said.

Then Cook, who rarely left her pots and kettles, came and gave Juppy a hug. The five little boys watched, astonished. Petey even forgot to scratch his rash. Mopsy raced around, frenzied with excitement, until Kate Berrybender caught him and insisted that he calm down.

"I hid him at Kit's," Jim admitted, when Tasmin wanted to know why he had shown up before her half brother. "He wanted to be a big surprise, and I guess he was."

Despite the fact that her mother and her aunts and even Cook were clearly fond of Juppy, Petal did not entirely lose her initial apprehension. What if the giant was only pretending to be good? What if his real purpose was to carry her off?

"So what's the news from Northampton-shire, Juppy?" Tasmin asked. Petey was sitting in Juppy's lap, a sight that greatly pleased her.

"The worst news is that Nanny Craigie died," Juppy reported—the news sobered them all.

"Not Nanny Craigie!" Tasmin exclaimed.

"I don't know why, but I thought she'd live forever."

"She didn't," Juppy said simply.

"Then who's looking after the younger brats?" Mary wanted to know.

"Nobody, they're running wild," Juppy admitted.

Tasmin felt a sudden stab of homesickness, a deep longing to be back in the home of her youth: back in their green and gray England. It was a brief stab, but intense. She leaned her head against Juppy's big arm.

"I'm so glad you came," she said. "We're all glad—very glad."

Petal soon came to be of the opinion that the big giant was harmless, after all. Ordinarily she would have gone over and shoved Petey out of his lap—on principle—but with her mother sitting so close she didn't quite dare. Her mother was too likely to take Petey's side. Petal had three times been spanked, for treating Petey roughly—an outrageous abuse. Still, it was not her way to allow anyone to deny her pride of place for long. After studying the situation for a moment, Petal moved. She marched over to the big man and squeezed into his lap, next to her twin.

"You have a big lap," she announced. "It can hold two."

"It sure can, little miss," Juppy said.

22

Even peasants gave way to hot impulse.

Julietta Olivaries had become Lord Berry-bender's mistress without hesitation—the very first time she was seated next to him at a formal dinner, she had signified her readiness by fondling him under the table. She even managed to get his cock out of his pants, and this before the dinner guests had quite finished their soup. Across the table Lord Berrybender's wife was watching them closely—very likely she had fondled him at table at some point herself. Lady Berrybender was a full-bosomed, beautiful woman, if a commoner. Julietta felt no overwhelming physical attraction to the tipsy old lord, but she did like his aristocratic manner, a manner that tolerated no scruples when it came to amorous activity. In Santa Fe only Lord Berrybender and herself could naturally assume the prerogatives of high aristocracy. Her own aunt, Doña Eleanora, was a settled housewife now. Lady Tasmin was certainly aristocratic, and looked to be a creature of hot impulse, but then, in Julietta's view, hot impulse was common. Even peasants gave way to hot impulse. What attracted her to Lord Berrybender was that his impulses were cool, not hot. He simply disregarded rules; he did as he pleased, not fastidiously but boldly.

Julietta felt just as privileged when it came to disregarding restrictions on her behavior. It infuriated her that she had been sent to Santa Fe—she meant to get back to Europe as soon as possible, but in the meantime, she meant to take her pleasures where she found them—and in the case most troubling to her aunt Eleanora, she found them with a blacksmith.

"A blacksmith—a peon! Surely not!" Doña Eleanora exclaimed, when Julietta casually confirmed a rumor that had been going around.

"We'll be disgraced," she added.

Julietta shrugged. "An Olivaries can be disliked but not disgraced," she pointed out. "We can do as we please. You've been

stuck in this little place too long. You're becoming dull."

"I'd rather be dull than give myself to a
blacksmith," Eleanora replied.

"But that's dull—be dull," Julietta retorted.

The blacksmith looked half Indian. He
was very dark; he had sturdy legs. He
worked with his shirt off—Julietta had often
watched him; sweat made his arms and
belly shiny. She watched him for two weeks
before she took him, looking down from her
window. Watching him work, all sweaty and
greasy, Julietta began to excite herself with
the thought of how it might be with a peon.
She watched him from shadows, gently exciting herself. Then one day at dusk, when
the Plaza was all but empty, she walked
across to the blacksmith's and simply lifted
her skirts. The blacksmith was so startled
that he burned his hand on a horseshoe he
had been straightening. Julietta pushed
past him, into the little dark room where he
slept. She waited for him to come. For a
bed there were only a few rags. At first the
man was so frightened that he couldn't
stiffen. His name was Joaquin; his experience with women had been brief and crude.

Julietta refused to let his nervousness defeat her. She took his balls in her hand; she bit his lip. Then she took off all her clothing—something none of the whores or native girls ever did. Instead of being as brief as possible in copulation, which was what Joaquin was used to, Julietta, once she had him in her, took her time. She did not seem to mind his sweat, his grease, the scratchy rags. She made him work, offered him her backside, made him lie down beneath her. She returned to her room filthy, soiled, her face and breasts red from the scrapings of the young man's stubble.

Every night for a week Julietta went to the blacksmith's—she offered caresses that Joaquin had never known before. Doña Eleanora thought her niece had lost her mind. She didn't bathe, her clothes were sweated through, she reeked. But when she attempted to remonstrate, Julietta merely looked scornful.

"You should try Joaquin sometime," she advised her aunt. "He's learning a few tricks. If you tried him you wouldn't be so dull."

"You're mad," Eleanora told her. "You should be locked up."

But she did sometimes think of what Juli-etta suggested.

Joaquin proved to be good for a week, but only a week. By the time he had be-come bolder, Julietta was bored. One night she abruptly left him; he was erect and pleading—but she left, went home, ordered the sleepy servant girls to draw a good bath. She threw away her sweaty clothes, bathed, slept soundly. Joaquin often looked at her window but Julietta didn't allow him even a glimpse.

A week later she told Lord Berrybender exactly what she had done with the black-smith. She went into detail, described inti-macies that she had not yet permitted His Lordship. Lord Berrybender was eating a bowl of green chili stew at the time. He looked idly up at his outrageous young mis-tress, but didn't lay down his spoon.

"So that's where you've been," he said mildly. "A blacksmith—sturdy specimens, I suppose.

"And younger than me," he added. "That's the crucial point. Age is rarely kind to lechers. I suppose he was a bit grubby, this fellow—part of the appeal. I enjoy a grubby girl myself, from time to time. Get my fill of ladies with their pouts. Juppy's mother was rather a grubby girl. Giantess from Santo Domingo. Juppy's nearly the size of his mother."

"Now there's a stallion," Julietta remarked. "I wonder what *he's* like."

"Juppy doesn't carry on with women," Lord Berrybender told her. "Never known him to."

"What a pity," Julietta said.

23

. . . for some hours she could not be consoled.

"I wish you'd just stop meddling," Jim told his wife. "It's better to just let people be."

Tasmin was in a mood to agree. She had made an attempt to settle the matter of Little Onion's divorce from Jim—in view of her obviously deepening bond with Signor Claricia—only to have everything go wrong. When Buffum, with High Shoulders' help, explained the matter to Little Onion, the girl burst into tears—for some hours she could not be consoled. Tasmin was horrified. She had meant to help the girl yet had only hurt her. That bringing up divorce might make Little Onion feel a failure had not occurred to her—and yet that was exactly what Little Onion felt. If her husband no longer wanted her for a wife, then she had not been good enough, and the only thing to do was go back to her people, a discarded woman. That Jim had never tried to be a husband did not seem very important to Little Onion—she had done her very best to be a good wife anyway—she had done the chores and kept the children. And yet it was over; she was not wanted, she had failed.

When it was explained to her that no criticism was intended, that they had merely supposed she might want to marry her Mr. Aldo, Little Onion looked even more horrified and burst into tears again. She shook her head vigorously; she wanted nothing of the sort. Mr. Aldo was her friend, and she wanted it to stay that way. Jim, finding himself in the middle of an unnecessary crisis, went to Little Onion himself and did his best to smooth things over. He assured her that she had been a fine wife—he had never wished to divorce her. Little Onion had already packed her few things, intent on leaving; but Jim persuaded her to stay, and Tasmin and the family, deeply embarrassed, lavished affection on her. Little Onion agreed to stay, but she was skeptical and, for a time, sad.

A little later she realized that her friendship with Mr. Aldo might have just confused the white people. She liked the old man and wanted to see that he took care of himself. She fed him, kept his clothes mended, doctored him when he was ill; but she did not want to lie with him—nothing of the sort. Lately, it was true, he had become feisty; she sometimes had to fight him off. But that was merely the way of men. Finally Little Onion realized that it was Mr. Aldo's behavior, not hers, that had confused the white people. Slowly, she recovered from her sense of hurt. Someone should just have asked her point-blank about her feelings for Mr. Aldo—then they could have all laughed about it together.

All the Berrybender women were sorry to have hurt Little Onion, but Tasmin was the one who felt the deepest self-reproach. Jim was right; she ought not to meddle. She loved Little Onion—she didn't suppose her children would have survived the dark months of her grief without her Little Onion's loving attention. She did her best to win back the girl's trust—and, in time, she did.

"I suppose it's hopeless, trying to know what others are feeling," she confessed to Jim. "I don't even know what *you're* feeling unless you hit me—then I know you're angry. I could have sworn a romance was brewing between those two—and I was completely wrong."

"You got enough to do—don't be worrying about Onion," Jim said. "She can take care of herself."

"I fear meddling is just what families do—particularly families crammed together in a foreign place," Tasmin countered. "In England we'd have drifted apart by now, most of us."

Then Buffum came in, looking tearful. High Shoulders had been gone on one of his hunts. He had not been seen in ten days—Buffum was overcome with worry, as she always was if her husband was absent more than a week.

"I need to know he's safe," she told them.

"Be glad you aren't married to this one," Tasmin said. "He thinks nothing of absences of six months or more."

Jim quietly left. He didn't want to quarrel about his absences. Only yesterday he had quarreled so violently with Tasmin that he struck her. She had suddenly informed him that she and the children were going to accompany him on all future trips, no matter how arduous they promised to be—yet she knew perfectly well he couldn't do the jobs he was assigned with a wife and three babies in tow. It was absurd—and yet Tasmin flared and he flared—Jim felt cornered, as he always did if he was inside a house.

As he walked past the nursery his daughter spotted him. Petal was still feeling her way with her father. He was a difficult conquest; he could not simply be bossed, like other people. Flirting and cajoling didn't work either, though they worked on Juppy, the brown giant her father had brought back with him.

Nonetheless she pointed a finger at Jim, in a commanding way.

"Come see me, I'm a spider," Petal commanded.

Jim did as ordered.

"Spiders sting," he said. "What if I don't want to be stung?"

"Then behave good," Petal advised. "Behave good, Mr. Sin Killer."

Jim was startled.

"Auntie Mary says that's your other name," Petal explained. "Only I don't know what sin is."

"It's stealing your brothers' toys," Jim informed her. She was holding a small leather burro that he had brought specially for Monty. Petal sat the burro on the floor.

"It followed me," she explained.

"Telling lies is also a sin," her father informed her.

"Fibbing—only fibbing," Petal insisted. "But I was good in the kitchen. I didn't turn over the pudding."

"If I was you I'd give Monty back his donkey," Jim advised.

Petal made no move to comply.

"You isn't me," she pointed out.

24

*Even as he and Kit stood
whispering . . .*

Unable to sleep inside the house, Jim usually spread his blankets behind it, near two Dutch ovens Cook sometimes used for baking. Tasmin sometimes joined him there, but not often, since the whole nursery was likely to follow her, trailing along like so many little ducks. All six of the children would soon be shivering in the cold, spoiling Tasmin's hope of spending a quiet hour with Jim. Usually she gave up and led the brigade back inside, leaving Jim in peace. The Plaza seldom quieted down early; horsemen, cavalrymen mostly, would clatter across it at all hours.

Kit Carson could move with stealth if he wanted to, and on this occasion he particularly wanted to avoid sentries and soldiers. He materialized at Jim's side, pressing a finger to his lips, indicating that Jim should follow him. Jim took his gun and did as Kit suggested, wondering what brought Kit to Santa Fe at that hour of the night.

They were on the far side of the sheep pens before Kit felt it was safe to talk. He came right to the point.

"They're arresting the bunch of you tomorrow in the morning," Kit told Jim bluntly. "Josie heard it from someone in the Palace."

Jim didn't question the information. Josie was usually reliable where matters in Santa Fe were concerned. She had lived in the Palace herself at some point. If she said the Berrybenders were being arrested, it was probably true. What it meant could be debated, but that the Mexicans meant to rid themselves of Americans and English alike he didn't doubt and had never doubted. From the Mexican viewpoint, it was get rid of the Americans before the Americans got rid of them.

Even as he and Kit stood whispering, the first hint of dawn showed in the east. Jim would have liked to slip in and warn Tasmin, but knew it might be a fatal mistake. Pomp had let himself be taken; Jim didn't intend to make the same mistake.

"They were already under house arrest," Jim pointed out. "I suppose arrest means they aim to ship 'em out."

"That's it—that's Josie's view," Kit agreed. "Charlie Bent thinks there's going to be a war for Texas anytime. I suppose the Berry-benders would make good hostages—the Mexicans might trade 'em for a general or two."

Day was breaking—Kit grew nervous.

"We better go if we're going," he said.

"I've no time to warn the family but I have to get my mare," Jim said. He crept through the sheep and soon was back with the mare. The tip of the sun just broke the horizon.

"High Shoulders is out hunting," Jim said. "I better go find him or he'll come back and get arrested himself."

In the distance Kit could already see a few soldiers, just waking up.

"I'm going," he said. "If you come to my house, come in the night."

"Thanks for the warning," Jim said. "Thank Josie too—don't let her whup you too bad."

Kit, suddenly nervous, was on his way to Taos—he felt he could not spare the time for gratitude.

25

Lord Berrybender, apoplectic . . .

"I'm so glad High Shoulders is hunting," Buffum said, as the whole Berrybender household, considerably disheveled, were being urged into wagons. Lord Berrybender, apoplectic at being disturbed so early, was allowed to use his buggy, with Signor Claricia to drive; but that was the only favor the English were allowed.

"I would have liked a word with the Governor—he's a friend, after all," Lord Berrybender said to the head of their escort, a graying major named Leon, a careful man, not brutal, not young, and not especially familiar with the English gentry and their ways. He had been allowed a skimpy escort of only eighteen young soldiers and was well aware that it might not be enough. Their destination, the port of Vera Cruz, was very distant; the country they had to cross was hard country. The essential thing was to get started.

"I will do my best to make you comfortable," Major Leon assured them—the English had been two hours assembling themselves, and one or another of the women was still darting into the house to search for some important article that had been forgotten in the haste and gloom of the dusty morning. The dog Mopsy was only remembered at the last minute.

"In fact, Major, you've only made us uncomfortable," Lord Berrybender grumbled. "Wouldn't have minded a bit more sleep."

"It's better to travel while the day is cool," Major Leon replied. He felt uneasy. With such talkative, grumbly people it was not easy to choose correct remarks, as Lady Tasmin at once reminded him.

"It's the fall, Major—that's not a summer breeze that's blowing," Tasmin pointed out. They were all swaddled in blankets, the children big-eyed and solemn at the prospect of departure.

Lord Berrybender, very annoyed, had not given up on protocol.

"I still think I ought to be allowed to say

good-bye to the Governor—he's been most generous with us," he asserted. "Besides, he's a friend."

"There is a problem," the Major admitted. "He may still be your friend, but he is no longer the governor."

He did not elaborate, but signaled to the drivers to get the wagons going. Soon a buggy, three wagons, and eighteen supply mules, and the escort, eighteen strong, filed out of the Plaza. Joaquin, the blacksmith, just stirring his forge, yawned as they went by.

"But where's Julietta? Stop!" Lord Berrybender exclaimed. It had just dawned on him that his mistress was not in the wagons.

The Major didn't stop.

"We seem to have forgotten Señorita Julietta Olivaries," Lord Berrybender insisted. "We must fetch her. I'm sure she'd want to come."

"Unfortunately that is not the case," Major Leon replied. "The señorita is in Santa Fe for her health. She is staying with her aunt."

The Major's eyes hardened. Who was this old English fool, to think that he could summon a lady of the Spanish nobility at will? It was intolerable. Hauling this old lecher away from Señorita Julietta was a pleasant part of his task.

Signor Claricia had not been feeling well—Juppy was driving the buggy. The reins looked like threads in his big hands.

"I think you better let that one go, Papa," he advised. "The Major wants to be making time."

"Thank you, señor," the Major said. "We cannot go back for anyone. The time for good-byes is past."

Then he trotted to the head of the column and led the party south, into the desert, along the Camino Real—the road that, if they could survive it, would take them to the City of Mexico and beyond.

26

Except for the biting, blowing dust . . .

"Travel is never as neat as one imagines it will be," Major Leon admitted. "Even military travel is rarely neat. One must heed these calls of nature."

"Indeed, and right now she's calling rather too often," Father Geoff allowed. "I've been twenty times. The water, I suppose."

Except for the biting, blowing dust which swirled around them constantly, chapping lips and irritating eyelids, reducing the children particularly to life beneath a kind of tent of blankets, the journey south had not yet been too harsh. Major Leon kept his word about trying to make them comfortable. He exhibited no compulsion to hurry, a relief to the mothers and to Cook, all still trying to organize their resources and equipment for what would surely be a long trip.

"One cannot hurry an ox," the Major pointed out. "We must remember the fine fable of the tortoise and the hare."

Stimulated by this reference, Piet Van Wely roused himself and gave an impromptu lecture on the differences between the tortoise, the turtle, and the terrapin. He too was suffering from bowel complaints—they all were. The precise, well-regulated columns that Major Leon liked to maintain ceased to exist, as the complaint attacked cavalrymen and hostages alike. The English were jumping out of wagons and hurrying desperately through the sparse vegetation, in hopes of finding a bush behind which to answer the frequent calls in private.

"It's quite clear that this is amoebic," Piet informed them, so weak by this time that he could scarcely sit up. "These waters contain bad amoebas."

"That's not very cheering news," Tasmin pointed out. "These are the only waters there are."

"Piet is merely speaking as a scientist," Mary replied—she was always quick to defend her Piet.

"Fine, I'm speaking as a sufferer," Tasmin told her.

Petal popped out of her tent community from time to time, surveying the weakened company. She herself had not been afflicted.

"But I don't see my Jim," she said. "Where is my Jim?" She had grown to like her Jim. But where was he?

"This wagon is too bumpy," she added, a complaint everyone could sympathize with. Her grandfather's buggy was better, but her grandfather seemed to be angry at the moment; he could tolerate no one but Juppy, who muttered soothingly while her grandfather grumbled.

"I'm surprised Albany didn't shoot somebody," Vicky said, to Tasmin. "Now he's without his pretty little mistress—and he's not a man who likes to have his pleasures snatched away."

"It means you'll be seeing more of him one of these cold nights," Tasmin remarked. "He'll be wanting a little coziness, pretty soon."

The fall weather continued cold. Tasmin's main worry was Petey—all six of the children were continually popping out of their blankets, despite the cold wind. Little Onion did her best to control them, but six small people with wills of their own stretched the attention of even the most competent nurse.

Buffum had hardly stopped sobbing since their departure. Though well aware that it was all to the good that High Shoulders had not been taken—undoubtedly he would have been chained again—she didn't like being without her husband.

"I miss him exceedingly—I can't help it," she sobbed. "I need him—it's been that way since the day we met. I should have let him take me to the Ute country—there'd be nothing to separate us there."

"Mortality might," Tasmin reminded her. "You're lucky you didn't mate with a rambler like Jimmy—he's been gone more than he's been present, in the years of our marriage."

"I don't suppose you're easy to live with, Tassie," Kate Berrybender remarked crisply. "If you were easier, Mr. James Snow would probably abide with us more often."

"Don't you miss him terribly?" Mary asked. "I would miss Piet bitterly, if we were ever to part."

"What a bunch of rampant sentimentalists," Tasmin replied. "Did you ever see the like, Geoff?"

The disorder in his bowels had left the priest exhausted, sallow, withdrawn. He managed only the smallest shrug.

"Major Leon says it's a thousand miles to Vera Cruz," he remarked. "It seems rather a long way to go."

"My question wasn't geographical," Tasmin complained. "Certain couples may not be well suited to constant proximity. What do you think?"

"All I know is that I've been twenty times," the priest said. "The person I miss is myself—the self I enjoyed before we entered this region of bad water."

Tasmin found that she could contemplate the long journey ahead of them with a certain degree of composure precisely because Jim Snow had been quick enough to avoid being taken, a fact that at first vexed the officials considerably. Jim had done what Pomp Charbonneau should have done—skipped away. Tasmin had no doubt that he was following them—he would appear and reclaim his family at a time he deemed best. She was confident of it. They would just have to deal as best they could with the vicissitudes of the day, whether bowel trouble or feverish babies, bad weather or a bumpy oxcart, until Jim came and got them. Talk of the great distance between Santa Fe and Vera Cruz did not dismay her, because she didn't expect to be going anything like that far. Indeed, on the whole, she was glad to be out of Santa Fe—it had served its purpose, which was to be a safe nursery.

Major Leon had not taken long to abandon his ideal of a parade-ground military appearance. Many of the young soldiers were so affected by the water that they could scarcely sit on their horses. Major Leon had ridden ramrod straight for the first week, but he gradually let go his formality and spent much of his time riding beside the oxcarts, chatting with one or another of the Berrybender sisters. Lord Berrybender he avoided, though he did sometimes chat with the large and amiable Juppy and the one-eared boy, Amboise d'Avigdor. Amboise and Juppy had become friends.

"I don't think we have anything to fear from this major," Tasmin told her sisters.

"Why do you say it, Tassie?" Mary asked.

"Because he likes women," Tasmin replied. "And we're women if we're anything."

It seemed to her that beneath Major Leon's amiability there lurked a deep strain of melancholy—of sadness even. It was unusual to find a military man who was so eager to have his captives like him. Sometimes, in the midst of conversation about something inconsequential—his bugler's inept bugle calls, or military medals, of which he had quite a few—Major Leon would suddenly pause and look vacant, almost as if he had received a punch that deprived him of breath. At these moments he would turn his horse and ride some distance from the company, alone with whatever memory he needed to be alone with. He seemed a lonely figure, struggling with a sorrow he could not share.

At such moments Tasmin found him touching, but she could not quite bring herself to ask the Major what his trouble was.

Kate too had become fond of Major Leon.

"Why do you think he looks that way, Tassie?" she asked.

"I don't know, but I find I like the Major," Tasmin said.

"I like him too," Kate replied.

27

To his astonishment she even bared a breast.

The day the Berrybenders had been rounded up and sent away, Julietta found that she had been locked in her room. Worse still, her shutters had been nailed shut. When she discovered this treachery on the part of her aunt she didn't waste energy in tantrums. Eleanora was not impressed by tantrums, and neither was her husband. The Governor, it turned out, had been replaced, and the new governor, a wizened old soldier, was not someone Julietta could appeal to.

Later, when the door was unlocked and the shutters opened again, Julietta learned from her sister that she was to be sent back to Spain. She had become yet again a bargaining chip on the gaming table of Europe—a pregnancy by the old English nobleman would have definitely upset the game.

Julietta was concerned with none of that, because she intended to leave Santa Fe at once, and she meant to leave with Joaquin, her blacksmith. As soon as her shutters were open she went to the window and emitted a keen whistle, the sort a hunter might use to call back his dog.

Amazed, Joaquin looked up—there was Julietta again, smiling at him. She blew him a kiss. To his astonishment she even bared a breast. Joaquin was transfixed. That evening at dusk Julietta came to him, back to the heat, the sweat, the bed of rags. Her acceptance was tepid, but Joaquin was too excited to notice. He was swept away. He told Julietta that he loved her. He promised to do anything she asked. If it was necessary to risk his life he would do it gladly.

Julietta visited Joaquin three times, slowly tightening her grip.

Very often the horses Joaquin was to shoe were stabled at the smithy overnight. A blacksmith could not afford to be lazy. The horses of the cavalrymen had to be properly shoed.

Julietta was no mean horsewoman. On

the third visit she made her selection, went briefly back to her quarters, and returned when it was fully dark with a bundle of warm clothes. She then reminded Joaquin of his promise.

"You said you'd do anything for me," she told him. "You said you'd risk your life."

"Sí," Joaquin replied, not without a certain alarm. "Whatever you ask."

"What I ask is two horses—we're taking them now, you and I, and we're going to catch up with the English," she told him.

"Steal horses?" Joaquin replied, shocked.

Stroking him gently, as she might a greyhound, she led him around to the horse stalls.

"I'll take the thoroughbred," she told him.

"But señorita, I'm only a blacksmith—I can't ride. Only my donkey, a little," Joaquin protested.

"I'll help you," Julietta assured him. Still, he looked horrified. She thought she might have to dispense a few more caresses, even take him quickly, to calm him down. But then she changed her mind. She had had enough of being mauled by this peasant. Let him just do as she commanded.

"But señorita, they hang horse thieves," Joaquin stammered, very frightened.

Julietta softened her tone a bit. Unless treated gently, he might panic and betray her. He was not a tall man, but the sorrel horse was small—he should be able to manage. The thoroughbred was more skittish. There were no sidesaddles in the smithy—because of the threat from Indians, the ladies of Santa Fe were not encouraged to ride. Ladies out for a canter might never be seen again.

"If they catch us they will hang me," Joaquin repeated several times.

"If you keep quiet they won't catch us," Julietta insisted. Avoiding the Plaza, she led the horses through the narrowest, darkest alleys she could find.

When it was Joaquin's turn to mount he swung himself onto the horse so awkwardly that the sorrel crow-hopped and threw him hard. Exasperated, Julietta dismounted and steadied the sorrel until Joaquin finally managed to crawl aboard and find his stirrups. The stars were still bright. Her aunt Eleanora was a notoriously late sleeper. It would be noon before anyone realized they had left. She thought the soldiers might conclude that Joaquin had accidentally left the stalls open, allowing two horses to escape; then he fled, for fear of punishment.

The only person who saw the two riders make their way south under the starlight was an old woman whose habit, on starlit nights, was to sit out beside her little hut with her tame goose. She liked to study the heavens; she was called Oriabe, though some of those whose fortunes she told just called her Grandmother. Her goose squawked twice, when the lady and the blacksmith rode by. "Be polite, you're just a goose," Oriabe scolded. She liked to sit out all night, until the stars began to fade. She wished she had not seen the two riders. A large owl was hooting from a nearby tree when the riders passed. Owls, of course, were harbingers of bad fortune—fatal fortune, in fact. She knew this owl, which often hooted from that tree. Oriabe meant to have a word with the bird, someday soon. She meant to ask it to find another tree to sit in. Owls were sure to scare away people who might need their fortunes told, and besides that, it was hard to make a proper reading of the stars with a big owl hooting all the time.

28

*If it seemed a good time to go north,
he went north . . .*

Jim Snow was usually quick to decide on a course of action; once decided, he worked efficiently to carry out whatever plan he had made. The ability to weigh options and act on his decisions had served him well all during the years when he had acted singly. If it seemed a good time to go north, he went north; and on the whole he preferred north to south. The water supply was too chancy in the south.

Now, though, having slipped out of Santa Fe ahead of arrest, Jim could not immediately decide on a plan. His family were already miles to the south—of course, one of the helpful things about travel in dry country were the dust clouds that any company threw up. Kit Carson was hardly out of sight before Jim spotted the dust of the first patrol—in the clear high air such dust clouds were visible many miles away.

Jim had no difficulty in eluding these young soldiers—he merely went higher into the rocks. The soldiers were not skilled at mountain pursuit. They explored a ridge or two and gave up. Soon the dust cloud was moving in the opposite direction, back toward Santa Fe.

Jim had gone north mainly because he wanted to intercept High Shoulders, who was hunting somewhere to the north. He wanted to prevent High Shoulders' arrest. Jim looked around for a campfire, or some evidence that High Shoulders was in the vicinity, but he found nothing. The hills were empty.

Finally he made a campfire himself and kept it going all night. If High Shoulders was nearby he would notice and investigate. High Shoulders had shown himself to be a skilled reader of country. Together they could easily catch up with the slow-moving oxcarts that were carrying their wives and children away south. Then a plan of rescue could be devised.

Jim felt a mild annoyance with Kit, for being so henpecked that he had gone scuttling back to his Josie when he might have been helpful to Jim and the Berrybenders. Thanks to his association with the Bent brothers, Kit could go in and out of Santa Fe at will. He might easily have found out how many soldiers were in the escort, and whether the officer in command was reliable or unreliable. Information of that sort would have been useful, but Kit had felt no need to secure it, a lapse Jim meant to tax him for, the next time he saw him.

Jim felt confident that he could catch up with his family and free them, but that would immediately create a real dilemma. Where was he to take them once he freed them? They could not go back to Santa Fe. If they went east to the Bents they ran the risk of being rearrested. The Bents were not strong enough to repulse a Mexican army. Besides, the Bents knew that they had to maintain good relations with the Mexicans—the very existence of their business depended on it. One wrong move and they might lose all their property, or even find themselves in jail.

Then there was Texas, where Lord Berrybender talked idly of starting a cotton plantation; Lord Berrybender took it for granted

that, one way or another, they would get
there, but Jim was less confident. He himself had never been much south of the
Canadian River. Hugh Glass *had* been there:
he did not paint a rosy picture. Between
them and coastal Texas lay hundreds of
miles of unknown country—unknown, that
is, to whites but thoroughly known to the
Comanches, the Kiowas, the Apaches—
all, so far as Jim knew, implacable enemies
of the whites. Oxcarts filled with women
and children would surely tempt them:
slaves for the markets in Mexico. At the
moment the Berrybenders had an escort of
soldiers, and Jim supposed the best plan
would be to keep the escort, at least until
they got past some of the Apaches. Reach-
ing Texas from the south might be safer
than trying to penetrate from the north-
west.

In the night Jim gave up trying to think
too far ahead. Life was unpredictable—Tasmin, unpredictable herself, insisted it was.
Jim could never figure out what Tasmin
might do, and the two of them together
could not really see what might be coming
next.

"Life happens day to day!" It was one of

Tasmin's favorite mottoes, and Jim had to admit that it seemed to be true. Even if he made, to his own satisfaction, a decision as to how to approach Texas, there was small likelihood that their arrival in that place would happen as planned. Crossing any hundred miles of country was sure to bring surprises.

Around dawn Jim began to get an uneasy feeling. Someone or something was watching him. He thought he would have heard a man approach, even a stealthy man—yet he had not heard the rustle of a bush—nothing. He wondered if it might be a cougar. He was wearing buckskins. Joe Walker claimed that a cougar had once jumped him while he was wearing buckskins—Joe thought the cougar had mistaken him for a deer. As soon as the animal realized its mistake it ran away, as frightened by the encounter as Joe had been himself.

Jim looked around him nervously—he didn't want a mountain lion to land on his shoulders by mistake.

He had camped beneath a steep hill—above him one hundred feet or so was a jumble of boulders—excellent hiding places for any man or animal that hoped to hide.

High up Jim saw something move—he thought it might be a bear. Jim reached for his rifle; when he did the figure above him raised his rifle too, in salute. The fellow on the mountain had a hunched look—it was not the first time he had been mistaken for a bear; in fact, he cultivated the look, because it scared away fools, a species which Bill Williams—usually called Old Bill—did not suffer gladly.

Jim was startled to see the man. Bill Williams was said to have moved into Ute country. What was he doing a day north of Santa Fe? It was the unpredictability principle again. Anyone was likely to be anywhere.

Jim had only met Bill Williams once or twice and had no particular opinion of him, though Kit Carson and other mountain men held very firm opinions about him—and the opinions were hardly positive. He was said to have a thunderous temper and to think little of killing, whether the man killed was friend or foe. That in itself was a failing common enough among the mountain trappers, who over the years, in violent brawls, did much to thin their own ranks.

Kit Carson, who knew Bill Williams well,

having once trapped with him in the Ute country, raised a more uncommon possibility. Food had been scarce. Two or three men had fallen, and exactly what had occurred to them in that harsh time had never been made exactly clear. Jim particularly remembered one remark of Kit's: "Nobody who knows Bill Williams walks in front of him in the starving times," Kit said. "Keep that in mind if you're ever with him when you're about the only thing left to eat."

Jim remembered the remark as he waited for the hulking mountain man to make his way out of the boulders and come to camp. He did hunch along like a bear and his buckskins were black with use. Cleanliness had clearly never been of major interest to Bill Williams.

"I hear you preach!" Bill Williams said loudly when he stumped into camp. He was of formidable size and had a wild mane of hair.

"No, I don't," Jim told him. "I cry the Word a little, once in a while."

"I've preached all my life—converted sixty heathen so far," Bill remarked, looking at Jim in a none too friendly way.

"When you've converted sixty heathen to

the Lord you can call yourself a preacher," Bill Williams continued, speaking loudly, as if daring Jim to challenge his claims.

"I don't know enough scripture to be able to convert folks," Jim admitted.

"And yet you call yourself the Sin Killer," Bill Williams said, tilting his head to one side and looking at Jim suspiciously.

"No, I call myself Jim Snow," Jim replied. "Some of the boys called me Sin Killer when I was younger. It's just a nickname."

"Well, I may borrow it, if I keep going with my converting," the man said. "You can get another nickname."

Jim was beginning to find the man's tone irritating. There was no friendliness in anything Bill Williams said. Jim didn't like his rude tone—he did not like being insulted at his own campfire.

"If you can't be polite, then I'll fight you," Jim told him. "I won't have rude behavior."

"You won't, eh! You puppy!" Bill said, his face coloring with fury. "I shot a sneaking Ute this morning and I might just shoot you, if you sass me."

"The Ute was probably my brother-in-law—did you kill him?" Jim asked.

"No, but I put a bullet in the sneaky

skunk," Bill replied. "He got in some brush and I didn't care to flush him out—I left him for the bears. And it don't mean a goddamn pickle to me that you're related to the man."

He leveled his rifle at Jim but as he did Jim stooped quickly, plunging his hands into the hot ash of the campfire—then he flung the ash and any coals that might be in it right into Bill Williams's face. The ashes were not particularly hot, but they blinded the man for a second, and two or three small coals went down his shirt, causing him to hop and yelp—he dropped his rifle as he attempted to shake out the burning coals. There was one fair-sized stick still smoking in the campfire. Jim snatched it and hit Bill Williams hard, right in the face, causing his nose to explode with blood. The man fell backwards, blinded, blood-smeared, and still writhing from the coals inside his shirt.

"If I let you live don't ever talk rude to me again," Jim told him. He put his foot on the man's throat and exerted just enough pressure to make him gasp. "You're just a walking bag of sin and I will kill you if I see you again."

He picked up Bill Williams's rifle and went to his horse.

"That's my rifle—I need it," Bill Williams managed to gasp.

"It was your rifle but you lost it through bad manners," Jim told him. "Santa Fe's just down the hill. You'll find plenty of rifles there."

"Down the hill fifty miles, you mean," the man said, sitting up. "A bear could get me before I make it to town."

"I hope one does," Jim told him. "If my brother-in-law's dead you won't have nothing to fear from bears because I'll come back and finish you myself."

"You're a sneaking rascal if I ever met one," Bill Williams told him. "Next time I meet you it'll be a different story."

Jim had been about to mount but he turned back, unsheathed his knife, and stood over the fallen man.

"The next time can be now," he told him. "Get up and get out your knife or else leave off your threats."

Bill Williams considered his assailant, trying to calculate whether he could make a lunge for Jim's legs and bring him down.

Jim waited, just out of reach of such a move.

"You stole my rifle like a common thief— I guess you would fight, goddamn you!" Bill Williams shouted.

The blasphemous phrase was too much for Jim—he felt the Word coming out, as it had not come since the day he yelled it at the four Osage warriors who were chasing him and Tasmin along the Missouri shore. He stood over Bill Williams and poured it out, a wild, unintelligible babble, shocking the mountain man so much that he began to scoot backward, alarmed. Jim still held his knife as the Word poured out.

Then he stopped, his chest heaving.

"Don't be cussing at me," he warned. "If you do I'll break your old scrawny neck."

Bill Williams, watching the knife, thought his hour had come. He had seen a terrible change—the mild young man had become the Sin Killer indeed. Bill Williams didn't say another word. Over the years he had fought and won many fights. When he let his violence out he was a powerful foe. But his violence, which had frightened many and flattened more, did not worry this boy—a boy who had thrown coals in his face and then flattened him with a hot stick. Bill Williams did not want to see what he might do if he used the knife.

Jim Snow put the knife away, got his horse, and rode slowly up the hill.

29

Jim found him, barely conscious . . .

High Shoulders, though not mortally wounded, had lost a great deal of blood— the bullet had passed through above his hip. Jim found him, barely conscious, in some thick underbrush well up the slope. Bill Williams had not been exaggerating about the bears, either. There was grizzly sign everywhere.

High Shoulders now knew a little English.

"My wife?" he asked. "Where my wife?"

"Headed south but traveling slow," Jim indicated. "We need to get this bleeding stopped—then we'll soon catch up with the folks."

The next day, though, a sandstorm struck, more severe than any Jim had experienced. They tore up a shirt and made dust masks, but the masks were little help. The

upper sky was an ugly brown and the sting-
ing, swirling sand thicker at ground level
than any Jim had tried to travel in. High
Shoulders, still weak, rode the mare, which
Jim led. When the reins were fully extended
he could only just see the horse's head.
Once he dropped a rein and thought he had
lost the horse—but for the fact that he
stepped on the dropped rein he might *have*
lost the horse. Even the most violent sand-
storms usually blew themselves out in a few
hours, but this one didn't; it lasted a day
and a night, and when it did stop the air was
so full of unsettled dust that it scarred the
nasal passages.

Jim had never been lost, in any weather;
he trusted his sense of direction as absolutely as he trusted his pulse. But for a
few hours at the height of the storm, Jim
wondered if, after all, he *was* lost. He
couldn't see the horizon or the sky and only
vaguely sensed the movement of the sun.
The feeling was unsettling—High Shoulders, in a kind of sick daze, could be little
help. When the storm struck they were due
west of Santa Fe. At first the wind came out
of the east, but then shifted north and later
south. It was in his face. Finally it became

so intense that he thought best to stop. He helped High Shoulders down, tied a rag around the mare's eyes, and waited, sheltered by a little bank of rocks. Tired, he sat and let the sand cover his lap. At one point, sensing movement, he saw a rattlesnake slither across his lap. Jim didn't move—in a moment the snake slithered away.

The wait proved beneficial to High Shoulders. His strength began to return. But he could not stop asking about his wife—he wanted to know when he could be back with her, a question Jim couldn't answer until the dust cleared. The young Ute's anxiety about his English wife was so intense that it was almost irritating. The plain, often woebegone girl had blossomed into a confident, appealing woman since joining her fate to High Shoulders'. Sitting in the sand, waiting for the air to clear, Jim wondered why some human linkages were so tight and others so loose. Mary Berrybender and Piet Van Wely were never apart for more than an hour, and yet her father, Lord Berrybender, seldom addressed a word to his wife, Vicky; he took no interest at all in the two healthy boys Vicky had borne him.

He himself liked being with Tasmin and

the little ones, but he was not driven by any need to hurry back to her. High Shoulders and Piet seemed to draw energy from their mates, but that was not the case with Tasmin and himself. Their conflicts were too frequent; they left Jim feeling worn out. What had changed in their situation was the children, all of whom looked at him with sad eyes when he prepared to leave.

Finally the dust did settle out of the air. They discovered that they were not far from the Rio Grande. High Shoulders even thought he could see the dust of the Berrybender party far ahead—perhaps fifty miles off. Jim was skeptical—many travelers used the Camino Real. High Shoulders wanted to travel all night, to catch up with his wife, but Jim preached caution. The country was broken and he didn't know it. In unfamiliar country it was best to go slow. More than once they came across signs of Indians: the remains of campfires, human scat, tracks here and there. Once Jim thought he saw a small man watching them from behind a ridge of rocks—he couldn't be sure, but he knew there was nothing to be gained by taking unusual risks. The Berrybenders were somewhere ahead. They would catch them in a day, two days, three.

"Better to be safe than sorry," Jim said. High Shoulders did not agree.

. . . there was no sign of Mopsy.

Tasmin woke to wailings, grief, six children awash in tears, with several whites also on the brink.

"Oh no!" she cried, when informed that there was no sign of Mopsy.

Even Major Leon had a weakness for the little mongrel. He dispatched his soldiers to search for clues—the soldiers rode in a wide circle but failed to find even a trace of the small dog.

"Let me go, I can find him," Monty pleaded. All six children tumbled out of their wagon, determined to locate their pet.

"But I need him, where is he?" Petal inquired.

Mopsy had been helplessly friendly. If he had an enemy it was only Cook, who found him too much underfoot when she was trying to make a meal under windy or gritty conditions. But even Cook was seen to weep.

"What could have *got* him?" Petal questioned, when the search was abandoned and the trek continued.

"An eagle, perhaps—he was quite small," Mary suggested.

"Or a wolf or a bobcat," Piet added.

"But I'm small and Petey is small and Elf," Petal pointed out. "What if an eagle got *me?*"

"It would soon spit you out—you'd be a difficult mouthful," Tasmin said.

"I think the eagle might get Elf next," Petal concluded. "He's the smallest."

Despite this reassuring thought Petal kept her eyes on the skies—she fled under her blankets with mouselike speed if a big bird showed itself.

The country they had to cross grew increasingly bleak, harsher, in Tasmin's opinion, even than the plains. She had begun to feel fearful for her children—anxiety, like a low fever, was never quite absent. She looked around her often, hoping to see Jim. Major Leon liked Tasmin—seeing that she was worried, he did his best to reassure her.

"For now we have the Rio Grande," he reminded her. "Water won't be a problem until after we come to the Pass of the North."

"And after that?"

"After that we will have to be careful," the Major said.

Tasmin felt a deepening anger at her father, who was grumbling and pettish because he was not allowed to hunt with his new guns. One of the things she liked about Major Leon was that he stood firm against Lord Berrybender's complaints.

"Your guns will be returned to you when you board the boat," Major Leon insisted.

"Board the boat—what nonsense," Lord Berrybender grumped. "What can I hunt from a boat?"

"For that matter, what could you hunt in this desert?" the Major asked.

When Tasmin needed to communicate with her father she did it through Juppy, who continued to drive the buggy.

"I suppose you can tolerate him because you've only had to put up with him for a month," she said. "We've had four years of this, and look where we are. In a desert. The sandstorm gave all the children nosebleeds and sore eyes. And I doubt that's the worst we'll have to put up with."

"You can't hurry life—just got to wait it out," Juppy remarked. "What are you going to do with Jim? Take him home?"

"Oh, don't ask me—I don't know," Tasmin said. "I think about it all the time, but I have no answer. He's used to all this space. I fear he'd feel rather cooped up, on our little island."

Juppy looked over Tasmin's head. He thought he saw a man, a very short man, half hidden behind some dry bushes. But when he looked again he saw only the bushes. Had he seen a man? None of the soldiers betrayed any anxiety. The peculiar thing about the country they were in was that there was so much light that it somehow made it harder to see things. A yucca might look like a man, or a man like a yucca. What at first seemed to be a deer might only be a bush. When he tried to peer into the far distance his eyes soon began to water, causing the horizons to blur. Only things that were close—the horses, the oxen, the soldiers—could be seen clearly. The strange hard light had a blinding effect. The greater the distances ahead, the less precisely it seemed one could see.

Juppy had become a great favorite with the children—sometimes all six swarmed over him at once, like so many little raccoons. During their noon break, while he was playing with them, Major Leon came trotting over.

"We have company," he said.

"Who? Where?" Tasmin asked.

"You won't see them, but they're here," the Major told them. "They may not be hostile but it's best to take no chances. Just stay close to the wagons."

"I thought I saw a small man," Juppy confessed.

"I haven't seen them but I feel them—they're here," the Major said.

31

Why must she look at him so scornfully?

The large mule deer burst out of the brush so suddenly that the thoroughbred bolted and Julietta was nearly thrown. The fleeing deer almost ran into Joaquin's horse, which threw him high. Joaquin came down in a jumble of rocks. He was a very bad rider— he had been thrown several times since leaving Santa Fe, but he was sturdy. The falls didn't hurt him, although Julietta's contempt, which she made no attempt to conceal, did hurt him. Why must she look at him so scornfully? He had helped steal the two horses, as she had asked. He could never go back to Santa Fe—he had lost his livelihood for her sake. Never again would he stir his forge in the morning. He knew nothing of horses, and the sorrel he had been assigned was nervous, shying even at rabbits.

Joaquin didn't know how to rein the horse properly; he was thrown and thrown again, and with each embarrassing debacle, Julietta grew more and more distant, more icy. At night she sat on the other side of the campfire, wrapped in a cloak. Her look was so haughty that Joaquin didn't even try to approach her. He sat by himself, dumb, cold, miserable, unable to fix his mind on the future. They had a little jerky and a sack of hard corn—it was not much to eat, but Julietta seemed indifferent. All day she said not a word.

After the scare with the mule deer Julietta walked the thoroughbred around a bit, to calm him. The sorrel had calmed down too; he was standing patiently not far from where Joaquin was thrown. Joaquin did not appear—Julietta began to wonder what could be wrong with the lout. Even if the fall had knocked the wind out of him it was time for him to get up. She was convinced that the Berrybenders were not far ahead. She wanted to catch them; she did not want to spend another cold night in the desert with Joaquin. The sooner she was rid of his company the better.

Still, Joaquin did not appear—could the

fool have been knocked out? She called his name but he didn't answer. Annoyed, she dismounted and walked to the rocks where he had been thrown. And there he was, his eyes open, flat on his back. He made no move to get up.

"Joaquin! Get up! Let's go!" Julietta demanded.

Still, Joaquin did not get up. He stared at Julietta helplessly, looking up into the sky. He had gashed his head on one of the rocks and his cheek was bloody, but the gash in his head was not the problem. The problem was that he couldn't move. He felt no pain—he was glad Julietta had come. He wanted to do as she requested, but he couldn't. He could see his legs but he couldn't move them. He could not even raise his head—he lay as he was, staring, numb, helpless.

Julietta suddenly realized the truth: Joaquin was paralyzed. He stared straight up into the empty sky. Julietta felt a moment of panic. Joaquin was not much help but he was somebody. She did not want to be entirely alone in this vast desert.

"Joaquin!" she called again, sharply— perhaps the sharpness of her voice would break the spell, enable Joaquin to stand up. But her sharp tone changed nothing. Joaquin was helpless, rigid. What had happened was not correctable. Without another look she turned and went back to her horse. Both horses seemed nervous again—Julietta had to will herself to be patient and gentle as she approached them. She might need both of them—she could not afford to spook them. She forced herself to move slowly, to talk soothingly. She did not want to be left afoot.

While she was talking soothingly to the horses Julietta noticed a curious thing. The mule deer that had frightened the horses had not run very far. It had stopped nearby. It seemed to be staggering. Then it fell. Julietta suddenly noticed two arrows sticking out of the mule deer's side. Panic hit her like a blow. There were Indians near—she had to flee. But when she jumped to mount, the thoroughbred shied and she missed the stirrup. Before she could catch the swinging stirrup, a swarm of small men began to clutch at her. She struck one of them in the face with her quirt, but the blow had no effect. The frightened horses fled, leaving Julietta captive of the swarm of men, who soon bore her down, the faces above her hard as hatchets.

For a long time, as the sun shone in his face and arched toward its setting, Joaquin lay in the rocks and listened to Julietta scream: terrible screams and high at first, but then less high as she weakened. In time Julietta screamed herself out and could only produce rough, grunting, gutteral moans. She had fallen silent altogether when one of the Apaches found him and pulled him out of the rocks. It soon became apparent to the men that this new captive could neither move nor feel. The entertainment was over, the boy useless. They merely cut his throat.

32

He too was still warm . . .

When Jim and High Shoulders found Julietta Olivaries her body was still warm—the
arrow that killed her fired into her chest at
close range only minutes before. A great
pool of blood had gushed from the blacksmith's cut throat. He too was still warm,
though dead. High Shoulders, fearful that
the Indians might do to Buffum as they had
done to Julietta, could not be restrained. He
rushed recklessly into the desert, brandish-
ing Bill Williams's rifle and yelling his Ute
war cries. And yet all his rushing and yelling
produced nothing. Neither he nor Jim, who
had ridden to the top of a nearby ridge, saw
anything except a few wheeling hawks.

"I doubt there was many of them," Jim
told High Shoulders, when the latter gave
up and came back. The Indians had not

taken time to butcher the large mule deer, suggesting that they had seen Jim and High Shoulders coming and probably feared attack by men with guns.

They scratched out shallow graves for Julietta and the blacksmith, butchered the mule deer themselves, and pressed on south beside the river. Jim was not especially worried about the Berrybenders. Five or six Indians were not likely to attack a well-armed body of soldiers. The girl and the blacksmith had been unlucky. He regretted that his skills as a tracker were so modest—his tracking was better than his birdcalls, but not by much.

Just before dusk Jim came upon the remains of the horses Julietta and the blacksmith had been riding. These had been thoroughly and carefully butchered, which suggested that there was a band somewhere near. Jim thought it best to hide, once night fell. He made no fire, hobbled his horse, kept his hand on his rifle. He remained alert but did not try to bore holes in the darkness, watching. Staring hard into darkness only made one see things that were not there. He dozed, but went unchallenged. What awakened him was a strange sound: bugle calls. An incompetent bugler was attempting to play reveille. Ahead Jim saw a bend of the Rio Grande and a troop of soldiers—perhaps about twenty. He also saw the Berrybenders. Cook was bustling around over a big pot of porridge. Jim was hungry; he felt like riding in and having a big bowl. But he felt he couldn't afford to be rash. If he rode in, would he be arrested? Or would the Mexicans welcome an extra gun? Then he saw High Shoulders, who had rushed ahead—he was moving about freely, unchained. That was enough. He loped on into camp—it was time to have himself some grub.

⇥ 33 ⇤

Small people living in small groups in difficult country . . .

Small people living in small groups in difficult country could not behave like mighty conquerors and hope to survive. There were only twenty-two in the band, counting babies and old men. Only eight were active warriors, and of those, only four were experienced and reliable. The others were boys, impetuous as boys are. Eight men could not attack armies of soldiers and hope to win. These things Cibecue explained over and over to the young men, though he knew that none of them wanted to heed him. The boys had heard that to the west there were bands of one hundred warriors or more, bands that had no fear of Mexicans and killed them where they found them.

"That may be true, but we don't live in that place," Cibecue explained. "We live here, and there aren't many of us. We have to be careful."

The boy named Ojo was particularly intolerant of Cibecue's words of caution. Ojo was convinced they could easily beat the Mexicans who were guarding the family of whites.

"They have guns—we don't," Cibecue pointed out. It was an argument that convinced the older warriors but it didn't convince Ojo or his three friends.

"Why can't we sneak in and steal some guns?" Ojo asked. "I would like a gun, myself, and I would like to catch one of those white women and do what we did with the Spanish girl."

Catching the Spanish girl had been a huge stroke of luck—the boys were all still excited by the memory of the things they had done to her—they had all been following the wounded mule deer and out of nowhere this girl appeared. They also found a boy with a broken back, farther up in the rocks. It had been a fine afternoon, but it was also a fluke. Cibecue was not young and yet never before in his life had the band caught a Spanish woman.

Catching a lone white woman who happened to be in the wrong place was one thing—attacking a column of Mexican soldiers quite another. Cibecue kept trying to explain to Ojo that luck was never constant. One day it might be good, the next day bad. The fact that they were able to kill the two horses was even luckier than having the girl to rape and torture. The women had done a thorough job with the horses; for once they had an abundance of meat. It was a time of plenty, but it wouldn't last forever. What Cibecue had to make Ojo understand was that he couldn't risk four young hunters in a foolish attack on some Mexican soldiers.

"Suppose they kill three of you?" he speculated. "You are all good hunters and you will get better. You raped that Spanish girl pretty good. You can make the band some babies when we need babies. If I let you go and they kill three of you, then we lose three hunters and three fathers too."

There was a silence. The older men weren't really listening. They were watching an eagle soaring over a good-sized butte to the west. They were thinking the eagle might have a nest there: they might be able to catch some young eagles, which would be a thing of power. They thought Cibecue was wasting his time, lecturing Ojo and the other boys. Young men never believed they could die—even less were they able to grasp that the whole band might die if they lost too many hunters. The band was small and poor, but at least the women were energetic, constantly at work gathering seeds and roots, growing a little corn, and snaring rabbits, which were unusually numerous just then. The boys were not men yet; they didn't want to think ahead. The band had always been there—in their immature heads it would always be there.

"Can't we just follow the Mexicans?" Ojo asked. "We can stay out of sight. The women have to make water sometimes. I bet we could catch one."

Cibecue decided it was hopeless. No matter what he said these boys were not going to be restrained unless he took them far from the source of temptation. They had been too excited by what they had done to the Spanish girl. He did not want to be sharp with them—they were good boys. He didn't want to flatly lay down the law, either. Boys were apt to feel that their pride demanded independence. Tell them not to do something and they would just be that much more apt to do it.

Cibecue was the leader, but he had to lead delicately—he didn't want to make Ojo and the other boys too puffy with rebellion. The simplest thing to do was just go west for two or three days, until the temptation of the white women was not so immediate.

"Are you counting eagles?" he asked old Erzmin, the oldest warrior in the band.

Erzmin had always been unusually attentive to the ways of birds. Once, in a bad time, when deer seemed to have vanished from the country, Erzmin had kept them from starving by collecting the eggs of various birds he had managed to follow to their nests.

"Just two, so far," Erzmin replied. "I think they may be a pair—they might have a nest over there but it's too early for there to be eggs."

"Let's go look anyway," Cibecue suggested. "Keeping up with eagles' nests is a good thing to do."

"The women are still cutting up that jerky—those were fat horses," Erzmin reminded him.

"We don't want the women with us,"

Cibecue said. "We can go hunt eagles' nests for ourselves."

He started west at a brisk pace—Erzmin and the older warriors right behind him. Erzmin knew what Cibecue was trying to do. He didn't want Ojo or the other boys getting themselves killed trying to steal a white woman.

Ojo and his three companions were bitterly disappointed by this development— but, alone, what could they do?

After a minute or two they fell in behind the older men.

34

. . . Major Leon did not have the aspect of a joker.

Major Leon laughed genially when Jim politely inquired about his status—that is, whether he could expect to be arrested at some point down the trail. Jim thought it best to be clear on that point—he did not mean to be arrested.

"In Santa Fe you might have been an enemy, but here you are an ally, Señor Snow," the Major told him. "We have a long way to go—we might need every fighter we can get—besides which it's my duty to tell you that I've fallen in love with your wife."

With that the Major smiled, made Jim a little half bow, and rode off.

Jim was so startled by the Major's last remark that he would have been hard put to reply. Probably it was meant as a joke, just a rather flowery way of saying that the Major liked Tasmin a lot. And yet Major Leon did not have the aspect of a joker. He had looked, on the whole, rather melancholy when he mentioned to Jim that he was in love with his wife. Jim could not believe that such an absurd statement was to be taken literally, and yet the Major had sounded rather matter-of-fact about it.

With Petal, Monty, and Petey all competing for his attention, Jim had little opportunity to think much more about the Major's startling declaration. It seemed that Major Leon was on good terms with the children too, even taking them one by one on short horseback rides. Petal particularly seemed to enjoy these rides, insisting that she could hold the reins herself and pushing the Major's hands away when he briefly attempted a correction of some sort.

"Take your hands *off!*" Petal insisted, and usually the Major complied.

It was late in the day before Jim finally had a chance to speak privately with Tasmin.

"That's a funny kind of a major," Jim remarked. "The first thing he said to me was that he was in love with you."

Tasmin blushed a little, nervously. She

made a little what-can-I-do gesture; she shrugged.

"It doesn't surprise me that he told you," she said, with a heavy sigh. "He's incapable of concealing anything from anyone—it's part of his problem."

Jim still didn't understand.

"Does he just mean that he likes you a bunch?" he asked.

Tasmin chuckled.

"No, he doesn't mean that he likes me a bunch, as you put it," she told him. "Geoff, after all, likes me a bunch."

She sighed again.

"It's different with Major Leon," she told him. "Major Leon *is* in love with me."

For a moment Tasmin teared up, at the thought of the absurdity of the situation. Here she was in the middle of nowhere; her captor was in love with her; she had three bouncy children, and a husband who was honestly puzzled.

"I hope you'll just excuse it," she said to Jim. "Nothing improper has happened— nothing improper ever will. But the Major *is* in love with me and it's best to just let it wear off. I can't seem to make him give it up.

"At least it's a benefit for the children," she said. "They get little horse rides."

Jim didn't know what to think. He didn't doubt Tasmin's fidelity—it had not occurred to him that anything sinful could have happened—surely not. Major Leon seemed sad and perhaps a little silly, but he hardly seemed like much of a ladies' man.

"I don't understand it," Jim admitted.

"No, you don't," Tasmin said mildly, irritated by the position she found herself in.

"You've never been in love with me, you see, Jimmy," she said, taking his hand. "I believe you do care for me—and then there's *this* that we have."

She moved his hand between her legs and at once felt an old quickening.

"There's this, and I'm glad we have it." She didn't move his hand, but she held it to her. Her boldness stirred Jim a good deal.

"Maybe it's more important than being in love—the poets aren't clear on that point," Tasmin continued. "But it isn't the same. Major Leon is in love with me, as Kit once was—you remember that, don't you?

Jim nodded.

"What's the Major get out of it?" he asked, not angry, just puzzled.

"Oh, I don't know," Tasmin admitted. "A chance to do me small kindnesses, or pay me small attentions," she said. "You remember how Kit was—he was always at his happiest when I gave him a chore to do—the harder the chore, the more it pleased him to do it."

Jim did remember Kit's infatuation. He had not been jealous of Kit's attentions to his wife; but he had thought Kit rather a fool, for doing so much of what was rightly Tasmin's work. Jim had supposed that Pomp was also sweet on Tasmin, though Pomp was far less likely to do her endless favors or hang on her conversation. At first, when he heard Tasmin and Pomp talking about some book or play, he had supposed it was only educated people who fell in love; but then along came Kit, who couldn't read or write a lick, and he was worse sweet on Tasmin than Pomp had been. If further proof was needed that all sorts of people fell in love, there was High Shoulders, a Ute who at first couldn't speak a word of English, and yet had been in a fever to be with Buffum from the minute they laid eyes on one another.

"Major Leon is a curious case," Tasmin

went on. "He confessed to me that he has only been able to be in love with married women—and yet he doesn't attempt to make love to them, in the common way. Instead he fetches me extra blankets for the children. Once he brought me a pretty rock. Or he might offer me a tidbit from the stores. He's not read me poetry, though—Geoff is still my only literary man."

Jim looked over at the Major. He always sat alone, apart from his men.

"There's plenty of things I don't understand," Jim admitted.

"And being in love is one of them," Tasmin said. She still held his hand and began to rub it against her.

"It's not dark enough," Jim protested.

"It's dark enough for *something*," Tasmin chided. "Leave me that hand."

Later, in the deep night, Tasmin woke from a doze and saw Jim sitting up—he still wore a look of confusion.

"Jimmy, don't worry about it—being in love isn't everything," she told him. "It can be a terribly painful condition. The poets are clear on that point."

"Kit can do it and Major Leon can do it and High Shoulders can do it—how come I

can't?" he asked. "It just don't seem necessary."

"Correct—it isn't," Tasmin agreed.
"We've done a bunch without it—though of
course I was as much in love with you as
you'd tolerate," she told him.

"Though I wouldn't be surprised if you fall
in love yet," she added.

"Why would I?"

"You might be given no choice—it might
just sweep over you one day. You mustn't
underestimate Petal—if any woman can get
you, I expect it's her."

"She's a baby," Jim replied—though he
did like Petal. She didn't readily allow anyone not to like her, once she took an interest in them, and lately she had taken a
strong interest in him.

But being in love with your own child
surely wasn't what they had been talking
about.

"Best not to think of it too simply, as just
being a thing that happens to people who
want to rut," Tasmin told him. "It just might
be that your own daughter is the only woman
capable of sweeping you off your feet.

"Time will tell," she added. "Time will
tell."

35

"This makes me feel rather dry and coldhearted . . ."

"Don't you be sulking, Geoff," Tasmin warned. "I have enough to do keeping this unruly lot in marching order. If there's one thing I don't need in my life right now it's a rude friend."

"I can't help it," Father Geoffrin replied. "I'm filled with dark forebodings anyway, and now this ridiculous little major has turned your head."

"Not a bit of it . . . my head's *not* turned," Tasmin argued. "My husband is here, re-member. Nothing untoward has happened. Major Leon is just a bit smitten, that's all."

"I could be smitten myself with a little en-couragement," Father Geoff told her. Then he shrugged and apologized.

"I'm sorry—it just irritates," he admitted. "I'm used to being the one you talk to—I'm jealous that you're talking to someone else."

"Incorrect—I'm mostly *listening* to someone else," Tasmin said. "Yesterday the Major finally told me his sad tale."

"And was it sad?"

"As tales of thwarted love go, yes," Tasmin told him. "He confessed to being very shy, a quality I had already detected in him."

"Prissy, I'd call it," Geoff complained. "He's always stroking his mustache—I notice these things, you see."

Tasmin gave him a stern look.

"You notice—and then you misinterpret," Tasmin scolded. "Major Leon is at ease with me because he doesn't expect to succeed. The impossibility of success is what it takes for some men to relax with a woman. That's common enough."

"Out with the sad tale—I won't interrupt."

"Major Leon was once in love with a girl of good family in Santa Fe," Tasmin began. "But because of his shyness he could not quite work up to proposing. The girl, of good family, who was not unreceptive to his suit, grew tired of waiting and accepted another. But the man she accepted quite abruptly died. There was a period of mourning, and then Major Leon tried again. This time he was just able to mumble out a proposal, which was immediately accepted. A wedding date was set—at last his love had been answered."

Tasmin stopped.

"Why don't you finish the story for me, Geoff?" she teased. "It's suitable for a tragedy. Your beloved Racine would have found it interesting."

"More likely Molière, if that prissy little man is the hero," Geoff said. "There he is stroking his mustache again.

"I suppose the girl died," he added, after thinking for a moment.

Tasmin nodded. "The girl died. Rather sad, don't you agree? He's a decent man, if limited. He finally wins the consent of a woman he could have—and then she dies, after which he has taken no chances in that particular line. He only falls in love with women he can't have, like my humble self."

"And yet you do *like* him, so it's not *so* sad," Geoff remarked. "He gets affection, at least. What does Jim think about the Major and his affections?"

Tasmin laughed.

"The Major told Jimmy right off that he

was in love with me—startling news to my Jimmy, who's continually puzzled by the odd twistings and turnings of human emotion. Now and then he attempts to puzzle out what romance might be, but it's so foreign to his nature that he can't quite grasp it."

"I can't see that this bothers you much," the priest said.

"That's because you don't see me when it's bothering me," Tasmin told him. "You may have noticed that I've started caring about my looks again, in the small way that's possible under present circumstances."

"So?"

"It's the result of Major Leon's attentions," Tasmin told him. "It's always nice to have a man who looks at you closely enough to notice small improvements.

"Very small improvements," she added. "But still it's nice."

"This makes me feel rather dry and cold-hearted, and I don't like the feeling," Father Geoff said. "I'm sure that's why the Major annoys me. His attentions may be shallow but they please you, and my attentions don't."

"Nonsense, your attentions have always pleased me," Tasmin assured him. "You're the one man I can talk to. At one point I could talk to Pomp, but then I fell in love with him and that spoiled that."

"I wish the man would quit stroking his silly mustache," Geoff said, looking at the Major.

36

Juppy, their giant . . .

Juppy, their giant, who sometimes pretended to be a great fish, rising from the water with all six shrieking children clinging to his back, died first, followed by Eliza—she would break no more plates—and Amboise d'Avigdor, ten of the skinny soldiers, and the shy, sad Major Leon. Signore Aldo Claricia died, even as Little Onion sought frantically for herbs to cure him. Cook was very ill but lived; Piet Van Wely was also at the point of death but survived. High Shoulders died an hour after Juppy; Buffum raged, cried, clung to him, prayed, but nothing helped: the cholera took him, though it spared his son, Elphinstone, spared Vicky's Talley but killed her Randy, spared the twins but took Monty. Jim held his dying son in his arms to the end, but Tasmin could not bear

the look on her son's shocked, silent face—
she grabbed her twins and ran far out into
the desert, convinced that they would all die
unless they fled the place of infection, a
small, filthy village where Major Leon assured them travelers on the Camino Real
often stopped to rest their animals. Jim had
not much liked the look of the place—a burial had been in progress as he rode in—but
they were short of fodder for the oxen, there
were goats that could be bought, and perhaps even a horse or two to replace some
of theirs that had gone lame.

"I regret that I left him so often," Jim said
to Father Geoffrin, when Monty died.

"None of us are free of regret," Father
Geoff told him.

Jim had not tried to stop Tasmin's mad
dash into the desert, but now he was worried.

"I wish you'd go find her," Jim asked the
priest. "There's Indians around—I wouldn't
want them to catch her."

As he sat with his son's body, he remembered what had been done to the Spanish
girl.

Lord Berrybender was weeping, stomp-
ing, occasionally crying out.

"Oh, my poor Juppy—come all the way from Northamptonshire, only to die like this," he exclaimed.

Vicky stared at him with hatred.

"I regret Juppy, but you might remember that your son Randy died too—a child you scarcely noticed."

Lord Berrybender merely shrugged.

"I loathe you—you will never touch me again," Vicky said. She picked up Talley and ran into the desert, in the direction that Tasmin had gone.

It was near sunset. Father Geoffrin hurried on his errand. He didn't like it. Cold sun shone on the stark mountains to the east. The landscape offered no welcome—it offered its sere implacability. Where was consolation to be found in such terrible country?

Tasmin clutched her two babies tight. She supposed Monty would have died; she wanted to know but dreaded to ask. She looked at Geoff, who nodded, sadly.

"What about Jim?" she asked.

"He's not dead. He wanted to stay with Monty. He thinks the village well is tainted."

He spoke mainly to fill the terrible silence.

"Is Monty gone'd?" Petal asked, nervously. "I don't see Randy—is he gone'd?"

She knew something had gone terribly wrong, but none of the adults would talk to her.

"You remember that tosh about love we were talking only last week?" Tasmin asked. "That talk about love. I will never forgive myself for being so frivolous."

Father Geoff had no wisdom to offer. The tragedy that had befallen them was beyond any words to correct. What were words, set against the deaths of young and old? And yet silence before the facts was terrible too.

"In casual times there's no harm in talk about love," he said.

"It will never amuse me again," Tasmin avowed.

Father Geoff didn't try to speak against her despair, or Vicky's.

"Children so often die," he said. "All three of my brothers died within a year. I suspect that's why I became so odd."

It was true, of course—Tasmin knew. Many children died in the Berrybender nurseries. Cousins died—the children of the servants died. Master Stiles, her first lover, lost a beloved young daughter. Her own aunt

Clarissa had lost no less than six children. What Tasmin, in the freshness of her grief, could not fathom was how Aunt Clarissa regained enough interest to keep making more babies. Tasmin certainly did not expect to regain it.

"Please, can we go back to the camp—Jim is afraid there might be Indians," Geoff asked.

"They're no worse than cholera, if they are around," Tasmin said. She felt a deep reluctance to take her two living children back to the place of death. Vicky seemed to feel the same way.

"Look where we are—nowhere!" she said. "That whole wretched village is dying. It seems impossible to go on."

"But we must! For the sake of the living," Geoff pleaded.

The surviving soldiers and one or two men from the village dug the graves. There was no wood for coffins—they sacrificed blankets to make shrouds. Finally everyone but Juppy was shrouded, not up to Cook's standards, of course. Crosses were made and fixed rather unstably in rocks. Tasmin sobbed until she was dry. So did Buffum and Vicky. It seemed terrible to have to leave a dear child, a dear mate, in such a bleak place.

"I hope to come back someday and get him," Tasmin said to Jim. "I want him to be in a proper graveyard."

Petal could not understand it. She thought that Monty and Randy must only be playing hide-and-seek. They were playing too long; she wanted them to come out, be found. She refused to believe that they were, as she put it, gone'd. For the next few days she kept poking her head under blankets, looking for them. "I don't think they're really gone'd," she repeated. The adults made no answer.

The morning after the burial two more soldiers died.

⊷ 37 ⊶

The soldiers supposed they were all doomed . . .

"Cholera's on the river—we have to get off the river," Jim told the company. Lord Berrybender had found a bottle of whiskey in Major Leon's baggage and was very drunk—he was shunned by all. Tasmin and Vicky were prepared to smash his fine new guns—they both held Lord B. responsible for the deaths of their boys and they meant to take revenge, but Jim stopped them.

"Best not spoil the guns—we might need 'em," Jim pointed out.

"Then I'll smash him!" Vicky said, overcome by a terrible bitterness. She rushed at Lord Berrybender and began to punch him as hard as she could. Soon he was all bloodied. Vicky kicked and punched at him until she exhausted herself. Buffum merely

238 LARRY MCMURTRY

stumbled along, rigid with grief—though she did help Little Onion get the babies fed.

Jim determined to take the party east, over the low mountain range east of the river. He didn't know the desert, didn't trust himself in it. He wanted to get back to the plains—there should be buffalo. One thing that worried him was their lack of fighting men. High Shoulders, the best fighter after himself, was dead. Juppy was dead, and Amboise; it left himself, Lord Berrybender, and Father Geoff. As things stood any sizable band of hostile Indians could finish them. With that problem in mind he decided to ask the six remaining soldiers to come with them. They had weapons—maybe they could shoot. The soldiers, exhausted by the grave digging, sat listlessly on their saddles.

"You had better come with us," Jim told them. "I doubt you could make it back to Santa Fe."

The soldiers supposed they were all doomed—they wished they had never decided to be soldiers.

Corporal Dominguin, now nomimally their leader, brightened at Jim's suggestion.

"We will be happy to come with you,

señor," he said. "We were afraid you meant to abandon us."

Jim had to pull Tasmin away from Monty's grave.

"Let me stay," she begged. "I'm useless now. Go on—save the twins."

She remembered how often Monty had seemed bewildered—in fact she was the part of his life that had bewildered him, kissing him one minute and ignoring him the next.

"You have another wife, and a good one—can't you just leave me?" she asked.

Jim made no effort to talk to her. He put her in the wagon and pulled Buffum off High Shoulders' grave.

Vicky refused to ride with Lord Berrybender, or to help him in any way. He finally persuaded Cook to ride in the buggy with him, and take the reins.

"Oh, Jimmy—I don't know—I wish you'd leave me," Tasmin cried.

"Hush about that," Jim said. For once, he thought he understood his wife. Whenever Monty's face came to mind, which was often, he felt a plunging sadness. He knew there were many things he should have done differently but now would never have the chance to do.

A blinding snowstorm struck as they were toiling up the low pass. Tasmin was almost glad of the pain of the cold.

"We're leaving a great many dead in Nuevo México," Mary remarked, sighing. "If Piet had died I would have died. I could not live without him."

"To think so is a very great luxury, very wrong," Buffum told her. "I thought the same myself but as you see I'm alive."

"Old Gorska killed himself, in despair for his son—I rather admired him for it," Mary replied.

"Shut up, all of you—you're making it worse," Tasmin told them.

"No, Tassie—I have to talk—it's the silence I can't bear," Buffum said.

"We have our young to consider," she added.

"I know that, but please shut up," Tasmin asked.

"It's too much snow," Petal said, popping out from under a blanket.

Tasmin felt a moment of resentment. How had this noisy child survived the place that killed Monty? And wouldn't this place—this West—finally kill them all?

"You're all young," Father Geoffrin told them. "There will be other children."

Tasmin slapped him—she couldn't help it.

"We don't want them, you fool," Tasmin yelled. "We want the ones we lost. Monty! Randy!"

"I was just . . . ," Father Geoff said, and then gave it up.

— 38 —

In the morning Jim rode back to find her.

Neither Tasmin nor Jim could sleep. Petey dozed in Tasmin's arms, Petal in Jim's. Little Onion was walking Elf, crooning to him in her own tongue. Buffum continually threw small chips of wood into the fire.

One of the young soldiers had a kind of tambourine—the soldiers sang songs around their own campfire. Everyone seemed to fear sleep, except Lord Berrybender, who was snoring loudly. They had bought three nanny goats in the village. Cook was milking one of them.

"I forgot my cello," Vicky said. "Come all this way with me, and I forgot it. I must just go back and fetch it."

Jim shook his head.

"It's the other side of the pass," Jim reminded her. "There's two feet of snow up there."

"But I must have my cello," Vicky said, in a voice that was high and unnatural.

"He's right, Vicky—let it go," Tasmin advised. She didn't like the look in Vicky's eyes.

"There are plenty of cellos in this world," Tasmin reminded her. "I personally will see that you have the finest in London, once we get back."

"It was the deaths—I forgot it—it's been my cello for such a while."

"Please forget it, Vicky—please," Buffum pled.

"I think we should tie her," Jim said to Tasmin, later.

"No—I fear she'd go crazy."

"She *is* crazy—grief crazy," Jim argued.

"So am I, or very nearly," Tasmin told him.

"She's worse," Jim insisted. "And she's got Talley to think of."

"And we have the twins to think of, and Buffum has Elf—but we aren't thinking of *them.* I'm thinking of Monty—I suspect you are too."

"I still think we ought to tie her—it's for her own good," Jim insisted.

"Doing what one can to dull this pain is for one's own good, Jim," Tasmin argued.

Despite Jim's vigilance, Vicky escaped. In the morning Jim rode back to find her. Fortunately it had warmed a little—she had only managed to stumble half a mile. One foot was frostbitten but Cook and Father Geoffrin rubbed it vigorously with snow and concluded that it could be saved.

"I'm only dubious about the little toe," Geoff concluded.

When the dawn mists cleared they looked down a long slope to the snowy prairies, almost covered with grazing buffalo.

Lord Berrybender, to his fury, was not permitted a weapon. The old man was bent on revenge for the beating he had been given by his wife.

"I fear he'll shoot Vicky, if we allow him a gun," Jim argued.

Lord Berrybender, in tears, appealed to his eldest daughter.

"But I've come all this way to hunt—and there's the buffalo," Lord B. insisted. "Why shouldn't I hunt?"

"You'll have no gun today," Tasmin assured him. "We've suffered grievous losses.

Two children are dead. Do you think we care a fig for your hunting?"

Lord B., infuriated, tried to slap Tasmin, who ducked and slapped him smartly hard.

"We are none of us at our best today—indeed, we may never be at our best again," she told him, fiercely. "But we *are* struggling to behave as civilized people. Your own behavior is disgraceful. Any more out of you and we'll have the soldiers tie you to your buggy."

"Not a bit of it, you insolent bitch!" Lord Berrybender shouted, enraged.

"Spent thousands on this trip—I suppose I *will* hunt when I want to—and no more damned impudence from you!"

He shoved Tasmin and hobbled to his gun cases. He tried to grab a rifle but Vicky seized the barrel and the two of them struggled in the snow. With a violent yank he managed to wrench the rifle from her and was just looking to his ammunition when Jim picked him up and flung him violently to the ground; then he dragged the old man to the buggy and pitched him into it. With help from Little Onion and Corporal Dominguin they soon had him tied in his seat. Lord

Berrybender was frothing and spitting in his fury.

"I'll have every man jack of you lashed at the cart's tail!" he yelled. "Don't care if you are my own blood. Put you in the stocks! Pelted with offal!"

"Maybe his mind's slipping, Tassie," Mary conjectured. "He's like he was that day Bobbety shot his horse."

"We've just lost seven people," Tasmin reminded her. "One was his son and two were his grandchildren—and yet he still wants to shoot.

"I think most of us are not far from crazy at this juncture," she went on. She meant it; she felt only just sane. It seemed to her she might just hang on to sanity if there was no more trouble, no more loss. But here they were again, facing a wintry plain—a plain that seemed endless. There would be more trouble and, very likely, more loss.

Suddenly they were all startled by a wild ululation from Jim—furious at Lord Berrybender. The Word suddenly poured out, frightening the old lord so that his hair stood on end. Tasmin remembered the sounds of the Word from the day the Osage chased them; to everyone else it was a shock. Lord

Berrybender thought his son-in-law must have gone mad. What did it mean?

Petal was extremely startled, but not frightened.

"Petey, listen at Jim," she commanded, and Petey did listen, amazed.

The whole camp fell silent until the Sin Killer finished his cry.

"As I was mentioning, Mary, some of us are not far from crazy," Tasmin said. Jim Snow gave her father a hard shaking before he turned away.

"That's only the third time I've heard you do that," Tasmin said, when Jim, calming, came to her.

"You missed Billy Williams—he's the one who shot High Shoulders," Jim told her. "I yelled him the Word, not long ago."

"Do it again," Petal demanded. "I like it. Do it for me. It's like a gobble bird.

"Some people call them turkeys but I call them gobble birds," Petal added.

Despite her cheerful request, Jim did not do it again.

39

"It just comes out, when I see bad sinning," Jim told his wife . . .

"It just comes out, when I see bad sinning," Jim told his wife, trying to explain his crying of the Word.

What he had done so startled the camp that, for a few minutes, they all forgot their grief. Soon enough sorrow edged back into their consciousness, but they looked at Jim differently. Petal was the only one in the company who tried to make him make the strange sounds on command—her command.

"Be the Sin Killer," she asked her father, but he wouldn't obey.

Lord Berrybender was so upset by what his son-in-law had just done that he got an attack of the shakes. He trembled so violently that Cook finally gave him a little whiskey, to calm him down.

"I wish I knew exactly what you think the bad sins are," Tasmin said. "I'm sure we'd all try not to do them if we just knew what they were."

Jim felt shaky himself. In his rage he had pulled his knife, just as he had with Billy Williams. It had been in him to cut Lord Berrybender's throat—he had just managed to stop himself, and yet all Lord Berrybender had done was make himself a violent old nuisance.

"I nearly killed your pa," he said, to Tasmin. "I had the knife out. It's lucky I stopped."

"I believe it made a profound impression on Papa," Tasmin told him. "On all of us, for that matter."

For a second night they scarcely slept. Jim untied Lord Berrybender but didn't speak to him. Lord B. looked pathetically at Vicky, hoping for a word of sympathy, but Vicky turned her back. Cook finally took pity on him. She had been His Lordship's cook for many years; his flaws and faults were abundant, but still he must be fed—though, as she worked, from time to time she found herself sobbing at the thought of dear Eliza and the little lost babies.

"Where will we go now, Jimmy?" Tasmin asked. "Are there no towns anywhere? We're all tired of this wilderness my father's selfishness has brought us to."

Jim had been asking himself the same questions. There were Mexican towns to the west but they would all just be arrested again if he took them to a Mexican town. He knew there were settlements in south Texas—but he didn't know the country and would have to feel his way along, hoping to strike one of the forks of the Brazos River, which he had been told led to the settlements. When he and Kit had come back along the Canadian River country after their trip to New Orleans, they had met numbers of immigrants, but none of them had any very reliable information to pass on. With luck, once they got east, they might chance on a party of immigrants and join up with with them as protection against the tribes.

Tasmin could not remember Jim being as doubtful about how to proceed as he was at the moment. Always before, he had seemed to know exactly where he wanted to go— when decisions had to be made, he made them without hesitation. His sudden lack of certainty filled her with despair. They were caught in a nightmare—a nightmare that had no meaning. If they had come to a place where even Jim Snow felt daunted, then the future looked dark indeed.

"Remember that first morning, when we met?" she asked. "You killed me a deer and we set out in the boat and I became rather impatient. I offered to put you ashore and proceed on my own, but you wouldn't have it—then the Osage got after us and you saved me."

Jim just nodded—of course he remembered.

"If you'd just gone ashore as I wished, none of this would have happened," she went on. "You'd have survived and I'd have been killed. Probably all of us would have been killed, and it would have served us right. We left our place—and a good place it was—for a place where we could not possibly belong. The Indians were right to try and kill us. We were just invaders—spoiled invaders."

She paused—she knew she was just confusing Jim. And yet it was how she felt: better to have died than to have lived to bury her child.

Jim kept his mind on the route. Past

times, such as Tasmin was talking about, didn't interest him. He meant to kill several buffalo and have Cook and Little Onion jerk the meat. They might pass out of the buffalo range—they would need meat.

"I wish Kit was here," he admitted. "Kit's been a passel of places. He might even know something about Texas."

Tasmin saw that he did not want to deal with the complexity of her regret, which was hers to suffer alone—yet she knew he grieved for Monty. As parent and child the two had got off to a slow start, but improvement had been rapid. Jim often took Monty up beside him on the mare—he had even tried to teach him one or two bird-calls—calls Jim himself didn't do well.

Jim after all had the job of saving them. Why should he care about her moody recollections? And yet the fact that he didn't made her feel lonely; she abruptly got up and walked away. She felt like giving up— what Vicky had done under the pretext of recovering her cello. Vicky could not stand what was—she had sought the cold, hoping it would all be over.

Tasmin stood at the edge of the camp for

a long time—not particularly thinking, just being alone.

"I wish you'd go talk to Tassie," Kate Berrybender said, to Father Geoff. "She might run away. Couldn't you stop her? She likes you."

Geoff got up and did what Kate asked.

"Go away, Geoff—can't you see I prefer to be alone?" Tasmin said at once, when he approached.

"Don't leave—we all depend on you," Geoff told her.

Tasmin looked at him so coldly that he turned and went away, fearing that he had failed in his mission.

Tasmin stood until her feet and fingers were numb with cold—the faraway stars were brilliant. Finally she went back to the wagon and made sure her children were covered up.

. . . an extremely irritating old fellow.

"His nose is too small," Greasy Lake told the Likeness Maker. "He's proud of his nose—I think you better make it larger."

George Catlin was both exasperated and frightened. He was attempting the portrait of a Comanche warrior named Flat Nose—the man had been kicked by a horse in his youth and was very flat-nosed indeed. But he himself was not a caricaturist—he did not like to exaggerate anatomical features and he also did not like to receive instruction from Greasy Lake, an extremely irritating old fellow. George had jumped at the chance to come out with the military to this great convening of Comanches and Kiowas on the southern plains, in an area of bumpy mountains, the prairies swarming with buffalo.

There was no real danger—he had Colonel Dodge's troops to protect him. And yet there was always an element of the gamble, when doing portraits of Indians. George Catlin had done nearly four hundred such portraits—the risk that a savage sitter wouldn't approve his own likeness was always there.

Still, he had come, and he was determined to paint—there might never again be such a gathering of tribes on the south plains. It was a golden, if a frightening, opportunity. He was, it was true, disappointed in Colonel Dodge, who had not brought nearly enough presents, and now, just as George Catlin was gaining the confidence of his subjects, the colonel seemed to want to leave. George had decided to take the dare and stay even without the troops. If anyone was to record the Comanches and the Kiowas in their undiminished splendor, it had to be himself and it had to be now.

He knew that he ought not to grumble about Greasy Lake—the fact that the tribes accepted him as a prophet made his own task possible. With Greasy Lake's protection the tribes would likely not bother him, even if Colonel Dodge did leave. Toussaint

Charbonneau, though much saddened by
the death of his son, Pomp, had nonetheless been kind enough to travel to the
Osage country, find Greasy Lake, and intro-
duce him to George Catlin—the presence of
Greasy Lake had been an immense help in
enabling the Likeness Maker to secure his
first sitters. The old prophet's purpose in
being on the plains had been to attempt to
locate a white buffalo, a beast that was said
to have been found by the Comanches two
years earlier. The white buffalo was said to
be as tame as a milk cow—the Comanches
kept the animal in a cave and brought people to see him one or two at a time.

George was convinced that he had Flat
Nose about right; he was convinced the sitter would like it. The great challenge, always, were the eyes. Flat Nose's look was
stony and suspicious—vanity had caused
him to sit for the likeness, as other chiefs
had sat—but like most of the native poten-
tates, he was suspicious of the Likeness
Maker. Early on George had learned never
to do natives in profile—the Indian was apt
to conclude that the Likeness Maker had
stolen half his face. It was full face or nothing, when painting Indians.

Another small technical difficulty was that the Indians insisted on painting themselves elaborately before George was allowed to depict them; getting his colors to match their colors was very important—and no item of decoration might be neglected: he must get the bear claws right, the feathers right, the furs right. Sometimes a warrior might insist on being painted with his lance, from which might dangle two or three scalps—these grisly trophies must not be scanted. To omit even one scalp from the portrait would mean trouble.

Greasy Lake was a keen observer of George Catlin's practice. He was not reluctant to offer advice, if he thought a portrait not bold enough. George Catlin seldom took his advice, it was true, and yet somehow, in most cases, the sitter liked the portrait and offered no violence to the painter.

In time Greasy Lake concluded that there had to be magic involved—magic and a kind of trickery. The painter managed to make the chiefs appear not so much as they were but as they liked to believe they were: noble, strong, brave, dignified. When he mentioned this aspect of the matter to Catlin, the painter laughed.

"It's better than that—I'm anticipating," George assured him. "I'm making them look like they *will* look, in a few years."

When he studied the pictures closely and compared them to the living men, Greasy Lake saw that what the Likeness Maker said was true. He was skipping ahead, through time, to capture something that the sitters would become.

Then Greasy Lake had a troubling thought. What if the men died before they became the men caught in the pictures? The pictures would then be pictures of ghosts—a frightening thought, one that made Greasy Lake very uncomfortable. It might be that the ghost of the man might come back and inhabit the picture itself. The spirits of dead men might find their way into these likenesses.

In the case of Flat Nose, George had judged correctly. The moment when he showed a painting to its subject was rarely without tension. Almost all Indians were at first startled to see themselves on a piece of canvas. It was a grave thing, an important thing—many had to sit and settle their nerves while they considered the situation. When they were calm enough they took a long time studying the portrait. After all, a human being was complex—there were hands, hair, ears, feet, chin to examine. Were they accurately drawn? Would the image, if it was wrong, affect their bodies? The making of likenesses was a new thing. The tribal councils were divided about it. They were mainly against it—but in the end many of the young men and even some of the old men were unable to resist this opportunity to see exactly how they looked.

Flat Nose sat with his portrait in his hands for many minutes. He brought his eyes very close to the canvas—he looked at every detail. When he was finished he nodded gravely and gave the Likeness Maker a dignified hug.

"See, I told you he'd like it," George told Greasy Lake.

"Flat Nose doesn't know how to look at a picture," Greasy Lake replied. "But it's just as well. If he had realized you made his nose too small he would have killed you."

41

An old, half-blind Kiowa woman . . .

When the Likeness Maker found out that Greasy Lake had traveled with the English party for a while he made himself a great pest, asking question after question about them. He wanted to know how many of them were still alive, and which direction they might be traveling. Greasy Lake knew they had been in Santa Fe for a while, and now, if Kit Carson was to be believed, were under escort and on their way to Mexico.

"I might need to go to Mexico myself," George said. "At least, I intend to go to Texas. I hope you'll come with me—I'd like to see a white buffalo too."

The two of them had lingered near the Wichita Mountains for a few days, after the big convening. George found himself attracted to the low, humpy hills. He wanted to complete a few landscapes before moving on.

An old, half-blind Kiowa woman had been left behind by her people when the big gathering broke up. She had a small camp and a little food. Her name was Na-a-me. Greasy Lake did his best to make friends with her, but it was not easy. Na-a-me was bitter that her life was over. She did not want to be old and abandoned. She wanted to do life over again and she tolerated Greasy Lake because he claimed to be a powerful prophet. Perhaps he knew some way to help a person start life over again.

Greasy Lake had a motive of his own, when he tried to make friendly talk with the bitter Na-a-me. He suspected she knew where the white buffalo was—the beast he had been looking for for almost two years. The white buffalo had been born during a great shower of falling stars. Obviously the band that had captured the beast wanted to keep its whereabouts a secret. Greasy Lake was not even sure that the white buffalo was in a cave. That might be bad information, meant to throw searchers off. Many bands would like to have access to such a powerful beast. Many would seek to steal it, if they knew where it was. The band that had it was said to be small and poor—their best bet for keeping the buffalo would be to hide it. He had a suspicion old Na-a-me knew more than she was saying about the whereabouts of the important beast.

Old Na-a-me, however, was a tough customer. She said it was all a lie some Kickapoos made up. There never had been a white buffalo. Some Kickapoos had come on a white skin of some kind, that was all— perhaps it had belonged to a buffalo calf that had been eaten by wolves and coyotes. Some said it was a buffalo skin but others claimed it was only the skin of a goat. Old Na-a-me considered it a joke. She had lived amid buffalo all her life and had never seen a white one.

Then Greasy Lake became absolutely convinced that the old woman was lying. Probably the reason she was lying was because it was her own band that had the white buffalo.

"If you can make a picture of how a person will be, can you also make a picture of how a person used to be?" he asked the Likeness Maker. "Can you look at this old granny and draw her as she was when she was young?"

The possibility had not occurred to George Catlin—it had never crossed his mind to reverse his normal practice—that is, to show what a sitter had been like in earlier life. Of course, it *should* be possible. The fate of a face, like the fate of a man himself, was to change. From what was there, it should be possible to recover what had been there.

"Paint the old granny as she might have been when she had twenty summers," Greasy Lake requested.

George squatted down and looked closely at the old woman—annoyed by the scrutiny, she glared at the white man. Why was he looking at her so?

"But she's blind—she won't be able to see my painting," George said.

Greasy Lake had been watching the old woman closely and was not convinced that she was so blind.

"She just pretends to be blind so people will wait on her," Greasy Lake concluded.

"Wait on her? They left her to die!" George pointed out. "Who do you think is going to wait on her?"

"I think she could see a picture if you painted one," Greasy Lake insisted.

"Even if she doesn't, it will be an interesting challenge," George said. "I should have thought of it myself. Perhaps I can even make it a profitable sideline, when I get back home. The society matron as young belle! Why, my fortune will be made."

At once he set to work, old Na-a-me glaring at him the whole time—she worked her gums and occasionally mouthed imprecations. George found the situation amusing; he wished Tasmin were with him to share the joke. He was trying to use his art to turn an old Kiowa grandmother into a young woman.

Despite the old woman's irritation George took as much time with this portrait as he would have if he had been painting a mighty chief. When he finished he handed the picture to Greasy Lake, who studied it carefully before passing it on to old Na-a-me. At first old Na-a-me was puzzled by what she was given. One of her eyes was gone but one was not quite so bad—peering at the picture, she decided the white man must be a powerful magician. From nothing he had made a picture of a Kiowa girl, such as her sisters and her cousins had been long ago. That the girl was meant to be herself, she did not grasp. Except for a rippling reflection in a stream now and then she had never seen herself as a girl. The Kiowa had no mirrors then—only lately had traders begun to bring them. The girl in the picture was only a girl to Na-a-me at first, and yet the white man had worked hard and brought it into being with his magic.

Then it occurred to her that the white man might be even more of a magician than she had supposed. Perhaps he was offering to make her into a girl again—young like the girl in his picture. Why would this strange magician want to do that?

After thinking about it for a few minutes Na-a-me decided it was all about the white buffalo. The old prophet was trying to bribe her with the gift of youth, if she would only help him find the white buffalo. He wanted the power of the white buffalo so badly that he had gone to the trouble of finding a magician who was offering her what appeared to be a second life. Perhaps this time she would find better husbands than she had found the first time—but if not, she would at

least get to live a great many more summers.

There was a problem, though: Na-a-me
had no idea where the white buffalo was—
nor was she even sure there *was* a white
buffalo. But she had always been an accomplished liar, easily deceiving her husbands and her lovers when it pleased her to.
It took no time at all for her to invent a big
lie about the white buffalo.

"He's in that big canyon over by the Rio
Rojo," she said.

"The Palo Duro, she means," George
said. "That's not far from here."

Greasy Lake was wary. He wanted Na-a-
me to be more specific.

"If the buffalo is there, where do they hide
it?" he asked.

"To the west, near the sunset," Na-a-me
told him glibly. She didn't like the prophet.
He reminded her of her husband Peta, who
was always asking questions, hoping to ex-
pose her lies. Greasy Lake was the same
kind of man. He wanted to pick her story
apart, but Na-a-me didn't let him. The buffalo was at the west end of the big canyon.
That was all she intended to say. The
prophet wanted to know if the white buffalo

was well guarded, but Na-a-me refused to elaborate. She considered that she had told them a perfect lie.

That night Na-a-me slept little. She was waiting to feel herself become young again.

Bitter was her disappointment to wake up to find herself still old. The white man and the prophet were leaving. She had seen the picture. Why wasn't she young?

Then it became clear to her. The white man was a clever trickster, but not clever enough to make old people young. He had tricked her into telling them about the white buffalo. Then she remembered that she had lied too. She had no idea where a white buffalo lived. The lies, she saw, had canceled one another out. She would just die, as the People had intended she die. There would be no second life, a realization that made Na-a-me bitter. She cursed and cursed, working her mouth in anger. The white man had left her some food, some matches, some tobacco. What he hadn't left her was a second life.

42

It was easy enough for Charlie to prance around . . .

"Charlie will think we're lazy if we give up and go back this soon," Willy Bent argued. "I expect he'll dock your wages."

Kit began to boil at the thought of such an injustice.

"If he tries to dock my wages I'll give him a lickin' he'll never forget," Kit said. "And if he tries to dock yours I suggest you do the same."

"He can't dock *my* wages," Willy pointed out. "I'm his partner. I own as much of the company as he does."

"Then you could dock my wages your-self—just try it if you want a lickin'," Kit told him, still indignant. The high-handedness of the Bents frequently put him in an angry state.

"You deserve to have yours docked,"

Willy observed. "You're the one who got us lost."

"I ain't lost," Kit protested. "Why are you standing there telling lies?"

"If you don't know which river this is, then we're lost," Willy insisted. "You're the one who wanted to follow it."

The day before they had dropped off a high escarpment into broken country of gullies and washes and salt cedar thickets. They had chosen the rough country because of the abundance of Indian sign on the plains. In the gullies and washes there were places to hide. Charlie Bent had sent them on a scouting trip to the country below the Canadian River, country that was controlled by the Comanches and the Kiowas. Charlie saw it as a major immigration route and was determined to put a trading post somewhere in it. Kit and Willy's job was to look for likely sites, and they had found several; but the likeliest site in the country didn't eliminate the real problem with such a venture: the real problem, still, were the Indians.

Charlie's notion was that they might locate some small poor band and lavish presents on them until they put aside their lances and scalping knives and began to see the virtue of having traders around. Maybe the small bands could then influence the big bands. It was easy enough for Charlie to prance around his secure establishment on the Arkansas and develop theories such as that one; but it was quite another thing, as Willy and Kit could testify, to ride around in constant danger trying to locate this ideal small band.

They had been scared enough just because of the overabundance of sign, but then they ran into Tom Fitzpatrick, on his way back from a trip to Mississippi, and Tom brought news of a bad new war chief, known as Wolf Eater from his habit of chasing down wolves and eating them in order to enhance his power. Wolf Eater had recently wiped out two small immigrant trains, leaving burned and mangled bodies here and there on the prairie.

"He's a bad un," Tom assured them. "Whatever you do, don't try to powwow with him."

"I have no intention of speaking to the man," Kit told old Tom.

It was worry about the Wolf Eater that had prompted them to leave the prairie and begin to traverse the badlands, on a day of light snow and cutting wind. In the distance a broadish, reddish river flowed east.

"That'll be the Rio Rojo, I guess," Kit said.

"What if it ain't?" Willy asked. "Charlie's going to want an accurate report."

"If he don't trust me, let him come look for himself," Kit replied hotly. The pickiness of Charles Bent was often hard to tolerate.

"If it ain't the Red, I suppose it could be the Prairie Dog Fork of the Brazos," Kit allowed.

"Whatever it is, it's no place for a trading post," Willy said. "You'd never get wagons through these gullies."

There was no disputing the fact that rocky gullies had a bad effect on wagon wheels.

"There's a big canyon around here somewhere," Kit mentioned. "They say a million buffalo can graze in it without even being crowded."

"I suppose that would be an exaggeration," Willy remarked.

"What's to stop us from having a look?" Kit argued.

Willy thought he might as well humor the

man. If he refused to let him visit the canyon he'd sulk all the way back to the Arkansas.

"We can look, but I have no intention of going down in it," Willy told him. "It would be easy to get boxed in by Indians in a hole in the ground like that."

The next day near dusk they found themselves looking down into the Palo Duro canyon—plenty of buffalo roamed the canyon floor, though considerably less than a million, as Willy was quick to point out.

Kit, as usual, was reluctant to give ground.

"I expect it'll fill up in the spring, when the grass is better," he said.

They were near the west end of the canyon when they spotted two horsemen who had stopped near the rim and were looking down into the shadowy gorge. One of the horses was white.

"I know that horse—it's Greasy Lake's," Kit said at once. "He got that horse from the Partezon, that bad old Sioux, remember him?"

"Never met him, which is why I'm now alive," Willy replied.

"Why, that other fellow is George Catlin— I'd swear it is," Kit cried, excited. "He's that fellow paints pictures of Indians. I was with him on the Yellowstone."

"Is the man a fool?" Willy inquired. "Who would want a picture of an Indian when there's real Indians all over the place, waiting to scalp anybody they can catch?"

"Why, easterners—the Indians there are rather tamed down," George explained, when he and Willy had been introduced. "Most easterners today have never seen a fighting Indian, and never will."

"I'm surprised life is so boresome that they have to look at pictures," Willy said, even as he edged closer to the painter's easel, where a fine rendering of a buffalo was nearly completed. The only thing wrong with the rendering of the buffalo that Willy could see was that the animal was yellow.

"Yes, yellow," George admitted. "It's a freak of coloration, I suppose. Greasy is mighty disappointed. He says the animal was born white but turned yellow before he could locate it."

Greasy Lake stood on the rim of the canyon, chanting—he looked wildly distraught.

"Why would a buffalo turn yellow?" Kit wondered.

"I don't know, but it's the only yellow buffalo I've ever seen—I thought I ought to paint it," the painter said.

. . . the ignorant Kiowas merely made rude sounds.

The trip to the canyon had been arduous, the weather bitter. Along the way they had been harassed by a band of surly Kiowas, who were not much impressed by Greasy Lake's credentials as a prophet. What they were impressed by was the white horse he rode. When Greasy explained to them that the white horse had been given him by the Partezon, the greatest of all Sioux warriors, the ignorant Kiowas merely made rude sounds. They had never heard of any Partezon. George Catlin saved the day by showing them portraits of some of the Kiowa chiefs he had painted at the great convening. The paintings startled the Kiowas very much—the fact that a white man was carrying around likenesses of their own chiefs disturbed them. Here was magic—possibly

negative magic. They decided they had better go find Wolf Eater and tell him about this
magic. Wolf Eater had refused to go to the
great convening. He did not like talking to
white soldiers.

"I'd be happy to paint Chief Wolf Eater, if
he'd care to pay us a visit," George told the
Kiowas, before they left.

Greasy Lake chided George for this invi-
tation. Wolf Eater's only use for white men
was to kill them. Inviting him to visit had not
been wise.

George took these strictures with a grain
of salt. Most savages he had painted in his
years in the West had been volatile fellows
who posed some danger—and yet usually
their vanity had been his protection. Somehow the ceremonial nature of the sitting had
exerted a taming quality that George had
begun to find a little boring. The closest he
had come to recording native life at its
bloodiest were not portraits at all but
sketches he had done of the Mandan torture ceremonies, and a few grisly buffalo
hunts. In the torture ceremonies young men
were suspended from the lodge poles by
cords strung through their pectorals. There,
in the faces of the old men watching, he felt

he had seen real savagery, rituals absolutely pagan in their character. He considered these sketches the crown of his dangerous work, and yet he could not neglect the portraits, because it was the portraits that gained him entry to the torture lodges.

The closer the two men got to the canyon where the white buffalo was supposed to be, the more convinced Greasy Lake became that the old woman had been telling them lies. Old people left to die sometimes sought final amusements, such as sending prophets off on wild-goose chases.

Still, seeing the great canyon would be worth it, even if no white buffalo appeared. Great canyons were important places in themselves—it was from the floor of these canyons that the People had emerged from the earth on the back of the Great Turtle that had brought them into the light.

The first shock came when the two of them ran into a small band of Kickapoos who informed them that they themselves, not the Comanches, had found the white buffalo when it was just a calf. Naturally they were overjoyed to see the white buffalo, a great gift from the spirits. They soon caught it and tamed it. They band was very small—only two of their women could still bear children, and yet once the white buffalo came, three other women immediately got with child, and the older men made several successful hunts. It seemed the band might be saved.

But then a bad thing happened, a thing that caused the whole band to lose much of its optimism. The white buffalo grew into a yearling, and when it did, not only did it not stay white, but it turned yellow, the unluckiest color of all. The whiteness of the buffalo calf had only been a temporary miracle, one that allowed the little band to increase by a few promising babies. They assumed the yellow buffalo was still changing and would soon become a normal brown buffalo.

But the yellow buffalo did not become normal and brown. It remained yellow. The little band had no prophet, no wise man. They had once had a prophet but he developed a disease of the bowels and quickly wasted away.

The yellow buffalo, as tame as a dog, stayed with the band. Some argued for killing it but others insisted that would be a mistake. Occasionally the yellow buffalo ran off with some wild buffalo for a few days, but it always came back.

George Catlin and Greasy Lake happened on the yellow buffalo before they met the Kickapoos who were its keepers. George considered it a fine curiosity, a freak of coloration that sometimes occurred in this or that species. He knew it was something that would interest his rival, Mr. Audubon, who was preparing a book on the quadrupeds of America. George felt happy to have stolen a march on his rival—he did several sketches and would have liked to continue to do them had Greasy Lake not become so upset. It was not easy to make out exactly why the prophet was so disturbed—he seemed to see the yellow buffalo as somehow connected to doom.

At first George thought he was merely predicting *their* doom, but then it emerged that the doom he had in mind was considerably more general.

The minute he saw the yellow buffalo Greasy Lake began to tremble—the oldest stories, the ones he himself was supposed to guard, all insisted that the coming of a yellow beast meant that the Ending was near. Seeing the buffalo was thus a cruel disappointment. Out of a white beast might have grown new hope; but from a yellow beast they could expect only decay and sickness, a trailing off, a diminishment into ever smaller and more hopeless bands, such as the little band of Kickapoos they soon met.

Seeing the yellow buffalo made Greasy Lake realize that the old Partezon had been right: the time of the People was coming to an end. Soon the women of the tribes would become barren, the warriors would lose their strength of arm, the old men would begin to forget the stories; then the game would gain mastery over the hunters, the ducks and geese would learn to elude snares, and even rabbits would disappear. Soon, in a few more generations, there would be no People at all; the circle would be broken, the stories would end.

George Catlin was prepared to admit that the yellow buffalo was ugly—but then, normal brown buffalo were not beautiful, and not smart, either. In the north the tribes would sometimes get them running so mindlessly that they would pour off cliffs, killing and crippling themselves in a mass of bellowing froth as the Indians waded in, hacking and stabbing until the last beast was dead, by which time the hackers would be covered with blood.

This buffalo, though a rather disgusting color, was at least a novelty. George could not understand why Greasy Lake was taking on so.

"I can't make out what's upset you so," George confessed. "I know you were counting on finding a white buffalo but I'm afraid that ugly fellow is as close as we're going to come. It's just a yellow animal with a rather peculiar coloration—it's not the end of the world."

Greasy Lake knew that his friend George meant well. George was kind, if not terribly bright.

He failed to understand that for the People the arrival of the yellow buffalo meant exactly that: the End of the world.

. . . a flock of wild turkeys, bursting from their roost . . .

It was a flock of wild turkeys, bursting from their roost, that caused the mare to stumble. Jim had been easing down a steep shaley ridge, his eye on two buffalo grazing in the flats about a mile away. He was being careful because the wind was acting as if it might shift. The company was almost out of meat, and here was meat, and Jim wanted to make sure of it. The capricious wind was not helping. He didn't see the turkeys and neither did the mare, who shied violently when the gobblers rose above them, their big wings almost brushing Jim's head.

The mare stumbled and went to her knees—Jim, trying to protect his rifle, attempted to jump clear but didn't quite make it. He hit with his left arm twisted under him—he suspected the arm was broken but didn't mean to allow the injury to distract him from what he had come to do, which was make meat. The buffalo were still placidly grazing. Jim dropped them both; butchering them with only one useful hand proved awkward in the extreme, but he took enough to feed the company—once his arm was set and splinted he could return for the rest of the meat. He felt sure that Father Geoff could set the arm—he could be back for the rest of the meat before the wolves and coyotes did too much damage.

The accident had occurred not much past dawn, which was why the turkeys were still on their roost. It was a chill, sleety day. Jim pushed the mare—he wanted to get his arm set and return to the two carcasses as soon as possible.

He had been pushing the company eastward as fast as he could—he still hoped to strike an immigrant train and perhaps join forces. But he was in unknown country—the first necessity was to keep the company fed. None of them had managed to put the recent deaths behind them—they were too low-spirited to travel as briskly as Jim would have liked them to. Indian sign was everywhere; Jim considered it almost a miracle that they hadn't been harassed.

Jim thought every day of Monty, so young and so innocent. Bad as the cholera had been, Jim knew that worse could happen. If they got through the Comanche country with no more losses they could consider themselves lucky.

It irked him that he had broken his arm because of turkeys, but then it was often the absurd and unexpected that led to injury.

When he returned to camp, Tasmin took the injury harder than anyone. A belief in Jim's invulnerability was one of the convictions that kept her going. By the time he reached camp with the buffalo meat he seemed feverish to her. Piet and Father Geoffrin quickly set the arm and made an excellent splint. Tasmin sat with the twins. She knew rationally that a broken arm was not a serious injury, but she still couldn't help worrying.

"It was just some gobble birds scared his horse," Petal reminded her, giving her mother a friendly pat on the knee.

Tasmin had just recovered a measure of calm when she saw Jim saddling the mare.

She rushed over and felt his forehead. He still felt feverish.

"Now where are you going?" she asked.

"Back to get the rest of that buffalo meat," Jim told her. "We can't afford to lose it—we'll soon be starving, if we do."

Tasmin knew he was right, and yet she had become increasingly anxious whenever Jim was out of camp for very long.

"I just worry so," she admitted. "I wish there was someone else who could go."

"There ain't," he said, speaking tolerantly. He himself was anxious now, on his hunts. The country was too dangerous—too much bad could happen, and quickly. Shy Petey worried Jim a lot. It wouldn't take much, by way of an illness, to carry Petey off. And yet he had to go: there was no one else capable of bringing in the meat. Corporal Dominguin seemed competent but he and the other Mexicans needed to stand guard.

"It's not that far—the meat," he told Tasmin. "I'll be back quick, if I can keep from breaking my other arm."

He meant it as a joke, but a shadow of worry crossed her countenance. After what had happened on the Rio Grande nothing seemed like a joke anymore.

"Jimmy, you're feverish," she told him.

Jim knew it was true. He had always been prone to fevers. When they were high he sometimes hallucinated, even dreamed that he was back with Preacher Cockerell. He knew he was a little feverish—and yet the fact that he might sicken made the recovery of the meat even more vital. He was taking a packhorse. He meant to bring back enough meat to keep them all fed if he was ill for a day or two.

Tasmin suddenly flung herself into his arms. She hated feeling so cowardly but since the deaths she couldn't help it. She felt scared for her children most of the time.

"This is an endless nightmare now," she told Jim. "We're nowhere—there's no safety. The Indians could come anytime. A blizzard could come. Just hurry—please hurry—we've a better chance when you're here."

"The sooner I leave, the sooner I'll get back," Jim told her. He could find no adequate words of reassurance. Everything Tasmin had just said was true. And yet they had to have the meat. All he could do was promise to be as quick as possible.

When he left, Tasmin sat down by Father Geoff. The priest put his arm around her.

"He's always come back," Father Geoff reminded her. "He wants to fill our larder—nothing wrong with that. I wish you wouldn't worry so much. It's making you thin."

"Shut up, Geoff. Just shut up," Tasmin said.

. . . everyone noticed that she was subdued.

"I was never Monty's only mother," Tasmin reminded Mary. "He always had two. When I was too weak from my labor even to lift him, Little Onion held him to my breast. She helped him take his first milk, and she closed his eyes when he died. Not a day in his short life but that she loved him."

They had been discussing Little Onion's changed demeanor. Though still as efficient as ever, quickly attending to the necessary chores, she was no longer cheerful. Her liveliness had brightened camp life on many a lowering day—now everyone noticed that she was subdued. Even Lord Berrybender noticed. Cook was very troubled. Since the death of Eliza, Cook had begun to feel old. There were mornings when she felt herself failing; always, from the moment of waking,

Cook had been resolutely on the move; yet now she wasn't. There were mornings when she could hardly force herself to throw off her blankets. Little Onion had always taken a keen interest in cooking—little by little Cook was teaching the girl her skills. It was a relief to think that there would be someone competent to feed the company if she herself fell by, as she put it. Yet now Little Onion ate little and had lost interest in the preparation of food, though she still kept an eye out for edibles as they traveled.

"I suppose you're right, Tassie—it's mother's grief she's feeling."

"There's more besides," Tasmin said, looking at Little Onion, who sat with the four children but did not seem to be really attending them. Now she looked after them neutrally. Even Petal, with all her wiles, could seldom get Little Onion to smile.

"They all like her but Monty loved her," Tasmin pointed out. "He rarely knew quite what to make of me, but with our Onion it was pure love. No wonder she misses him."

"I've conceived," Mary said, quietly.

Tasmin supposed she had misheard. She looked at her sister in surprise.

"You heard me correctly—I've conceived," Mary said. "Piet and I have at last mastered sexual intercourse."

"I see," Tasmin remarked. "That always seems to mean babies, if a Berrybender female is involved."

"Piet is pleased," Mary said. "I expect him to be an ideal father."

"I expect so too," Tasmin told her.

"Piet likes to do it from the rear, as quadrupeds do," Mary confided. "It's his belief that the seed has easier access to the womb if that approach is adopted."

Tasmin snorted.

"The seed seems to find our eggs with very little difficulty," she said. "Personally I like to face my customers. I feel like a bitch often enough without going on all fours to mate."

"I'm hoping Little Onion will help me as she helped you," Mary said. "I'm rather unconfident when it comes to babies."

"The confidence may arrive with the child," Tasmin told her. "Hard to be maternal in advance."

Petal, getting nowhere in her play with Little Onion, noticed her mother and aunt in conversation and hurried over to inject herself into the situation. Kate Berrybender, who was helping Cook scour some pans, glared at Petal as she passed. Petal generally kept clear of Kate, her youngest aunt.

"Mary is going to have a baby," Tasmin told her daughter, without preamble. "A fresh victim for you to torment."

Petal's hair was a cascade of black curls, defiant of the hairbrush.

"No, there's enough babies now," Petal assured them.

Tasmin wondered if she and Jim had seen the end of baby making. They had been closer since Monty's death, but it was a sad closeness, lacking in conjugal heat. She remembered her aunt Clarissa, who had somehow kept on reproducing after six deaths in the nursery. Tasmin didn't consider herself much like Aunt Clarissa. She got up suddenly, leaving Petal to bicker with Mary, and went over to Little Onion, who looked at her gratefully, though the look came from sad eyes. Tasmin sat down beside her, two mothers of a lost boy. No words needed be said; none were. Petey came and sat in his mother's lap. Petal ran back and tried to shove her way into the same lap, but Tasmin held Petey tight. Petal let be. Something seemed to be amiss with the adults. She accepted Little Onion's lap and began to hum a song Vicky had taught her.

Little Onion liked it that Tasmin had come to sit by her. She knew that Tasmin was her friend. They were both, after all, wives of the same man—good wives too, in Little Onion's opinion. They didn't quarrel—and even she and her sister Sun Girl had quarreled.

She meant to do her best for Tasmin and the other children, and yet the ache of the loss of Monty was a pain not easily endured. Of course, many children died. In the tribe many infants died even as they were born. They were not alive long enough for many people to cherish them, as she had cherished Monty. Such an ache as she felt could only heal slowly—it was there like a sore tooth that throbbed if one bit on a nut too hard. In the case of Monty, the nut was memory. She could not stop remembering him as he had been at his happiest, playing with the simple toys she made him, from corncobs, sticks, scraps of leather.

It made it hard to go on with this journey that seemed without purpose, into country that was far less pleasing than the country of her own people. It was perplexing to her, that whites must be always moving. In her own country she felt confident—she understood the country and could always find sufficient food to eat: roots, berries, nuts. When she was in her country she understood she did not much fear hunger. If her husband was wounded she felt she could find the bark or the herbs that would cure him.

But how could one be sure of anything, in country one has not been able to study? It took thorough knowledge of a place before its secrets could be understood—and yet survival depended on knowing the secrets of the land.

Little Onion felt she might confide these worries to Tasmin at some point; she had already confided a few of them to Buffum. But it wouldn't stop the men. Even in her own tribe the men sometimes insisted on foolish trips.

When the twins wandered off to play with Talley and Elf, Tasmin gave Little Onion's hand a squeeze and told her Mary's news. Little Onion opened her mouth in surprise. Mary was the only one of the whites who was skilled at finding edibles. She and Little

Onion often foraged together. One reason Little Onion was so protective of Tasmin was because Tasmin knew so little about feeding herself; and Buffum and Vicky were just as unskilled. None of them could even find a rat's nest, in a place where rats were plentiful. Mary knew that rats were easy to catch and good to eat, but the other women were horrified by the notion. Little Onion could not imagine why most of the whites had been trained so poorly. Mary could find berries or tubers or wild onions but even she knew little about the plants that could be used as medicines. Piet, though, was very interested in medicinal plants and as knowledgeable about them as Little Onion. Buffum and Vicky could not muster the interest, a mystery to Little Onion, who could not understand why they would not want to be able to cure themselves or their children if they got sick.

Little Onion meant to do all she could to protect her friend Tasmin and the others, but often, at night, she worried. The Mexican boys were not good sentinels. When Jim was out of camp hunting, Little Onion felt obliged to be especially alert. She could do nothing against enemies like the cholera

but she did know how to watch for attack-
ers like the Pawnee boys. She was always
urging the company to stay closer together
when they traveled—it was the fact that
they were so spread out when the Pawnees
attacked that enabled the raiders to kill four
of them. With High Shoulders dead and Jim
often out hunting, the group needed to stay
compact and ready.

It only made sense, and yet it was clear
to Little Onion that the others didn't know
how to guard themselves, or be sensible.
Perhaps it was because they were so far
from their own country. She was baffled
herself, much of the time, by cacti or
bushes that she had never seen before.
Was the plant useful? Or was it deadly? She
would have liked to know but there was no
one to teach her. She tried little experiments
with this plant or that, but she had to be
cautious. She didn't want to poison herself.

*. . . she showed him a heron,
standing on one leg . . .*

Petey loved birds. He tried to chase the
speedy roadrunners, but they soon outdis-
tanced him. He liked to watch the sparrows
that sometimes lit near the campfire, peck-
ing at little seeds or kernels of corn someone had dropped. He would sit for long
hours, watching hawks soar in the sky.
Sometimes Little Onion would point up-
ward, directing his eye to high skeins of
geese. Once she showed him a heron,
standing on one leg in a small pond, the end
of a frog's foot sticking out of its mouth.

The day his father went away Petey was
playing with a small wooden bear Jim had
carved for him. Petal was always stealing
the bear, but at the moment she was with
Cook and Little Onion, eating porridge. His
mother and Buffum were trying to fix his

grandfather's crutch, which the old man had broken in one of his fits. It was a cold morning—Little Onion was building up the campfire. Talley and Elf were with Vicky. Petey thought it was safe to play with his bear and he was doing just that when the little blue quail were passing near—the quail were chirping and Petey heard them. He saw them slipping through the grass just behind them. They moved so quickly that he couldn't get a good look at them. But this time they were very close—he began to creep toward them but the quail sped on. Only now and then did he get a clear look as the blue quail stopped to peck at a seed or bit of gravel. Petey wished he could make one of the blue quail into a pet. They didn't have Mopsy anymore, and he longed for a pet. He decided to follow the quail and perhaps catch one; he wouldn't hurt it.

Petey had been out of the camp only a minute or two when Little Onion missed him. She did frequent surveys of the four active children. One thing all the women were in agreement about was that it only took a minute for a child to get in trouble. If there was a snake anywhere near they would find it. If there was a wasp in the vicinity they would get stung.

Little Onion had a good eye—she just glimpsed Petey as he hurried after the quail. She had heard the blue quail chirping earlier and had been thinking of trying to trap a few. Fat quail were good to eat. But blue quail were speedy—she would need to make a good trap.

Tasmin, though exasperated with her father for cracking his only crutch in one of his violent distempers, surveyed the children herself and failed to see Petey, but before she could grow alarmed Little Onion waved at her and left the camp; evidently she knew where Petey had got to and was off to retrieve him. Tasmin forgot about it. She and Buffum were trying to wrap the splintered crutch with some light cord—the task was not made easier by Lord Berrybender's surly mood.

"I insist that you speak to my wife," he told Tasmin. "Shameful the way she neglects me. Wives have duties—they are not just free to indulge themselves. Selfish of her to abandon the conjugal bed."

"I don't recall your minding her neglect

while your Spanish mistress was available," Tasmin told him.

"Not a bit," Buffum seconded. "Then you didn't give Vicky the time of day. No time for old familiar Vicky then. You'd rather do gross things in the buggy with that Spanish girl."

"Shut up, damn you both! She was a saint!" Lord Berrybender spluttered.

Just then Elf came rushing up to Buffum, who kissed him. Elf was a tiny mite of a boy, but quick on his feet and possessed of merry black eyes.

Tasmin smiled at Elf and looked around for her twins. Petal was with Cook, making a great nuisance of herself. She had captured a vital spoon and refused to surrender it. Vicky sat with Talley, a quiet boy who rarely said much.

Vaguely, at first without alarm, Tasmin registered an absence. The picture wasn't complete. Something nagged at her. Then she remembered that Petey had wandered off, with Little Onion in pursuit. He had been sitting by himself, playing with his bear—but now where was he?

"Seen Petey?" she asked Cook. "I

thought Little Onion went to get him but I
don't see them. That was some time ago."

Wasn't it some time ago? Time had
passed, but how much time she couldn't
say. Where was Little Onion?

"Probably gathering firewood—it's chill,"
Cook said. She looked around. Where *was*
the helpful girl?

Tasmin hurried over to Corporal Dominguin, the friendliest and most reliable of the
soldiers.

"Corporal, we seem to have lost Little
Onion," she told him. "I can't seem to find
my boy Petey, either. Have you seen them?"

Startled, Corporal Dominguin shook his
head. He had been idly rolling dice, and
watching Buffum, whom he greatly admired.
Whenever he could, he did her favors, performed little chores. He had not seen the Indian girl or the little boy but he liked Tasmin
and readily agreed to take one of his men
and go have a look. Two of the soldiers were
cleaning their rifles—they were hopeful that
they might see game to shoot at. Lazily they
got up and followed Corporal Dominguin.

Tasmin wished desperately that Jim
would show up. For some reason she became frightened—the vast, empty place,

filled with perils, was enough to frighten her. She had an urge to race off and find Petey herself, though she realized that she would probably only get lost.

When Corporal Dominguin came back he just shook his head. In his hand he held Petey's little bear.

☞ **47** ☜

. . . trying to call the blue quail . . .

Blue Foot hated whimpering children. He had not wanted to take the child at all but Tay-ha insisted. Women were easier managed if they were allowed their children. Tay-ha was not sure how the brown woman happened to have a white child, but many whites now passed through the country— mixed pairs were not uncommon. They were all disappointed because they had only managed to catch a brown girl when there were at least five salable white women in camp. But there were only four of them, and a number of soldiers with rifles guarded the women.

"You hit her too hard," Blue Foot insisted.

Tay-ha was very good at ambushes. If he didn't want to be seen he wasn't seen. He was already swinging his club when the girl sensed him. She turned and the blow took her in the temple, which was not where he meant to hit her. He swung hard because they were close to the camp and he didn't want her to scream, but he had meant to hit her in the back of the head. Her own movement caused his miscalculation. They had thrown her, inert and unconscious, over the spare horse and put ten miles between them and the camp before they stopped.

Still, Tay-ha was ready to admit that he had hit the girl too hard. She had been lifeless as a sack when they raped her. She had not opened her eyes.

"Draga won't like this—she wanted us to catch some white women," Blue Foot complained.

"I can't do everything right," Tay-ha told him.

The old man, Snaggle, bent over Little Onion, looking at her closely.

"She has blood in her eyes and more coming out her ears—she's dying," Snaggle told them. "It's pointless to take her any farther."

Little Onion faintly heard the talk, which seemed to come from a great distance. She tried to stroke Petey, to make him stop whimpering, but her hands wouldn't fully obey her. She and Petey had been squatting, trying to call the blue quail, and the blue quail were listening. They had stopped, listening to Little Onion's call. Only at the last second did she sense the man with the club who had somehow got behind her. Then she fell into deep darkness, in her head a pain far worse than any she had felt before. In the blackness all she could do was try to soothe Petey so the men would spare him. If they could only survive a day her husband might come.

Blue Foot was thoroughly disgusted. The white women in the camp would have made them all rich, if they could have caught them. But Tay-ha had to go club a brown girl who was making birdcalls with the child. They would have to go back to Draga's great slavers' camp with nothing to show. Any of the white women would have brought big money—but now that prospect was all spoiled. He had wanted to grab one of the white women while she was making water, but the soldiers were too close.

"Are we going to wait all day?" Snaggle asked. "This girl is ruined."

Blue Foot knew it was true. She had

blood in her eyes. She could have been a useful slave, but that was not to be.

"Just finish her, since you ruined her," he said to Tay-ha.

He caught the little boy by the ankle, swung him a few times, and threw him as high as he could throw him. While he was swinging the boy, Tay-ha killed the girl. It only required another hard rap.

The little boy hit the frozen ground. Blue Foot intended for the fall to kill him—he didn't seem like a strong boy. Old Snaggle went over and inspected him.

"He's still breathing," Snaggle reported.

Enraged—why couldn't anything go right?—Blue Foot looped his rawhide rope around one of the little boy's feet—then he jumped on his horse and rode off as fast as he could go, through some rocks and some cactus. When he came back Snaggle was quick to report that the boy was dead.

"This has been a wasted day," Blue Foot complained, as the four of them rode south.

"More than that," Snaggle reminded him. "We watched that camp for three days."

"There were just too many soldiers," Tay-ha said.

"We might catch somebody if we went to

Mexico," Bent Finger suggested. He was
the youngest slaver—no one paid much attention to him.

"We are not going to Mexico," Blue Foot
said, in a tone that suggested to Bent Finger that his comments were unwelcome.

They rode south, under a full moon, for
most of the night. Here and there they saw
campfires—Comanche campfires, probably. They were on the great war trail that the
Comanches used when they made their
raids into Mexico. A day's ride west of the
war trail was the big slavers' camp known
as Los Dolores. There, at the moment, the
old woman Draga reigned—a woman cru-
eler but more efficient than most of the
other slavers.

"I wish you hadn't hit that girl so hard,"
Blue Foot chided. "I hate going back with
no captives to show."

"Shut up about it," Snaggle told him.
"Tay-ha didn't mean to kill her, but what's
done is done."

48

. . . Tasmin came running out, panic in her face.

"I'm eager to see Tasmin and the rest," George Catlin said.

"Me too," Kit Carson put in. "We'll have us a regular reunion."

Old Greasy Lake had refused to leave the yellow buffalo, so Kit and Willy had thrown in with George Catlin and set out in search of the Berrybenders. A few days later they had the happy luck to run into Jim Snow, who was packing home a sizable load of buffalo meat, a welcome sight.

"It's just like Jim to have buffalo when the rest of us are making do with prairie dog," Kit remarked.

Then Tom Fitzpatrick, who had been trapping on the south Canadian with little luck, drifted in, and he also was looking for the Berrybenders.

"I thought I might court that pretty cook a little bit more," he told them, "Absence makes the heart grow fonder, they say."

Kit Carson felt that the sentiment was very dubious.

"It don't make my wife's grow fonder," Kit said. He knew Josefina would soon be throwing things, once he got home—mad because he had been away so long.

Jim was glad to see them all, though he was surprised that George had risked himself in the Comanche country.

"I had a military escort, you see," George said. "And after that I had Greasy Lake."

Jim supposed that the arrival of so many old friends would throw the camp into an uproar of welcome—but he soon saw that there had been trouble. All the soldiers had their rifles at the ready. Before they were even in camp Tasmin came running out, panic in her face.

"Hello, George—I'll hug you in a minute," she said, going straight to Jim.

"Little Onion has been taken, and Petey," she told him. "They've been gone since yesterday. None of us saw or heard a thing. Can you please go find them?"

"I doubt it was Comanches—you'd have

heard plenty if it had been," Tom Fitzpatrick remarked.

"Please go find them," Tasmin repeated, her eyes on her husband.

George Catlin was shocked by how the years had roughened Tasmin—roughened all the women. Beauty was still there, but they were no longer peaches-and-cream English girls, fresh off a boat.

While Jim and the others were debating what to do, Tasmin gave George a kiss and a long hug.

"George, I'm frightened—really frightened," she said. "We lost Monty to cholera and now one of my twins is missing—it's very hard."

"I'm sure," he said. "But who's that little girl I see with the wild curls—she must be yours?"

"Yes, that's Petal—make what you can of her," Tasmin said, before rushing back to Jim.

"Tom thinks it's slavers—there's some big camp south of here where they trade captives," Jim told her. "That old Draga, that once had Buffum, is there."

"Slavers steal people to sell," Jim pointed out. "They might be alive."

It was almost night, and the only clue to the direction was the little bear that Corporal Dominguin had found south of the camp.

"Will you and Willy go with me for a day?" Jim asked Kit. He knew the two of them were anxious to get home to their wives—and home was north, not south.

"We'll go with you—you got that bad arm," Kit told him.

Willy Bent saw the trouble as confirmation of what he had been telling his brother all along: that Texas was too raw and dangerous for a trading post to work. If the Indians didn't steal the goods, the slavers would steal the help.

None of the Berrybenders could stop thinking about Petey and Little Onion. Petal was disturbed by the continued absence of her twin.

"I need Petey to come back *now!*" she said several times.

Cook broke down in tears as she was serving the buffalo roast—the little boy had been her favorite of all the children.

George Catlin attempted to amuse the children by drawing whimsical sketches.

"Here's a fairy and here's an elf," he said.

Petal studied the drawing critically.

"That's a fairy but that's not an elf," she said, pointing at her cousin. "That's an elf."

"Why, I didn't realize you had an elf," George said. "I'll just change this fellow into a leprechaun."

Tasmin and Jim were far too tense to sleep. They both found the night endless, the tension wracking. Jim knew it was unlikely that Petey was alive—slavers couldn't sell a child that young. Little Onion was resourceful—she might escape. But a tiny boy had no value to slavers, or Indians either.

Tasmin trembled with rage and fear.

"I'd like to tear whoever took them apart with my teeth," she said. "If there's a bad storm I fear Petey won't survive."

The three men left at dawn. Willy Bent, the best tracker of the three, soon found the tracks of five horses, all of them unshod.

"I make it four men—the fifth horse is probably a packhorse," Willy said.

Ten miles on they found the two bodies. Petey's small corpse was filled with cactus thorns. Blood had frozen on Little Onion's eyes.

"My God," Kit said, looking at Petey.

Willy's stomach flipped—he vomited.

The horse tracks continued southwest.

"They're not in a hurry—we might catch them," Willy told Jim.

"No, I'll catch them, in time," Jim said. "We have to take these two back. Tasmin will want to clean them up and bury them proper."

"I don't know that I'd take 'em back," Willy said, still shaken by the violence of his revulsion.

"She'll want to clean them up," Jim repeated.

He felt hatred rising in him, but he was determined to try and contain it until the hour of his vengeance came. He also felt guilt. He had not really much known his little boy; he had never found a tone that allowed him to give proper credit to Little Onion's virtues—after all, she had died trying to protect Petey.

George Catlin had never witnessed such grief as racked the Berrybender family that wintry afternoon. The Berrybender sisters—Tasmin, Buffum, Mary, Kate—took turns with Father Geoffrin's one pair of tweezers, easing the fine cactus thorns out of Petey's small body. Tasmin worked as if turned to stone; the others wept and wailed. Petal raced around in wild despair. "Petey got too many stickers!" she cried. "He's got too many stickers!" She crawled up in Father Geoffrin's lap and cried herself to sleep. Cook fainted—Tom Fitzpatrick helped her up when she came to.

Vicky, holding Talley, was pinched and silent, but the old lord wept and blubbered.

"Dastardly of them to kill our Onion— such a fine lassie," he said, more than once.

"I suppose it's no matter that they killed your grandson," Vicky told him. "After all, you can get plenty more of those."

"Bad of me, scarcely knew the boy," Lord Berrybender admitted.

Tasmin remained stoical as they cleaned Petey and wrapped him in a little shroud, but a river of grief swept through her when she set about cleaning Little Onion's broken head. She couldn't manage it—couldn't see for crying.

"You've lost your best wife, Jimmy," she cried. "*She* was your best wife!"

The two were put in one grave, Petey in Little Onion's arms.

Tasmin ran sobbing out of camp. Jim let her go, but Father Geoff and George Catlin, fearing that she might go too far and be taken herself, followed her.

"What can anyone say?" Geoff asked. "Our two purest souls have been taken from us."

Tasmin came back, passively.

Petal kept insisting that Petey had just got too many stickers.

Vicky, without her cello, could only sing a little Handel.

Tasmin held Jim's arm while Vicky sang. His look was the old flinty look she had first seen the day she met him. He wasn't yelling out incomprehensible words, but he had become the Sin Killer—he was going to avenge the terrible thing that had been done to Petey and Little Onion. She herself could expect no comfort from him—not then.

As soon as the service was over Jim went to Lord Berrybender.

"I need to borrow one of your new rifles—and a fair bunch of ammunition," he said.

"Why, of course, Jimmy—take what you need. I hope you slaughter the devils," Lord Berrybender said.

"I need that spyglass too," Jim said. "I need to see them before they see me."

When Kit and Willy realized that Jim

meant to go after the killers alone, they tried to remonstrate with him.

"There could be twenty slavers around that camp, for all you know," Kit told him.

"I hope there are," Jim replied. "It'd be good to kill twenty slavers."

"Jimmy, are you sure about this?" Willy asked. "What about your arm?"

"By the time I'm ready to strike, my arm will be healed," Jim told them. He was loading a packhorse—Cook was wrapping up meat.

When the horse was ready Jim went over to Corporal Dominguin and asked a question.

"Didn't you keep Major Leon's sword, when we buried him?"

"*Sí,*" the corporal said.

"I'd like to borrow it," Jim requested.

The corporal went to his kit, took out the sword, and handed it to Jim.

Kit and Willy were uncertain about letting Jim Snow go off alone. Both of them felt it was wrong not to support a colleague on such a quest—and yet clearly Jim didn't mean to take them.

"You've both got wives," he reminded

them. "I've no doubt you've already been gone too long to suit them."

"I guess I won't be told when I can take off and how long I can stay gone," Kit said, in Tasmin's hearing.

"What a rooster you've become, Kit," she protested.

"He's a rooster but his hen can whip him up one side and down the other—and he knows it," Willy told her.

A little grumpy because Jim wouldn't have them, the two finally left.

Jim's next task was to seek an understanding with Tom Fitzpatrick.

"I want you to take 'em through to the settlements on the Brazos," Jim told him.

"That's where I'll come, when I'm done."

"I'll do it," Tom assured him.

Tasmin felt shaky—hot with fury one moment, despairing the next. She would have liked the comfort of her husband's affection, but knew he couldn't give it once the Sin Killer began to rise in him. He only wanted to be off, alone, free to be the killer that he was.

"*You* stop him!" Petal said to her mother, when she saw that Jim was leaving; but then Elf wandered by with a corncob doll that she coveted and she forgot Jim and went to chase him down. Elf was a match for her, though. He climbed up a wagon wheel and tried to push Petal down when she followed.

"I don't know how to say it, Jimmy—but when you turn into the Sin Killer I feel as though I don't exist—we all feel that way," Tasmin told him.

Jim had no answer to make to that. He tucked the sword carefully into his pack.

"I promise I'll come and find you, if I live," Jim said. He knew Tasmin was wracked with grief—and what could you say to grief that would be any help? Putting a son in the ground was the hardest thing anyone was likely to be called to do.

Impulsively Tasmin kissed him—she jumped toward him as if released by a spring. It was a quick kiss—it surprised both of them.

"We're out of boys, Jimmy," she said. "We made good boys, too."

She had seldom felt so divided, at one moment wanting him to go and kill, the next wishing he would just give it up and lead them on to safety.

Jim felt no confusion. He meant to kill all

the men who had hurt Petey and Little Onion. He made sure his gear was secure, said good-bye to the family, and left.

Tasmin felt fearful, deeply fearful. Would she ever see her husband again?

Petal had had no ambivalence—Jim kissed her, but then he rode away. It was dark and she couldn't see him.

"Jim went—you go get him!" she demanded of her mother. Then she burst into tears.

49

"It's a long way to a madhouse, Tassie."

"I suppose Geoff's annoyed with me, now that I've taken up with you again," Tasmin told George Catlin.

"Why should that annoy a priest?" George asked.

"Because he likes to be my only comfort and counselor, and he has been for two years," she said. "He's sulking right now."

"Two friends are better than one—he should look at it that way," George told her.

"That isn't the way men are—no wonder you're a bachelor," Tasmin remarked. "If you were more determined on exclusive privileges, you'd do better with women."

"I was madly in love with you for months, and what did it get me?" George asked. "You remember how jealous I was of Jim."

"I suppose you were, but you merely irritated me, in those days," Tasmin remembered. "I wanted a wilder man and I got one—and what it meant and mostly still means is that I'm alone. It's my friends who see me through—you and Geoff."

She gave the painter's hand a squeeze.

Yet the next evening the combined efforts of painter and priest could not keep Tasmin from despair. Images of her dead sons rose to haunt her.

"If only memory were an organ like an appendix," she said. "I'd dig it out, or cut it out. I don't think I can bear my memories. If we were home I'd ask to be put in a madhouse."

"It's a long way to a madhouse, Tassie," Buffum reminded her. Quietly, Buffum saw to Petal; she gathered firewood, with Petal and Elf trailing after her. Tasmin, who had thought little of her younger sister for much of her life, now came to admire her. As long as High Shoulders wasn't mentioned, Buffum held up. She took over many of the chores that Little Onion had done. Whenever she would allow it, Corporal Dominguin helped her.

"I believe I see something beginning," Father Geoff commented. "I believe our good corporal is falling in love with your lovely sister."

Tasmin was of the same mind. When High Shoulders died, Buffum despaired. She talked of taking the veil. Yet now she was seldom apart from the shy, polite Corporal Dominguin. Perhaps something *was* beginning.

"Renewal is normal—that's an old wisdom," Father Geoff said.

Tasmin made no retort. She didn't expect renewal for herself, although she had felt it more than once, when Jimmy returned from some scout. The men she sat with, George and Geoff, were both of them dry seeds— yet they stayed by her and they accepted her despair. When she was at her worst they didn't try to talk. They merely sat with her.

"I'll make it up to you two, someday—I swear I will," she said.

Tom Fitzpatrick made little progress with Cook, who still seemed set against him, and yet he kept the company on the move. They had reached what he claimed was a fork of the Brazos River, a narrow stream whose water was reddish. There were, he claimed, American settlements not far away.

In the camp, children quarreled and men

and women courted. Vicky had even begun to stay with Lord Berrybender again.

"I never supposed she'd relent," Father Geoff admitted.

Tasmin shrugged.

"It's hard to keep refusing a husband," she said. "They wear you down."

The wind was keening so that she could hardly think. Petal was asleep with Elf, and Buffum was watching them. Tasmin went over and sat a bit with Mary, as Piet snored by the flickering campfire.

"Do you remember when we first walked beside the Missouri, the night you threw that turtle into the boat?" Tasmin asked.

"Of course. Bobbety tried to put a frog down my dress and I was vexed. Why?"

"Buffum was declaiming about there being no schools in the American West. Do you remember?"

"Yes—it was rather silly of her. Papa would never have wasted money on a school, for the likes of us."

"My own view is that the Americans would do far better to forget schools and just build madhouses," Tasmin said. "I could use a madhouse right now, if you want to know, and I'm sure I'm hardly the only woman who can say that."

"But you're not the mad one, Tassie—I was always the mad one," Mary reminded her.

"It's been necessary for you to be the normal one, so the rest of us can pursue our vagaries," Mary went on.

"I've lost two children—you're about to bear one," Tasmin told her. "I've a husband who's a killer first and last. I've seen one lover shot dead. You have a nice man who adores you. You can't claim to be the mad one anymore.

"If there's a madwoman in the family just now, it's me," Tasmin assured her. "And yet for the lack of a madhouse I have to go on," she continued.

Mary didn't answer.

For the rest of the night Tasmin stared into the fire.

50

In a reddish or dun landscape . . .

Jim traveled southwest at a pace so slow that the little mare was puzzled—she kept jingling the bit impatiently. But Jim meant to be as careful and deliberate as possible. Some days he hid himself and his horses and merely watched the trail. Several times he saw Indians, some moving south, some returning north, but the Indians did not see him. One of his worries was that he was too white. In a reddish or dun landscape his color might betray him. He began to rub himself with dirt every day, to make himself brown. He was not fearful, but he meant to take care not to be seen until he was ready. Big camps were rarely static—people were always leaving or arriving. He didn't want someone to spot him and give the alarm. He had an excellent spyglass, borrowed from

Lord Berrybender. Several times a day he used it to scan the country. He moved through rocky places, where his tracks would be less likely to be seen. He had sufficient jerky; he made no fires. His intention was to become a phantom.

When Jim did find the slavers' camp, in a long shallow valley, he first studied it at night. There were more than a dozen campfires. Just to the west was a bluff, at least two hundred feet high and, he first thought, almost sheer. The bluff was pocked with caves but he was not sure he could reach any of them. He circled the bluff at night, hoping to find a crevasse where he could shelter the mare and the packhorse. One morning just at dawn he saw a flash of white, high up. The flash of white was a mountain sheep—it seemed to be walking on air. The sheep, a big ram, disappeared into one of the caves.

That night Jim hid the horses and attempted to investigate on foot. What he discovered was an extremely narrow ledge around the face of the bluff, invisible from below. Jim thought the mare, which was exceptionally sure-footed, might negotiate the ledge, but it would be too risky for the packhorse. The bluff sported little vegetation but there were forested hills to the west, only a few miles away.

As Jim predicted, people came and went from the slavers' camp, but none seemed to go in the direction of the scrubby hills. Jim found a copse on the back of one hill where he thought the horses would be safe. Then, with a rifle, his spyglass, and some meat he slipped into one of the caves. The camp was spread out below him: he could study his enemies at leisure, with no risk of discovery. The cave he was in could not be seen from below.

It took only a little study to convince Jim that, at the moment, the slavers outnumbered their captives. The only captives he could see were six bedraggled white children, two women who appeared to be Mexican, one white woman, and three Indian girls about the age of Little Onion. All the captives wore hopeless expressions: they were in hell and didn't expect to get out. In the course of an afternoon the white woman was raped four times.

While the fourth rape was occurring, Draga appeared, from a house made of sticks and brush—she took no notice of the rape but knocked one of the children down with a stick because the child had been slow in fetching her tobacco.

Jim counted fifteen slavers, camped in groups of three or four some distance from Draga's brush house. After studying each group for a while Jim felt confident that he could identify the four men who killed Petey and Little Onion—the main evidence was that one of them carried a heavy club—Little Onion had been killed with a club.

Most of the slavers looked as tired and half starved as the captives. The main food in the camp seemed to be dog—skinny dog at that, though on one occasion a hunter brought in a wild pig. There was a creek nearby—it wasn't running but there were pools of water in it, here and there. From one such pool, well away from the camp, Jim watered his horses every day.

After three days of careful watching, Jim noticed that activity in the camp suddenly increased. Two men, each leading a pack-horse, rode in from the north. One of the men was Malgres, the quick killer with the thin knife whom he had first seen with the trader John Skraeling, near the Mandan villages years before. The other man had been with Obregon, the slaver Jim had pounded so hard as they were marching into New Mexico. The packhorses carried some rusty-looking muskets and a variety of small trade items. The two presented themselves to Draga, clearly the mistress of the camp. The old woman sat on a heap of hides, smoking a long-stemmed pipe. Malgres and his friend were allowed to make camp.

The next day, though, Draga was quick to take note. A party of seventeen Comanches rode in from Mexico, leading ten captives, mostly half-grown children, though one grown woman was with the group. The captives were immediately inspected by the slavers, but they weren't abused, not until the Comanches got their price, which required a whole day of haggling.

The Comanches were more watchful than the slavers—Jim kept well back in his cave and did not use the spyglass for fear that a glint of sunlight off the glass might give him away. That night he moved his horses farther away.

By the next day several of the Mexican captives had been acquired by various slavers. The white woman was gone—one of the Comanches had traded for her. Mal-

gres's stock of muskets was reduced but he
and his friend still had ample trade goods—
they idled around the camp, evidently waiting for more arrivals from Mexico.

The four men Jim had marked as his
killers did not seem to like Malgres. They
kept to themselves. The slaver with the club
was much taken with one of the Mexican
women, a shapely brown woman who had
not yet lost her dignity of bearing. Twice in
one day Jim saw him take the woman out of
camp in order to copulate with her. The
woman submitted passively, her face turned
away.

Another small group of Indians appeared
from Mexico—this group had only five captives, all children. Jim heard Draga's voice,
raised in complaint. In this instance no deal
was struck. The Indians rode on with their
captives.

Jim supposed Draga must feel that she
already had more children than she had
customers for—and yet only a day later
more children arrived and Draga took them.
Jim watched the exchange, which involved
a little silver and a great deal of tobacco.
Many of the children were boys, just old

enough to do field work, the use they would be put to once sold, Jim supposed.

The day the new party of Mexicans rode away Jim concluded that he had seen enough. It was almost time for the Sin Killer to begin his righteous work.

51

He had come rather to fear his wife.

"I fear our Tasmin is falling off," George Catlin said to Mary. "I can hardly get her to hold a conversation, and neither can Geoff."

"We all fear for her," Mary told him. She too was alarmed by her sister's sunken cheeks and vacant eyes. Tasmin seldom walked now—she sat in the wagon all day, staring. Petal, by the application of her fierce will, could sometimes get her mother's attention for a few moments now and then, but most of them saw their efforts ignored.

"Can't think what's wrong with Tassie," Lord Berrybender said, nervously, to Vicky and Buffum.

"It's how one feels when a child dies," Vicky told him. "I felt that way when Randy died, but you didn't notice."

"Busy, I suppose," Lord B. said. He had

come rather to fear his wife. She had not lately flown into violent rages, and yet he knew she was capable of them. He was much troubled by the lack of drink. When drunk one could overlook the danger of one's wife. Sober, it was a fear that preyed on the mind.

George and Geoff and Mary gathered around at night and considered what they might do. They had all, in different ways, come to rely on Tasmin's strength. And yet now she wasn't strong—sometimes she stumbled when she tried to walk, and she never made spirited remarks. She didn't complain and she didn't cry—yet she seemed scarcely there.

"There's no helping anyone that deep in grief," Piet Van Wely told them. "We must go on attending to ourselves. Tasmin will finally recover."

Unable to bear Tasmin's silent despair, George began to sketch Petal in her various moods. Petal had been spending more time with Buffum and Elf.

"I like to be with my aunts because they *speak* more," Petal said. She herself spoke, and she was tired of asking her mother questions and getting no answers.

"I feel that somehow I left myself behind, George," Tasmin finally told him. "There's a promise I want you to make, in case I die."

"Anything . . . of course," he agreed.

"My sons lie in separate graves—I can't bear it," Tasmin told him. "If Jim is killed I want you to hire Kit or someone and get them and bury them together in a nice graveyard."

"I doubt Jim will be killed," George said.

Tasmin looked at him.

"If the history of this sad expedition proves anything it's that it's very easy to be killed," she told him. "Drummond Stewart was an able man, yet he was killed. Pomp was also able, yet he too was killed. Jim is the ablest of them all, but it doesn't mean he can't be killed."

"You're right, of course," George said.

"If I live I'll get Kit to help me and do this myself," Tasmin assured him. "I want my boys together, that's all.

"You were once jealous of Jim, weren't you?" she asked, unexpectedly.

"Of course," George admitted. "At first it seemed most unlikely that you'd suit one another—it seemed distinctly improbable. And yet I suppose you *do* so suit one an-

other—and I can never feel that I suit anyone—so far I haven't, at least."

"I can't bear to think of Jim right now,"
she told him. "Perhaps we do suit—though
not steadily. But right now I'm not strong
enough to bear the uncertainty of having to
wonder if he's alive. I have to put him out of
my mind, or lose my mind. There may be
months and months of waiting, this time.

"Just don't forget about my boys," she
said again. "If I should die, you and Kit have
to do that for me. Promise me. Promise
me."

"Certainly—you have my promise,"
George said.

"I shall probably charge Geoff with the
same mission," Tasmin told him. "The fact is
you could die yourself, George Catlin."

"I easily could," he admitted.

Tasmin gave him a grateful look.

"I fear you sell yourself rather short,
where women are concerned," she told him.

"Oh, I suppose—certainly I've had no no-
table successes," he said. "Why do you
mention it?"

"Because I believe I might have made do
with you, in a pinch," Tasmin said. "I fancy I
might have made do."

52

Draga had learned about poison in the faraway time . . .

Draga didn't like trading in Mexican captives—she longed to return to the Mandan country, where she had had her best years. Of course, it had been necessary to leave when the smallpox struck down the Mandans and the Rees. No traders came from the north in those grim years—the river no longer supplied her with captives, as it had for so long. In those rich years she had been able to count on a steady stream of white captives: French Canadians, Americans from across the Mississippi, the wives of white traders whose husbands had died from one cause or another.

Draga considered that she knew better than anyone how to handle captives, particularly women captives. She knew ways to make them submissive that didn't involve disfiguring beatings or tortures. A few women with strong spirits had to be broken by tortures, which of course excited the spectators and sometimes got out of hand, resulting in the death of the captive. But such losses didn't occur often. The Bad Eye, when he had been the main prophet of the Mandans, discouraged the burnings and tortures that had been common in earlier times. The Bad Eye, in Draga's view, had been more merchant than prophet. The Mandans held the choice spot on the Missouri River—in the years when the fur market was high, furs poured in from all directions. The Bad Eye discouraged violence because he didn't want the trappers to be frightened. He wanted the furs to keep pouring in.

But the smallpox ended that time. Draga had reluctantly gone south, where the work was harder and the pickings less interesting. Compared to what she had known with the Mandans, the southern Indians seemed dull; and she found the mostly squat brown captives dull too. There was little variety. Most of the Mexican children soon got sold back to Mexico, to provide help in the fields.

She had heard from many sources that

the white immigrants to the east would soon begin to push the Mexicans out. Malgres and even Blue Foot claimed this, and yet none of them brought her any of these abundant whites, as captives. The one white woman she had traded lately had been brought in by an Apache—the woman was sold within a week to a Kiowa chief. She had already been used so heavily that her mind was dislodged. The Kiowa wasn't going to get much for his money.

Because of this lack it was irritating to have Blue Foot and Tay-ha show up and brag about the big party of whites they had followed, a party that had several young white women in it. Draga thought from their description that it must be the same family of whites that had gone up the Missouri a few years before. What they had been doing all that time was a mystery to Draga, but she was highly irritated with the men for failing to bring in even one salable captive. It was a poor show, so poor that Draga idly considered poisoning all four of those worthless men. Or three of them, at least. She saw no point in wasting poison on old Snaggle, who was on his last legs anyway.

Draga had learned about poison in the

faraway time when she had been a girl in California—an old woman in one of the missions taught her a few simple poisons; later, at the Mandans', she had provided herself with strong chemicals brought down by a French apothecary who sometimes visited. These she kept carefully stoppered and concealed. In her opinion there was no quicker or safer way to get rid of men who had become obnoxious than with poisons. The first man she poisoned was Guillaume, an old trader who had once been her lover—Guillaume had caught Draga in the bushes with a young warrior and had had the temerity to beat her: she poisoned him that very night. He woke up with his belly on fire and was dead before the sunrise.

Now she thought she might poison Malgres, an envious man whom she had never trusted. Besides, Malgres was an indifferent slaver who never brought in interesting captives. Merely having him in camp filled her with a vague sense of menace. Draga considered Malgres a coward, and yet the fact was cowards sometimes made more effective killers than brave men. She never allowed Malgres to get behind her—he might kill on impulse, in hopes of finding the money and jewels she was supposed to have brought with her from the Mandans. She had hidden the money and the jewels under a black rock—but there were hundreds of black rocks in the desert and only she knew where her treasures were hidden.

As the sun set Draga rested on her heap of buffalo hides, thinking about whom she might poison in the next few days, when a strange cry, of a sort she had never heard before—a kind of rising ululation—suddenly filled the air. It seemed to come from the big bluff, and yet there was nothing to be seen on the bluff except the last rays of the evening sun, shining on the reddish rock.

Draga was not easily frightened and yet for a moment the hair stood up on her neck. Everyone in camp was suddenly scrambling for their guns, looking, listening to the strange, indecipherable sounds floating above them. Draga at first doubted that the sounds were human. She had heard that panthers sometimes made strange screaming sounds. Certainly there could be a panther near camp, hoping to kill one of the horses. But she had glimpsed panthers often in her life and had never heard one of them scream.

As abruptly as they began, the strange cries ended—though the echoes of the last call seemed to curl off some cliffs to the south.

The cry stopped, the sun slipped under the horizon, winter dusk closed in, and yet no one in the camp of slavers had moved. The men all waited with their guns. The captive children huddled together. The Mexican girls began to pray to the saints.

Draga forgot about poisoning anyone.

She walked over to consult with Malgres and Ramon, both of whom looked scared.

"Was it a panther?" she asked.

Both men shook their heads.

"It was no panther—it was the Sin Killer," Malgres said. "He's here somewhere."

"Where? I don't see him," Draga remarked.

Of course, she had heard stories about the ferocity of this Sin Killer, but she supposed most of them were lies. It took very little to get people started lying. She knew the Osage claimed that the Sin Killer had eaten the lightning and so could not be killed by ordinary weapons. Others said he was married to one of the English girls from the steamboat. Still others claimed his wives were Ute. The conflicting stories just convinced Draga that he was probably an ordinary frontiersman who had made a few lucky kills, after which a legend grew up about him.

"He's no legend," Malgres insisted. "In a second he destroyed Obregon."

"But Obregon was always slow," Draga reminded them. "He thought too much of himself."

"If it's the Sin Killer I think we should leave," Ramon proposed. The sound reminded him of how Obregon had moaned and screamed from the pain of his splintered jaw—they had finally killed him, to rid themselves of his cries.

"Obregon could not stand pain," Ramon said, distractedly, fingering his own jaw. A broken face must be extremely painful. What if the Sin Killer still had his club?

Malgres at once disagreed with Ramon about the business of departure—if the Sin Killer was close by, the last thing he intended to do was flee into the desert. The two of them would be easy prey if they tried to do that.

"Here, we are at least a dozen guns,"

Malgres argued. "Surely he wouldn't attack a dozen well-armed men."

"All of us put together couldn't kill him," Ramon declared gloomily. "He is quick as a panther when he moves. Remember how he jumped at Obregon?"

Malgres did remember. He considered himself a fast man, but the Sin Killer might be faster.

"Can't you make a bad spell?" Malgres asked Draga.

Draga thought it might be wiser to make a bad poison and feed it to Malgres and Ramon, for being such worthless cowards. She would just make them coffee one morning, pretending to be helpful. Then she would dribble a few drops of her strongest poison in the murky coffee—after a few swallows Malgres and Ramon would be writhing around like lizards whose backs were broken. Before the coffee cooled they'd be dead.

But how could she poison the Sin Killer, a creature whose existence she only half believed in? How did one go about poisoning a phantom?

"Sure, you go bring him here and I'll poison him quick," she said. "I'll put barbs in his belly for sure."

Ramon shook his head vigorously at this suggestion.

"I don't want to bring him here—I want him to go somewhere else," he said, so frightened that his knees were knocking together.

Disgusted, Draga turned and stumped back to her pile of hides. Ramon looked as if he might die of fright: how worthless could a man be?

53

*He had been holding in his anger for
days . . .*

Jim knew that he had been lucky to find a
perfect hiding place from which to cry out
the Word. If he hadn't seen the white ram
crossing the face of the cliff he would never
have found the small cave where he hid
himself. His hideaway was under an inslop-
ing curve of the cliff. It could not be seen
from below. He had been holding in his
anger for days, ever since he found the
bodies of Petey and Little Onion—finally he
let it out for a few minutes, listening to his
cries echoing off the distant hills.

Mainly he cried out to relieve the anger
and sorrow he felt—but he also wanted to
see what effect it had on the slavers.

All the men in the camp grabbed their
weapons, but none of them fled. They heard
the Word, but didn't know what the cries

meant, or what was best to do. The old slaving woman, Draga, had seemed bewildered at first, but she finally went and sat back down on her seat of hides. Jim had no worry that she might spot him—few women who had spent their lives in Indian lodges could see well in old age—years of having smoke in their eyes had dimmed their sight.

The men Jim meant to kill first, the four who had taken Petey and Little Onion, jumped up and grabbed their weapons, but they slowly calmed down and resumed playing dice. They were not worried enough to run—there seemed to be plenty of liquor in the camp, so probably most of the slavers were drunk, or half drunk.

Jim meant to kill all the slavers, but he had not planned his assault in much detail. Battle was too unpredictable—it was best just to do what had to be done when blood was up and the fighting fierce. One thing he did do was sharpen the sword he had borrowed from Corporal Dominguin. He had never fought with a sword, or even owned one, but he thought the weapon might be useful if he found himself in the middle of the slavers' camp. In close quarters, during a fight, many men got flustered and fired their guns foolishly, as Signor Claricia had been prone to do. A sword sharp enough to sever a limb or split a head would be a decided advantage when the time came to strike.

In the afternoon Jim got out his tattered copy of the Book and fumbled through it. There were two verses that he felt sure were in the Book, but he couldn't find them. One was "Vengeance is mine, saith the Lord." The other—he only half remembered it—was "Blessed are the meek, for they shall inherit the earth."

Jim wanted badly to find those verses, but his copy of the Book had so many pages missing that in the end he had to give up. The first seemed to mean that he should let the Lord manage what vengeance need be—but he wasn't going to heed that verse.

It was when he remembered Petey and Little Onion that he thought of the second verse. They had been the meek, as he understood the word, but they hadn't inherited the earth. Instead they had had painful deaths. He had been raised to believe that every word in the Book was true but he couldn't make that belief jibe with what had just happened—much less with what was about to happen.

Jim decided it would be best just not to think about the Book until he got back to the company and could talk about his confusion with someone who was educated. He was about to go into battle, and he didn't plan to hold back. Confusion of the mind was not something he could entertain—not then. The Sin Killer was going to fall upon the heathen, screaming out the Word. His sword and his gun would then accomplish what needed to be done.

⇥ 54 ⇤

At once everyone fell silent.

Malgres suddenly had a thought—a notion about the Sin Killer.

Ramon, still frightened, had bought some liquor from Draga, who kept some in her brush house. He was now in a stupor, not quite asleep but too drunk to be talkative.

Malgres gave him a shake.

"What?" Ramon asked, apprehensively.

Malgres pointed to the men who were camped with old Snaggle, the most ancient person in the camp.

"Weren't those men arguing about killing a girl?" he asked. "The one with the club did it—he hit the girl too hard, and she died. I think they killed a little boy too."

"So what? Nobody wants to drag a child around!" Ramon said.

"The girl and the little boy came from that

big party of whites—the one the Sin Killer was with when he hit Obregon," Malgres went on.

"I want to go to sleep—I hate talking about the Sin Killer," Ramon told him.

"I think that girl they killed was the Sin Killer's wife," Malgres concluded. "The boy must have been his son. He has come for vengeance."

"I thought he had a white wife," Ramon said.

"Yes, and an Indian wife too. I tell you, he's come for his vengeance. That's why we heard that cry."

"Then let him kill them—I don't like them anyway," Ramon remarked.

Malgres, convinced that the Sin Killer was near, and convinced, also, that he had come to kill the four slavers, at once went over to warn the men. Maybe they would want to try and outrun him.

But the men proved to be rude fellows—they were playing dice and resented Malgres's interruption.

"Can't you see we're gambling?" Blue Foot asked.

"Yes, I can see that," Malgres said. "In my

opinion you ought to get on your horses and go. The Sin Killer has come for you."

Tay-ha had begun to develop his own uneasy suspicions on that score. What Malgres said might be true. How could such a sound come from a bare cliff? Probably there was a cave they couldn't see. He tried to talk Blue Foot and Bent Finger into going with him to see if he could spot the cave, but they weren't interested.

"There must be a way up it," Tay-ha said. "We ought to go have a look."

"We'll just kill the man when we see him. What does he want?" Bent Finger said. He was losing at dice—his mood was sour.

"I think he wants the men who killed his wife and baby," Malgres declared.

Blue Foot took offense at once.

"How do you know so much about it?" he asked.

"I don't know much about it—I just had an opinion," Malgres said—he didn't know why he had troubled to warn this quarrelsome bunch.

"He knows because you bragged," old Snaggle said to Blue Foot. "You told everybody you killed a girl and a child."

"I doubt they were the Sin Killer's," Blue

Foot answered, but he was beginning to feel shaky. Why had this Malgres been so rude as to interrupt their game?

At once everyone fell silent. Then Blue Foot rattled the dice, but didn't roll them.

"I think the Sin Killer's dead," Tay-ha mentioned. "Some Utes caught him and took his hair. I heard that from somebody."

He didn't know why he had made the remark, because it was the opposite of what he believed, which was that the Sin Killer was in a cave, watching them, probably studying their weaknesses, which were many. Somewhere up there the man was watching, making his plans to kill. It was a bad thought to live with.

"You spoiled a good game and I was winning," Blue Foot pointed out.

"You're too rude—you deserve to be killed," Malgres told him. Then, feeling that his advice had been scorned, he went away.

55

A white man was standing there . . .

Tay-ha had begun to want to own the Mexican woman, whose name was Rosa. At least once and often twice a day he led her a little way from camp and copulated with her. Rosa didn't resist but she refused to look at him while he was about his pleasure; as soon as he finished and withdrew she stood up and walked wearily back to camp.

Rosa belonged to Chino, a small halfbreed slaver who was well known to put very high prices on his merchandise. He owned a dozen captives and kept them longer than was normal because he refused to lower his price. Tay-ha offered Chino one hundred dollars for Rosa, an offer that irritated Blue Foot. Not only was the price ridiculously high, but having to take a woman with them would seriously limit their mobility. Chino, however, refused the offer; he sometimes took his own pleasure with Rosa and was not going to let her go unless he got a high price.

Tay-ha believed he could finally talk Chino down, and if he couldn't, he might just kill him. The thought of owning Rosa excited him more and more. He led her out and kept her till late afternoon, playing with her breasts, probing. Rosa still refused to look at him, and she left at once when he finished. Tay-ha had laid his club down while enjoying Rosa's body, and when he turned to pick it up he received a terrible shock. A white man was standing there— the white man had his club and was raising it. The man had covered his body with brown dirt, but it was clear from his hair that he was a white man.

Tay-ha was too stunned even to cry out. Was it the Sin Killer? Already his club was coming toward his face, thick as a log, and fast.

Using the well-sharpened Mexican sword, Jim cut Tay-ha's head off. It was smashed and bloody, as Little Onion's had been. Jim left it for the coyotes and badgers. But he hoisted Tay-ha's small body and carried him to the bluff. As soon as it was dark he carried the corpse along the ledge to his cave.

The next morning, just at dawn, the people in the slavers' camp heard the cry of the Sin Killer for a second time—they heard the Word, emanating from the face of a cliff.

Then, from the same spot, a body flew out and fell with a thud on the hard desert floor.

"I thought so," old Snaggle said, when he went with the others to inspect the headless body. "It was not like Tay-ha to stay out all night. He had already sent that woman back."

Blue Foot suddenly felt seriously worried. Tay-ha's head had been cut off—this suggested that the killer had a plan. He had come for vengeance.

Malgres called for unified action.

"He's just in a cave up there," he said. "If we all go after him we can kill him."

None of the other slavers had the slightest interest in climbing the cliff.

Draga lumbered over and looked at the headless body. She studied the cliff for a long time. An enemy was around. But her eyes had been smoked to dimness. All she could see was rock.

"Maybe we should leave?" Blue Foot suggested.

Ramon approved of that plan.

"If we leave as a group he won't dare attack us," he said.

"He attacked Obregon when we were fourteen against him," Malgres reminded him. "Then he didn't even use a gun, just a club. I think he could have killed us all."

"Let's just leave," Ramon said, almost pleading.

Draga had no intention of leaving.

"There'll be Comanches along in a day or two," she reminded them. "We'll get the Comanches to hunt him down."

"What if no Comanches come?" Blue Foot asked. "What if they're late?"

They all strained their eyes looking up at the cliff, but it just looked like an ordinary red butte, very sheer. That a man could be up there didn't seem possible—and yet Tay-ha's body had been flung down.

"Tay-ha wanted to buy my captive," Chino remembered. "I wonder if there was any money in his pocket."

He began to search Tay-ha's pants, but

found nothing. Old Snaggle watched with amusement. He knew where Tay-ha hid his money—he meant to get it for himself when nobody was looking. He had come to admire the Mexican woman—perhaps he would buy her, with Tay-ha's money. It would be a fine joke on Tay-ha, although one he couldn't appreciate, due to being dead.

"What if he kills us all, one by one?" Ramon asked.

Blue Foot was outraged that one white man could disrupt their business so much. It was true that at present he had no slaves to sell himself, but he and Tay-ha had intended to go to Mexico and catch a few pretty soon. Now he would have to go with Bent Finger and old Snaggle, neither of whom was particularly skilled when it came to catching young Mexican slaves. With Tay-ha he could count on half a dozen captives; with the others he would be lucky to get three.

Later, drunk, Blue Foot decided it was all Tay-ha's fault, for carelessly hitting that Ute girl too hard; and as if that were not vexation enough, his own rope was missing. His rope had been right on his saddle but now it wasn't there. Annoyed, he accused old

Snaggle of stealing it, but the old man just shrugged. Angrily, Blue Foot made a tour of the whole camp, looking for his rope. It took a long time to braid a rawhide rope—its loss put him in such a foul mood that he cuffed two or three of the captive boys. Then he asked Chino if he could use the Mexican woman and Chino refused, a very annoying thing.

"You let Tay-ha use her often enough— why not me?" Blue Foot asked.

Chino didn't bother to reply. Rosa sat with her eyes downcast; she was tired of being summoned by men but she was a captive. If she refused she would just be beaten and then dishonored anyway. Only her thoughts were private; no man could have those. She was glad someone had cut off the head of Tay-ha, the man who dishonored her most often, but Rosa had forgotten how to hope. She was a poor woman—who would bother to rescue her from such a place? And yet when she saw Tay-ha's headless body she felt a little hope. Someone was up there—the slavers were afraid. She hoped whoever it was would kill all the slavers—then she would never have to accept their stinking bodies again.

56

*They gambled and drank; they posted
no guards . . .*

Jim could scarcely credit the carelessness
of the slavers. One of their own had been
killed—decapitated, in fact—and yet they
made little change in their habits. They
gambled and drank; they posted no guards;
they staggered around drunk; they didn't
even heed the warnings of their own dogs.
Jim had crept in in the night and stolen the
rope without being challenged, though
several dogs barked. When a dog barked
in an Indian camp all the warriors were on
the alert immediately. But the slavers only
kept dogs to eat—they just ignored the
barking.

Jim had studied the camp thoroughly and
was ready to attack. The rawhide rope had
been the last piece of equipment he
needed. He meant to drag its owner to

death at the end of it, as Petey had been dragged; then he meant to kill the rest of the slavers and attempt to guide the shivering captives to a place where they would be safe.

Jim had prepared one more demonstration—he wanted to spread a little more terror, enough to cause the drunken men to panic—and when they were panicked, the Sin Killer would come among them.

In the night he led the little mare up the narrow ledge to his cave. She snorted once or twice, probably because she smelled the ram, but she didn't falter.

That night he made sure that his sword was still sharp.

At dawn he was ready. He mounted the mare and rode her carefully along the ledge—as he did, he let the Word pour out. Below, slavers and captives struggled to come awake. When they did they saw a man riding across the face of the cliff, seemingly upon air. It was only just dawn: the sun was not up. As Jim yelled out the Word, men scrambled for their guns. Chino even fired a shot, though he knew the distance was too great.

Jim and the mare were off the ledge in

two minutes—then he loped a wide circle to the east. He wanted to come at the men when the rising sun was in their faces.

Malgres, Ramon, and Blue Foot decided to flee, but half drunk and gripped by fear, they made a mess of it. Blue Foot's horse was notably skittish—it had to be approached calmly and patiently, but Blue Foot was too frightened to be calm—he rushed at the horse and the horse bolted. The panic communicated itself to Malgres's horse, and then Ramon's. The three men found to their shock that they were afoot at the worst of all times. Ramon fumbled with his gun. Malgres, looking around for a horse he might steal, drew his thin knife and began to stumble toward Draga's hut. But then, to his horror, the Sin Killer came racing directly out of the face of the rising sun.

"A long knife beats a short knife every time," Jim said, as he cut Malgres down.

Ramon dropped his gun. The Sin Killer came racing past him, after Blue Foot. For a second Ramon felt hope—perhaps the man only wanted Blue Foot.

Jim killed Ramon with a backhand slash as he rode by. The mare closed with Blue Foot in only a second. Jim dropped the rope over the man and jerked it tight around his legs. Blue Foot's face hit the stony ground so hard his teeth cracked. Before he could try to free his legs Jim turned and raced directly at the slavers' camp, crying the Word as he came. Blue Foot bounced in the air, hitting rocks, hitting cactus; then he was dragged through a campfire: ashes filled his eyes, coals burned his hands. Jim poured the Word out in full cry, louder than he ever had. He dragged Blue Foot through every campfire as he slashed at the stumbling men. He cut Chino down where he stood. The Word had never poured out of him so strongly—it excited the little mare. Here was her chance to run, and she did run, bursting through Draga's brush house as if the sticks were twigs. The old woman just managed to crawl out of the way. Too late, the slavers tried to flee—Jim cut them down as they ran. One managed to mount and run but the mare overtook the slaver's horse as a greyhound might overtake a coyote. The fleeing slaver's horse threw him. Jim killed him as he struggled to his feet. What was left of Blue Foot still bounced at the end of his own rope. The Sin Killer was still crying out the Word; he turned back toward the camp, racing down on Draga, who faced him bitterly. No one could stop this man—he had cut through her slavers as if they were merely vegetation, and now he was charging at her. Draga felt a poisonous bitterness: a hard life hers had been, and now this sudden end.

The Sin Killer split her head; he could not stop. He had brought vengeance to the heathen and there were several more, huddled together in terror, screaming. The Sin Killer raised his bloody sword, still crying the Word. He could think of nothing but killing and was about to urge the mare into a last charge into the midst of the heathen, when the Mexican woman sprang in front of him. She grabbed his bridle, fought him for the little mare's head.

"Señor, no mas!" she said. *"No mas!"*

The Sin Killer found it hard to stop; he wanted to keep killing until there was no one left to kill. But the Mexican woman was stubborn; she hung on to the bridle.

"No mas, señor—they are only captives," she cried, clinging to the frothing, sweaty mare who wanted to run some more. The wild sounds excited her.

The woman would not let go—he would

have to kill her to free himself—and he didn't want to kill her, though he had raised a dripping sword. The Word ceased to pour out of him; he began to stop being the Sin Killer. One of the huddled little boys in the group before him looked like Monty. He saw a terrified girl the age of Little Onion. He remembered his children, his dead children, his dead wife. What the woman said was true. The group he had been about to charge were captives, not slavers. Only this stubborn Mexican woman had kept him from cutting them all down. He began to shake, as he realized what he had almost done. The struggle to stop himself from killing was the hardest he had ever fought. The captives still looked terrified. The sword he carried still dripped with Draga's blood. Jim dismounted, shaking, and broke the bloody sword over his knee. Toward the captives he felt a sudden shame.

"It's all right—I won't hurt you," he stammered.

When he snapped the sword he cut his hand on the sharp blade. The brown woman found a little of Draga's whiskey. She washed the wound and bound it. One or two of the captives began to lose their fear.

Jim saw that Blue Foot was dead, filled with thorns as Petey had been—it no longer seemed important. For an hour he felt too weak to walk. The captives were cautiously probing among the corpses of the slavers, taking a knife here, a little money there, a belt, a shirt.

Rosa saw that the white man had exhausted himself with his terrible rage. She herself had known rage, but only for a short time. She had raged at her husband for his drunkenness before he died. She raged at her neighbors for letting their goats into her squash. She had raged at God when her two babies died. But she had not raged as this man raged. He had killed every single slaver, and if she had not stopped him he would have killed the captives too—and killed her as well.

Rosa was cautious with the man. It took time to recover from such terrible anger. Meanwhile she did her own canvass of the destroyed camp. There was a boy named Emilio who was good with horses—she made him go catch the ones who had belonged to the slavers. She set one of the girls to assembling pots, and what food had been in camp.

All this time Rosa watched the white man. He seemed spent, able only to sit. His hands still shook. But he did notice that Emilio had managed to bring in the horses.

"Señor, will you help us—we are far from home?" Rosa asked finally.

Jim had never felt such weariness. He felt almost incapable of movement, yet he knew he had to move. He nodded at the woman. Of course he would help them, once the weariness passed.

"Señor, we should go," Rosa told him. "Too many Comanches come here—they are always coming and sometimes they are many."

Jim nodded again. He liked the looks of the boy who had captured the horses.

"That boy's good with horses," he told her. "My packhorse is tied just behind that bluff. If he'll go fetch him we can load up and leave."

Emilio started at once but Jim stopped him.

"You don't have to walk—take the mare," he said.

The mare had calmed too. She snorted when the boy mounted but Emilio spoke to her soothingly. Soon he returned with the packhorse. Jim would have liked to sleep, but he knew it was not the time. The brown woman was directing the packing, helping the captives assemble supplies. They should be able to make good time—or they should if only he could shrug off his strange weariness.

"I don't know your name," he said to the woman. "I'm Jim."

"My name is Rosa," she said. To her surprise the man stood up and offered to shake her hand. The gesture was so awkward that Rosa smiled—she had not expected to smile again. But she took the man's hand and shook it. He did not want to turn her hand loose, but finally he did. He acted like a badly wounded man, and yet he had received no wound. Rosa kept an eye on him, as she worked. She saw that he was dazed. There was a little of Draga's whiskey left. Rosa took the jug to Jim.

"We have a little whiskey—it might help," she said.

"I might turn sinner if I get drunk," Jim told her. But then he felt silly. He had killed a whole company of men. Surely killing was a worse sin than drunkenness. He took the jug and swallowed two mouthfuls of the burning liquid.

"That's like drinking fire," he said. But he felt a little energy return. A few minutes later he led the group out of the camp.

57

He felt a constant need to rest.

The next days were the hardest Jim Snow had ever spent on the trail. The country itself was no harsher than other country he had traveled through—the problem was that he had no energy and no drive. He felt a constant need to rest. He knew he needed to move the freed captives off the great Comanche war trail—and he did lead them east; but compared with other treks he had made, it was a fumbling, uncertain process. He could not seem to keep his head about him: he kept going back in memory to the terrible moment when he had been about to slay the innocent captives with his dripping sword.

After all, he *hadn't* done it—Rosa's stubborn action had brought him out of his killing frenzy just in time. The crisis had passed; yet he couldn't forget it, couldn't quite come back to himself.

"It's a good thing no Comanches found us today," he said to Rosa, as they sat by the campfire the first night out.

"I've got no fight in me now," he added. "We'd be easy pickings."

"The Comanches will see all those dead men—they may not want us," Rosa told him. "You even killed the old witch. She was a cruel woman—you did good to kill her."

Jim knew that was true—Draga's cruelties had been practiced on his own sister-in-law, Buffum, and countless others. Still, he seemed to have no strength and he could not get his mind off the terrible thing that he had almost done.

Three times in the next days they saw Indians—and yet the Indians didn't come close. Probably Rosa was right. The Indians had seen the massacred slavers, Draga with her head split, Blue Foot dragged to death. Rapidly news of the massacre of the slavers spread across the southern plains and deserts—in weeks it spread all the way to Canada. The Assiniboines knew the Sin Killer. They called him the Raven Brave and it did not surprise them that he had killed a bunch of miserable slavers. The Raven Brave was a man to be feared.

Of the captives only the boy Emilio, who was so good with horses, felt at ease with Jim. The two of them talked about the problems of horses. The other captives kept to themselves. They could not forget that this man had been about to kill them. They weren't sure they could trust him. The young women held back.

Rosa managed the trek, managed the camps they made, managed the other captives—most of all, she managed Jim. She was efficient. She knew to make well-banked campfires. With Lord Berrybender's fine new rifle Jim made a lucky shot on an antelope. Rosa took a horse and packed the animal in. She butchered it, fed the others, dried some of the meat.

Jim could not hide how disturbed he felt. He did not like to be without Rosa's company—she steadied him. She rode beside him all day and sat with him at night. There was little talk. Only once or twice did he return to the moment of conflict, when she had jumped forward and stopped the killing.

"'Vengeance is mine, saith the Lord'—it

says that in the Bible," Jim told her. "I expect that's the right way."

Rosa didn't answer. She had never liked
priests or followed their debates. What she
wanted to tell Jim was that she had never
been as glad of anything as she had been
when she watched him kill the slavers. She
didn't intend to speak of it to Jim—it was
better not to speak of one's shame—but
she had been particularly glad when he had
killed Tay-ha, the man who dishonored her
most casually, treating her as no better than
an animal, even taking her in her bowels.
She could never speak of such shame, or
hope to be an honorable woman again, but
she did not agree that vengeance should
only be the Lord's. She was alive because
Jim had been vengeful. It was true that he
lost himself in a blood frenzy and had almost gone too far—but she had stopped it,
and it was over. She was not going to regret
the deaths of slavers. In fact she had gone
and spat on Tay-ha's corpse, and was
happy when she did it.

She saw, though, that Jim was troubled
in himself, and she did what she could to
help. She brought him his food, sat with
him, administered the trek, settling little

quarrels and seeing that Emilio took good care of the horses. She saw it as a miracle that they were alive at all, and Jim, sad-eyed now and awkward, had made the miracle. Rosa meant to devote herself to him, to the extent that he would allow it.

One night, to her surprise, Jim asked how old she was.

"Old enough to have buried two babies and a husband," Rosa said.

Jim didn't press her. He had merely wondered. Rosa's silences were comfortable silences. She seemed to have no need to question him, as Tasmin did. When Tasmin went away after some discussion Jim usually felt relieved; but when Rosa went away, to attend to some chore, he felt anxious, and the anxious feeling only left him when Rosa came and settled herself by the fire. In settling herself she seemed to settle him. In a while he would stop feeling anxious. He found it to be a comfort of a sort he had not had in his life before. The thought that, once they were safe, Rosa might wish to go back to her home was unsettling. He began to wonder whether there might be a way to keep her. And yet he was a married man—he had a wife. Why was he thinking such things?

58

Was this ribbon becoming? Would this petticoat show?

"Goodness! A ball? What are you thinking about, George?" Tasmin asked. Buffum, Vicky, and Mary were all likewise taken aback. A ball, when they had been in the safety of the settlements only a few days?

"Mr. Austin absolutely insists that you come," George Catlin informed them. "There is much war stir—Mr. Austin feels that a little entertainment would not be amiss. There will be music—even dancing, perhaps."

"All things we once took for granted but have since put behind us," Tasmin said.

"Not so behind us—we danced in Santa Fe, Tassie," Buffum remarked.

"I didn't—I mourned—but never mind," Tasmin said. "I wouldn't mind consenting if I had a dress. What does Mr. Austin propose that we come to the ball *in?* We've all emerged from barbarism very nearly naked, it seems to me."

"Well, you aren't naked but you are perhaps a little begrimed still," George allowed. "Mr. Austin is sensitive to the problem of attire. Some nice Texas ladies are being dispatched to the rescue. They may desire to loan you frocks. Also, there's a kind of haberdashery here in Washington-on-the-Brazos. Not up to London standards, of course, but you might be able to obtain some cloth that would do to be sewn."

"I guess it's not a very long step from barbarism to civilization, down here in Texas," Mary remarked. "I would like to take one hundred baths before considering the matter of adornment."

"I suppose that means you'll be wearing your tiara," Tasmin said in jest—but at the mere mention of a ball their mutual spirits *did* rise.

"I suppose, after all, it's what we were bred to do—go to balls," Tasmin remarked.

"I hear it will be quite thick with heroes," Father Geoff put in.

"Oh, Davy Crockett's here," Lord Berrybender informed them. "I quite hit it off with

him in Washington. The man likes to drink—
so do I. He's quite the hunter, too. A killer of
bears, I believe."

"And then there's Mr. Bowie, who's in-
vented quite a formidable knife," George
told them. "It's the kind of weapon your
husband, Jim, could put to good use."

"I shall want to bring Juan—I hope it will
be no problem," Buffum announced. It was
now understood that she and Corporal
Dominguin were betrothed.

"Mr. Austin is a man of great sophistica-
tion—I'm sure your corporal will be welcome," George said.

A hasty trip was made to a tiny general
store, where cloth of various kinds was purchased. Cook was soon sewing. When the
local matrons showed up with frocks for
loan, all were in the end rejected by the very
particular Berrybenders.

"When we go to balls around here we
must manage to be queens of them," Tasmin instructed; but then, as she was trying
to pull a brush through her recalcitrant hair,
she suddenly put down her brush and burst
into tears.

"But Tassie, what is it?" Kate asked. She

found her sister's tendency to tears something of a trial.

"It's too soon—much too soon," Tasmin sobbed. "Two days ago—forty-eight hours—I hoped for nothing more than to keep my daughter alive. I had buried two sons. And now Mr. Austin gives a ball and I'm expected to care how my hair looks, and to observe that my frock is too tight in the bosom? I can't do it! I can't care about these fripperies. I've lived where it's life-or-death too long."

Then she began again to brush her hair.

"You are wrong, Tassie," Mary told her. "Those who survive *should* dance—it's a blow for life! Right, Geoff?"

Mary considered that she herself looked rather elegant, her pregnancy just showing.

Father Geoffrin, having seen the Berrybender women in all their states, had been permitted access to their boudoir so that he might advise about certain perplexities of fashion. Was this ribbon becoming? Would this petticoat show?

"Mary's right," he said. Tasmin's frock *was* too tight in the bosom, but then, she had a splendid bosom.

"It's a strike for life!" the priest agreed. "It

may feel like disloyalty to the dead, but it isn't."

Buffum was not quite able to resist her own looks, now that she had freshened up a little.

"I wish Juan had better shoes," she said.

At the last minute, as they were all making final adjustments to their wardrobes, Cook, in a panic, announced that there had been an escapee from the nursery: Petal could not be found.

For a moment Tasmin felt a wild flutter of panic—children were sometimes kidnapped even from the villages by clever Indians. But Petal?

Fortunately the miscreant was at once plucked from her grandfather's buggy. She was determined not to miss this exciting ball and negotiated a compromise: she would attend the ball for one hour and then be returned to the nursery. In fact Petal charmed so many of the officers that Cook waited long in an anteroom before the little minx was finally surrendered. Even the austere Mr. Austin was seen to be reciting Petal a rhyme.

Tasmin danced a dance with Davy Crockett but did not warm to the man—his breath was so heavy with brandy that she felt she might be made drunk.

The Berrybender women, though feeling themselves much reduced in vivacity by their recent ordeal, nonetheless swept the young men of Texas before them. Piet sat rather forlornly on the sidelines, watching Mary dance dance after dance with the lively young blades.

Tasmin allowed a few of the young blades too, but then found herself being gracefully led round the floor by James Bowie—his look was melancholy but his dancing expert.

"My goodness, Mr. Bowie," she said, "I'd forgotten how pleasant it is to dance with a man who can dance. I wouldn't be surprised if you were the best dancer in Texas."

James Bowie smiled—a happier light came into his face for a moment.

"My wife would not tolerate inept dancing," he said.

"Of course not—is she here?"

"She's dead—cholera—and my two daughters as well."

"Then we have tragedy in common," Tasmin replied. "I lost a son to cholera—he's buried in New Mexico. Lady Berrybender also lost a son, and my sister Elizabeth a husband."

"It's a wearying thing to see loved ones go so quickly," he said. "It's because I couldn't fight the cholera that I'm here to fight the Mexicans, I guess."

"And do you think the Texans will win?" she asked.

"Oh yes, they'll win—and it won't take them long, either," Bowie said. "If you stay around a few weeks you'll be guests of the Republic of Texas."

"My husband's behind me somewhere—I intend to wait for him," Tasmin told him. "We lost a second boy—this one to slavers. My husband's gone for his revenge."

Jim Bowie merely nodded. Though his dancing remained graceful, the melancholic look was back on his face.

Buffum came hurrying over, in some distress.

"Tassie, you must talk to father—Mr. Crockett is trying to persuade him to go fight the Mexicans," she said.

"What nonsense! Papa's a cripple—he'll just be in the way," Tasmin declared. "I consider old Crockett a bore, and he's nowhere near as good a dancer as Mr. Bowie here."

"Davy's feet are too big," Bowie said, with a smile. "We used to call him Bucket-foot. No fun dancing with Bucketfoot."

By the time they reached Lord Berryben-der, their persuasion was useless. Lord Berrybender's blood was up—he was de-termined to go.

"Father, that's ridiculous," Tasmin said. "You're too old for the barricades."

"Not a bit of it—stirs my blood just to think of a good fight," Lord B. told her. "Can't wait to see action, in fact. The blare of bugles, the thud of cannon. Bowie and Crockett and I will go tomorrow—Crockett assures me it will just be a skirmish—be back in a day or two. The place is called San Antonio."

Tasmin went at once to Davy Crockett and attempted to persuade him to leave her father, but Davy Crockett showed more in-terest in her bosom than in her opinions.

"Oh, we won't have much of a scrap in San Antonio," he assured her.

"Why not?"

"The big battle will be farther east," he assured her. "Sam Houston's over on the plain of San Jacinto, getting ready. He'll show General Santa Anna what's what—no question of that."

"Still, it seems foolish to take a crippled man into battle," Tasmin persisted.

"Nonsense—it'll be a tonic for your father," Crockett said. "He was just telling me about some of his adventures in Spain. Nothing like the smell of gunpowder to get an old warhorse stirred up."

"Getting Father stirred up has never been a problem, Mr. Crockett," Tasmin told him. "I think you would have done better to leave well enough alone."

Davy Crockett was taken aback. Young women with fine bosoms seldom talked to him so brashly—and from the look in this one's eye, worse might be to come. Though it was not his way, he strove to be diplomatic.

"I assure you there's no danger, madam—nothing serious is likely to happen at all," he told her. "The fact is I like your father's company. If he doesn't come I'll have to ride seventy miles with Jim Bowie, which is like riding seventy miles with a mute. Jim's run out of conversation. With your father along we can get drunk and tell lies and we'll be there in no time. There's nobody there but Billy Travis and a hundred or so of his men—hardly enough for Santa Anna to bother with."

James Bowie was of the same opinion.

"I've no great opinion of Billy Travis, which is why I felt Crockett and I ought to lend a hand."

"It all seems very casual, I must say," Tasmin told him. "It seems that Mr. Crockett anticipates a picnic—or better yet, a carouse—rather than war. What if he's wrong?"

"You've hit it!" Bowie told her. "Davy's whole life is a picnic or a carouse. He'll fight well enough, though, if he can find a fight."

Later, Tasmin allowed George Catlin a dance, which was not a success.

"Stop stepping on me, George—good Lord, why can't you dance?"

"I don't know—it's a puzzle," he said. "I do keep trying, though. I've noticed that ladies seem to reserve their greatest contempt for men who won't even try to dance. So I try."

"I don't like Mr. Crockett," Tasmin said. "It seemed to annoy him that I questioned his decision regarding my own father. Every time I ask a man a question I'm greeted with annoyance, if not worse. I don't see why that should be."

"I can't deal with these philosophical questions when I'm doing my best not to step on your feet," George said.

Later, dancing with a young soldier who didn't step on her feet but who didn't utter a word during the dance, either, Tasmin found herself thinking of Jim. She tried to imagine him dancing and couldn't. The surroundings were hardly fancy, just a half-formed army base near the Brazos River, and yet Tasmin could not picture her husband joining in even such a primitive soiree—much less some grander ball in Washington or London, or even Saint Louis. It was a perplexing dilemma. Jim had the skills that enabled him to pursue killers in a wilderness, and yet, she considered, how much easier it would be for her to be happy with him if he could just dance with her at a party—only something as normal as that.

"If we ever get anywhere where there's a dance instructor I mean to insist that you take dancing lessons, George," she told her friend.

"I could try, if you insist," George said.

"But it won't do any good. The flaw is within."

The next day in midmorning Davy Crockett, Jim Bowie, and Lord Albany Berrybender set off for San Antonio. Lord B. was in the best of spirits. It was decided that, once General Houston routed Santa Anna, the Berrybenders would proceed on toward Galveston and look into the possibility of getting a ship.

"I'll catch up with you, never fear," Lord Berrybender assured them. "I just want a whiff of battle one more time—takes me back to the great days of the duke."

"What do you think about this, Vicky?" Tasmin wanted to know.

Vicky had received so much attention from young soldiers at the dance that she had become a little flustered, fearful that she might have exposed too much bosom.

Nonetheless she was not happy to see Lord Berrybender drive away.

"Impossible as he is to live with, I still wish he hadn't gone," Vicky said.

"I feel the same," Tasmin told her.

⇒ 59 ⇒

. . . signs of settlement began to appear . . .

When signs of settlement began to appear—a farm here and there, some already abandoned—Jim reckoned that the worst of the danger was over. They were on the Brazos. One grizzled farmer met them with rifle in hand, offered no food, but did tell them where they needed to go.

"You're on the right river," he said. "Another week and you'll come to Mr. Austin's colony. I expect your people are there—they came by a week ago."

Jim was heartened by that news. Tom Fitzpatrick had brought them through. He himself still felt his strange fatigue. He led the party, but Rosa did most of the work, making the campfires, cooking, keeping the captives in order. One wintry day she went off with Lord Berrybender's rifle and came back with two wild turkeys.

As they drew nearer and nearer to the settlements Jim realized he would soon have different problems to consider. He had rescued eleven people, including Rosa. They were all Mexican, their clothes were rags, they had not a cent, although Rosa had collected what money she could find on the slavers. What was he to do with them? More particularly, what was he to do with Rosa? He had become so needful of her that he couldn't imagine being without her. Somehow her presence was comforting to him, easing, as no other woman's had ever been. The best times of the day were at night when all the chores were done and they just sat by the campfire. They spoke scarcely at all in those times; and yet her presence was a deep comfort. He did not want to lose her; but she had been kidnapped: she might want to go home. The others, perhaps, could find employment of some sort in the Texas settlements. Even if they succeeded in getting back to their homes, the raiders might take them again.

Jim found it hard to reconcile his need for Rosa with the fact that he had a wife and daughter not many days ahead. What could he do? What would Tasmin want? What would Rosa want?

Rosa knew that Jem, as she called him, was troubled. He had told her that he had a wife and daughter. He had made no move to use her, as the slavers had used her. She herself felt sad—what could she do, when Jem returned to his family? Her home was far—even if she could find it, it was no place she wanted to be. Her husband's wicked old mother blamed her for his death. His sisters hated her. Vaqueros she didn't want were pressing her to go with them. She had to fight them, and some of them were strong. If she went home she would finally have to accept one of them, or she would starve.

Rosa had come to be fond of Jem—but since he already had a wife he wouldn't want to stay with her. Besides, she had been dishonored. How could she be a wife to a good man after the stains she bore? She even worried that Jim might have witnessed her shame. He had a spyglass. He might have seen her when Tay-ha led her out. She didn't want to ask him.

Jim, in his years with Tasmin, had rarely

been able to figure out what she was feeling, except when she was angry. But now he had a sense that he *did* know what Rosa felt. When she sat by the campfire at night she wore a look of quiet sadness, as if she felt that her prospects were very bad. She did not want to look beyond the chores of the day. She would be happy to serve Jem, be a servant in his household, but probably his wife would not want such a thing.

Jim knew he was not a good talker, when it came to explaining things; and yet he had become so dependent on Rosa's company that he felt that he had better try. He didn't like the sad looks he saw on Rosa's face. Also, he didn't believe he could ever be at ease with Tasmin, in the way that he was with Rosa.

Besides, the Berrybenders were tending homeward. He didn't want to go to England and he doubted Tasmin intended to stay in America. The two boys' deaths had cut her too deeply. He didn't know how it would all work out but he knew he did not want to lose Rosa. He wanted to keep Rosa. One night he looked up and told her so in the simplest words he could find.

"I don't want to send you home," he told

her. "I want you to stay with me and go where I go."

Rosa was shocked. What was Jem thinking? He had a wife. Was he asking her to stay with him as his whore? Her face showed her disappointment.

"It's not what you're thinking," Jim told her. "I guess my wife and I will be parting. She's going to England and I can't. She won't be my wife always."

Rosa was too startled to respond at once. She had not let herself hope that Jem might want her as his woman, but that seemed to be what he did want. And yet it didn't seem credible. Why would he want to leave a rich woman for a poor Mexican who had been misused?

"I am . . . surprised," she told him. "You are no longer to be with your wife?"

Jim shook his head.

"You saved me when you grabbed that bridle," he told her. "Otherwise I would have killed all these people."

"Yes, I did that—but it's past," she told him. "You are not killing anybody now. I expect your wife is a good wife. Why would you leave her for a poor woman like me?"

"I'm better with you than I am with Tasmin," he said.

Beyond that he couldn't explain.

Rosa waited, but he said no more. Yet she thought she must make him be clear.

"Jem, are you asking me to be your woman?" she asked, watching him closely as she said it.

Jim nodded.

"And you mean to send away your wife?"

He nodded again.

Rosa said no more. Jim waited, nervously. He wanted an answer, but Rosa didn't immediately give him one.

"Will you, then?" he asked.

"I don't know," Rosa said quietly. "I am glad that you want this, but I don't know."

"When will you know?" he asked.

Rosa took his hand and squeezed it, to show that she was not being hard.

"When I've met this wife you want to send away—then I'll know," she said.

60

Davy Crockett, sober and somber . . .

"You know, Crockett, it's rather odd," Lord Berrybender said. "I started my military career attempting to shoot small brown men through the dust and the smoke, and here I am at the end of my military career, still attempting to shoot small brown men through the dust and the smoke. There's a certain symmetry to it, wouldn't you say?"

Davy Crockett, sober and somber, mainly wished the old lord would stop talking. The siege of the Alamo had lasted almost two weeks, and the mood inside the old mission was not optimistic. Inside the walls of the mission's courtyard Mexican bodies were piled in heaps; and yet there seemed to be an endless supply of soldiers, ready to fling themselves at the Texans as Santa Anna commanded. Jim Bowie was sick, they were almost out of ammunition, and yet old Albany Berrybender went on babbling end-lessly about battles he had fought in Portu-gal and Spain. Probably half of what he said were lies, Crockett thought; but then per-haps the old fellow was wise to relive old battles: it might distract him from the fact that he was likely to die in this one, a fact for which Davy Crockett knew he bore some responsibility.

"I fear I rather misled you, Albany—I sup-posed this would be mainly a lark," he ad-mitted. "I would never have supposed General Santa Anna would have come at our little company in such force—not when he has Sam Houston waiting for him on the plain of San Jacinto."

James Bowie, very weak from typhus, sat up on his cot and began to sharpen his knife—the big knife with the handle guard that he had designed himself.

"Why, Crockett, this is just a warm-up," he said. "Santa Anna thought he'd get an easy victory—probably wanted to get his soldiers' blood up. I doubt the man sup-posed we'd be this tough."

Around the shadowy interior of the old church, Texans were grimly counting bullets. William Travis, their leader, spent his day at a little lookout post, with his spyglass. What he was looking for was some slight sign that Santa Anna might be tiring of the siege. He knew he could overrun the Texans eventually, but on the other hand, the cost in men was not small—Travis had no time to count bodies but he supposed the Mexican casualties must be approaching a thousand men. The Texans had most of them lived by the rifle—they could shoot, and they had, day after day, for almost two weeks. A wise general would not sacrifice a thousand men to overrun a force of less than two hundred; and yet generals were not always wise, and the men were being sacrificed. The wisdom of generals was a topic Lord Berrybender was happy to expound upon, on chill evenings, in the old church.

"Napoleon—brilliant of course, but hardly wise," he said. "Got cocky after Austerlitz and let the Russians suck him in. I suppose that's what we've done with General Santa Anna. We've sucked him in and your General Houston can mop him up."

"Rather rough on us, of course," Lord B.

added. "Fortunes of war and all. Luck bound to run out sometime."

The last remark set Davy Crockett grumbling.

"Speak for yourself, Albany," Crockett said. "I'm not ready to have my luck run out. I didn't come to Texas to die—always rather fancied dying in a brothel, if you must know."

"An original choice, certainly," Lord Berrybender replied. "I expect we could find a few whores around here, if only the Mexicans would give us a pass. Easy enough to get passes at such times in Europe—officers' honor and all that, but it doesn't seem to have caught on here."

"Nope, they mean to have our gizzards, and no entertainment allowed," Jim Bowie remarked.

"If we're to be slaughtered I hope it happens before the brandy runs out," Lord Berrybender remarked. "I have rather an enviable reputation as a drinking man. I'd hate to be sober when I draw my last breath."

Davy Crockett didn't like the cheerful tone in which Lord Berrybender spoke of the likelihood that they would all be killed. It might be true enough, but why talk about it? The thing to do was keep one's focus on life.

"Well, America's a grand place—my only regret is that I never got to shoot a grizzly bear," Lord Berrybender said. There was every sign that another charge was coming. The Texans had repulsed many, perhaps they would repulse this one—and yet, perhaps not.

"Deplorable uniforms!" he yelled, when the Texans' guns had all but fallen silent—the brown men, at last, began to pour in.

"I'd speak to somebody about those uniforms—they make you look like clowns!" he yelled to the fellow who was rushing at him with the shining bayonet. Jim Bowie, he saw, was up and whirling like a dervish, jabbing and striking with his big knife.

Lord Berrybender just managed to parry the bayonet with his rifle, but another soldier came rushing just as fast and this time the blade went into his chest with a thunck, as if someone had stabbed a big ripe melon. Very surprising it was, that melon-struck sound. He thought he must remember to mention it to Vicky; but then, as he sank down, he realized that he would not be mentioning much else to his Vicky—how he had always liked that long, slim body of hers. The soldier in the clown uniform was trying to pull the bayonet out of his chest, but the bayonet seemed to be stuck. It was all more surprising than painful. He remembered the look on Señor Yanez's face when the Pawnee boy ran at him and stuck the lance deep into him. Surprised was how the small gunsmith had looked: perhaps that was how *he* looked at the moment—surprised. Then the boy did jerk the bayonet out and Lord Berrybender sank to his knees. All around him men were struggling, but he himself felt rather like stretching out. Time for a nap, gentlemen, he thought— time for a nap.

*. . . dark rumors began to reach
them . . .*

The Austin colony was all in a turmoil,
would-be soldiers arriving almost hourly to
fight for the Texas Republic—volunteers de-
parted at an equal rate, hoping not to miss
the glorious fight, though uncertain as yet
which battle offered the best chance for
glory. Petal and Elf particularly enjoyed the
confusion. Both were popular with the soldiers—they were given frequent horse rides
by men homesick for their own children.
George Catlin was impatient—he wanted to
press on to Galveston and see what boats
were going where, but Tasmin and Vicky
were reluctant to leave without their husbands. Vicky expected to see Lord Berrybender come up the road from San Antonio
any day.

Then dark rumors began to reach them—

the Texans were said to be besieged in something called the Alamo; the Mexican army was said to have an overwhelming advantage. And yet the news was all vague. It was reported that William Travis had drawn a line in the sand with his sword, with all those prepared to die for Texas independence on one side of it while those on the other side, who didn't care to commit themselves, were free to leave. Some said Jim Bowie was with the stalwarts, some said Crockett was with him, but no mention was made of Lord Albany Berrybender at all.

Vicky Berrybender became deeply apprehensive—her husband, after all, was notably reckless. When Mr. Austin, even more grave than usual, came to deliver the sad news—not only Lord Berrybender but nearly two hundred defenders of the Alamo all dead—Vicky was not really surprised. What surprised Lord Berrybender's daughters was the depth of Vicky's grief. She not only sobbed, she screamed so loudly that her frightened son, Talley, ran to Buffum for reassurance. Tasmin could do nothing with Vicky, nor could Father Geoffrin or anyone else.

"What do you suppose she would do if

Father had ever been nice to her?" Tasmin asked.

"Perhaps there was something about him that we missed," Buffum suggested. "After all, Mama had all of us by him."

"The ability to get women with child is a very common one," Tasmin remarked. "It's useful insofar as it keeps the race going, although whether that is a good thing might be debated."

"*Is* debated—that's what philosophy is all about," Geoff told her.

"Drat you, I don't care about philosophy!" Tasmin told him. "That old brute, my father, has now left us stranded in a place we have no reason to be. I'm his daughter. I wish I could feel something positive, but I can't. His life was one long selfish folly, and we're the victims of it."

"That's harsh, Tassie," Mary said. "Speak no ill of the dead."

"An absurd sentiment," Tasmin answered. "I cannot subscribe to it."

In fact she felt bitterness, not grief, when she thought of her father. The roll call of those who had died because of his selfishness—which included three of his grandchildren—would not be short, once it was tallied up.

"Almost two hundred heroes died at the Alamo," Mr. Austin intoned, in his sententious way.

"If you're counting our father, make it one hundred ninety-nine," Tasmin said, not caring if the comment shocked her sisters. "I'm sure he shot plenty of little Mexican soldiers before he died—children most of them, like our Corporal Dominguin."

Mr. Austin was deeply offended.

"Hardly a patriotic view, under the circumstances," he said, frowning.

"Not meant to be patriotic—but not unfair, either," she retorted. "What could you know about the trail of dead we've left behind us?"

"I merely meant that it would be an inconvenient thing to say just now, when everyone is hot to kill Mexicans," he said, shocked by the Englishwoman's temerity.

"Not everyone *is* hot to kill Mexicans—it's just you intemperate Texans," Tasmin told him, whereupon Stephen F. Austin turned on his heel and went away.

Geoff, George, and Tasmin's sisters all seemed stunned by what they had heard.

"Well, am I expected to be polite to a fool like that?" Tasmin asked. "I suppose I ain't polite enough for this fine new republic."

"I ain't polite either," the cheerful Petal said.

62

She felt a stir of unease.

Vicky didn't try to explain to Tasmin why she grieved so when the news came that her husband, Lord Berrybender, was dead. She found it easier to talk to Buffum, who, after all, had lost a husband also—perhaps a better husband than Albany Berrybender could ever have been. There were men who dissembled and men who changed, and then there were men who could only be what they were. Lord Berrybender was a man of the latter sort. He had been many things that were not nice. He had been violent and he had been cold; he had been drunken, unfaithful, and brutal; he begged shamelessly when she refused him, yet he thought no more of lying to her than he would have of lying to a fly. Cruelest of all, he had shown no interest in their children, had scarcely ever invited either boy into his lap, where Tasmin's brash Petal installed herself without bothering to ask permission.

"There is always more than people on the outside can see," Vicky told Buffum. "He was so sweet sometimes, Buffum—so infinitely sweet. I vowed a thousand times not to forgive him, and yet when he looked at me in a certain way I could not hold to my purpose. I forgave him countless times. Do you think I'm wrong?"

"No," Buffum said. "When men are sweet there's no holding out."

"They say the flesh is weak—it's a true saying," Vicky told her. "And yet if one is not weak—if one is strong, like Tasmin, it seems one must be mainly alone."

She sighed.

"I was not made to be alone," she said.

"Nor I," Buffum told her. "I fear that Tassie is very likely to end up alone. She is so very unbending."

"I'm certainly nothing of the sort," Tasmin said indignantly, when Mary repeated the remark to her. "How dare she say that? I've yielded, I've compromised, I've abandoned position after position in order to avoid being alone. I don't know what Buffum means. Even now all I can think of is when my husband will appear. I've spent more than half my marriage waiting for Jimmy to appear. I won't have Buffum telling me that I don't bend."

Cook was out early the next morning, hoping to find a few eggs—the hens in Washington-on-the-Brazos were skinny things. Cook felt it was better to rely on them for eggs than to attempt to cook such wiry specimens.

It was when she looked up from a nest with a single egg in it that she saw Mr. Jim coming. Behind him, on other horses, were some very ragged people. Riding beside him, at his elbow, was a brown woman. Something in the way the two looked at one another caught Cook's attention. She felt a stir of unease.

Nonetheless she at once woke Tasmin, to give her the news.

"What? Where is he?" Tasmin asked, jumping out of bed.

"He's just stopped to speak to Mr. Fitzpatrick," Cook said. She was in rather a quandary about what it was best to say.

"Why do you look that way?" Tasmin asked. "Is Jimmy hurt? Tell me."

"No, he's not hurt," Cook assured her, wishing she had never spoken. But Tasmin had known Cook so long that dissembling was impossible.

"There's a woman with him," Cook at last said.

"A woman? What do you mean, a captive?" Tasmin asked, more puzzled than concerned.

"Just a woman—I shouldn't have mentioned it," Cook said.

63

*She had been fearful of being
scorned . . .*

Petal, friendly as could be, put her short
white arm next to Rosa's brown one, com-
paring the two tones.

"I wish I was brown—it's prettier," she
concluded.

"You better just stay white," Rosa told
her. "If you're white maybe you can be the
queen someday."

"Yes, and she'd certainly like that," Cook
observed. "She acts like a queen already,
this little miss does."

"I boss her," Petal said, smiling. "I boss
everybody. I even bossed my grandpa, only
now he's gone'd."

"Your pa's dead?" Jim asked, very startled, when Tasmin told him the news. "I
didn't think anybody could kill that old
man."

"There were said to be five thousand soldiers with General Santa Anna—I suppose it was enough to do the job," she told him.

Tasmin refrained from asking Jim about Rosa, who had met all the Berrybenders and now sat with Petal and Cook. Jim was just back. Tasmin intended to resist her impulse to be the prying housewife. Tasmin assumed Jim had rescued Rosa, and then came to like her. It was easy to see that he *did* like her. Meeting the Berrybenders had made Rosa a little nervous, but not very. What they all noted about her was that she seemed very calm.

"I suppose it's because she's had to put up with worse things than meeting a bunch of half-addled Europeans," Geoff remarked, trying to put his finger on the quality of Rosa's calm.

"But does she want my husband?" Tasmin wondered. "It's clear that Jim wants her—but it's not clear that she intends to accept him. What do you think, George?"

"She was taken by slavers—undoubtedly a rough experience," George said. "Remember what happened to Buffum at the Mandans'. These hothouse questions probably mean nothing to the woman. She's far from home—she has nothing but the clothes on her back. What Jim wants or doesn't want may be the least of her problems."

"But it's not the least of mine," Tasmin told him. "I'm not criticizing her, George. I think I like her. Whatever she is, one can see that she's not cheap. Jim didn't bring back a whore."

Though Tasmin didn't say it to the company, the questions she wanted to ask did not all have to do with Jim. The man who had ridden away, flinty faced, to revenge the murder of a wife and son was not the man who had come back, leading ten captives and a dignified Mexican woman. Jim had always been lean—it was one source of his appeal. Tasmin had always disliked fleshy men. Master Stiles had been lean, Pomp had been lean, Jim was lean. But now he seemed a skeleton, hollow-faced, haunted. He wore a look of deep unhappiness, which only changed when he looked at Rosa, or sat by her for a moment. Tasmin felt perplexed. Jim had fought fierce battles before: with the Piegans, with the Pawnee boys, with Obregon and his men. He blazed with rage, became the Sin Killer, then slowly came back to being Jim. Only this time it was clear that he had *not* come back. He was not the old Jim—even Petal could not quite reach him. Whatever they had gone through together had left Jim in great need of this quiet woman.

Despite her curiosity, Tasmin felt hesitant about trying to get the story from Jim—he never liked it when she questioned him. While he was busy with the horses, listening to Tom Fitzpatrick fill him in on what was known about the terrible massacre at the Alamo, Tasmin saw an opportunity and sat down by Rosa.

"Will you tell me what happened?" she asked. Why not be direct? "My husband doesn't seem quite like himself."

Rosa was relieved that Jim's wife could speak to her in a friendly, frank way. She had been fearful of being scorned, perhaps even beaten, although she had done nothing sinful with Jem. But a wife wouldn't know that—a wife might have suspicions. She had had plenty of suspicions about her husband—and well-founded ones, too.

"I was taken by the slavers, like the others," Rosa said. "They were very bad men, cruel. Jem came in the morning and killed them all, every one. No one escaped him."

"That's no surprise," Tasmin told her.

"He spilled much blood—he couldn't stop," Rosa went on. "He was going to kill everybody—those women—even those children."

She nodded toward the other captives, who were sitting listlessly nearby, waiting for someone to tell them what to do.

"I was able to stop him," Rosa told Tasmin. "I grabbed his bridle—in time he came back to himself. When he realized what he had been about to do, he broke his sword. Now Jem thinks I saved him."

"It sounds to me like you *did* save him," Tasmin said. "You kept him from killing innocent people. So it's no wonder that now he needs you very much."

"Yes, he needs me," Rosa agreed. "I don't know for how long. He saved my life. He killed the men who dishonored me. He kept us all from starving. He told me he had a wife. I'm glad you are friendly toward me. I am not a husband stealer. I told Jem I would be his servant. I can cook and make fires and do the things a servant does."

"But do you have a home to go to?" Tasmin asked.

Rosa shook her head. "My little ones are dead," she replied. "So is my husband—he was no great loss. So if you and Jem need a servant I will stay and work for you, to show that I am grateful."

Tasmin didn't immediately answer, because she didn't know what to say. That Jim wanted to keep Rosa was obvious. What was less certain was whether he wanted to keep his wife. He had not kissed her, not touched her. He *had* kissed Petal, but that was all.

Cook soon took to Rosa, who immediately set about making herself useful. Tasmin could only brood and wonder.

Jim was aware that he needed to explain things to Tasmin. She *was* his—when night came she would expect him in her bed. And yet he meant to do as he had been doing, spending his nights by the campfire with Rosa.

Finally Tasmin bearded him—indecision and uncertainty were states not to be born.

"Jimmy, I'm not angry—I just want to know what you want."

"I have to stay with Rosa," Jim said, relieved that Tasmin didn't seem angry.

"She saved me, now I need her," he added. "I guess we should marry."

"Well, that might work in the Ute country, where men are allowed various wives—but it won't work here," Tasmin said. "It would make you a bigamist, and bigamy is a crime, I'm sure—besides, I imagine Rosa's Catholic, and the Catholic Church certainly frowns on bigamy."

"Rosa saved me from slaughtering the women and children," Jim said. "She's the real Sin Killer—she killed the big sin I was about to do."

Tasmin walked away, perplexed. She needed to talk to her counselors—George and Geoff.

"Jim's been through a crucible—the slaughter in that camp must have been terrible," George said. "He's had a moral crisis and it's left him not himself. He badly needs Rosa to lean on, but of course that may be temporary."

"She seems a nice woman," Geoff added.

"She is, but I don't know that *I* am," Tasmin told them. "It's so complicated. She's

very grateful to Jimmy, of course. She offered to be our servant, to show her gratitude. Besides that, she has no place to go.
I don't think a servant is what Jimmy wants.
I think he wants to take her to wife. He said
as much. And yet here I am, the old wife but
hardly the easy wife. Rosa seems to want to
be as Little Onion was. She's been misused,
and Jem, as she calls him, saved her. So
she wants to help him. I don't think she
means to mate with him."

"That could change," Geoff told her.

"Of course, given enough time—but
enough time might mean years," Tasmin
said. "What am I to do right now?"

Her counselors looked stumped. They
ceased to counsel.

"It's very peculiar, the situations life presents one with," Father Geoff reflected.

Night fell, the company ate. Tasmin slept
alone. Rosa built a campfire, and she and
Jim sat beside it.

⇥ 64 ⇤

. . . Tasmin woke up tearful . . .

In the night Tasmin woke up tearful, from an aching pain—but the pain was not because her husband was sitting by a campfire with a quiet Mexican woman. She cried from the grief that woke her two nights out of three— her grief for her boys. It was a grief she had come to doubt she could bear and remain sane. If Jim had known how to help her, she felt she might get better—but Jim didn't know how to help her—never had. When, yesterday, he had casually said that he wanted to marry Rosa, Tasmin suddenly re-alized that words such as "marry," "hus-band," "wife" had, for Jim, neither legal nor sacramental weight. Those words didn't mean to Jim what they meant to people brought up in settled societies. All he meant by "husband," "wife," "marry" was that he

and the woman in question might travel together for some while. But his scanty reading of his tattered Bible had given him no
sense of holy matrimony as it was understood by settled people. His agreeing to get
"hitched up" with her had been, for him, a
light thing. He was a mountain man; he saw
no reason not to add wives when a pleasing
new woman came along—it wasn't a fault
exactly, merely the fruit of his unparented
upbringing. Tasmin didn't hold this against
him—how, under the circumstances, could
it have been otherwise?—but it did make
her feel lonelier when she woke up in the
night grieving for her boys. She now considered that she should have known all this
at once, on their first night together, when
she had got slapped for attempting to explain what theology was. Jim had no theology, just a notion or two: that sin, whatever
it was, should be punished; that wives
should be silent and obey their husbands.
He had the merest scraps of belief and he
couldn't help her when she felt sad in the
night.

When dawn came she went straight to
the fire Rosa was already building up.

"Excuse me for inviting myself into your

company this early," Tasmin said. Jim looked tired and a little wary. Rosa offered Tasmin coffee.

"I've got to say this, Jim," she told him, trying to control her voice, trying not to begin to cry.

"I can accept the death of our boys because I have to—they're dead," she said. "What I can't accept is how they're buried."

Jim looked perplexed. The boys were buried where they died, as most travelers were buried.

"Here it is, Jim," she went on. "I can't bear to think of them buried lonely and far apart, far from either of us. I want them buried together, in a churchyard we could visit. A nice churchyard, with grass, and a headstone for each of them."

"I buried my girls that way," Rosa said. "I put up little crosses.

"If I am ever in my village again I will visit them," she said sadly. "But I don't know if I will be."

"You see, Jimmy?" Tasmin said. "That's how any good mother would feel."

Jim waited, not sure what the women were telling him.

"I think I have the resources to be happy

again, sometime in my life," Tasmin told him. "If I can just visit my boys from time to time and know that they're together in a proper graveyard I can reconcile myself to what's happened and go on. But if one poor tyke is over by the Rio Grande and the other I know not where, in time I think I'll go mad. It's a thing I just can't bear."

"You should go get them for her—you can find them," Rosa said. "If you buried them you can find them—it will help her."

"That's just what I intended to ask—that you go gather in our boys," Tasmin told him, grateful to Rosa for smoothing the way. "I haven't asked you for many favors—I'm sure you'll agree. But I'm asking this."

Jim thought the request strange, but had no objection to doing it so long as Rosa would come along.

"I would be grateful if you'd go with him," Tasmin said, to Rosa. "As their mother I know it's my job. But it would mean leaving Petal in the lap of this infant republic and I fear she would soon bring it down. They'd be trying to recall General Santa Anna if they had to cope with Petal for a month."

"You mean you want to wait here?" Jim asked.

"No—not here," she said. "I mean to leave Texas and I hope never to come back. I'll wait for you in Saint Louis. I'll make George or Geoff wait with me, and perhaps Buffum and her young corporal as well."

Jim looked at Tasmin several times—she had a wild, desperate look, like a mare that had been locoed. Her face was thinning, making her eyes even larger, wilder.

"Please, Jim," Tasmin asked. "We've got Petal to think of. I don't want to become a crazed mother. If you can't find the time to bring them all the way to Saint Louis, then take them to Bent's Fort. I'm sure Kit would bring them the rest of the way."

Jim thought he could see the right in it, brothers laid together in a settled place.

"No, I won't send them by Kit—they're our boys," he told her. "I'll go get them and bring them wherever you want them."

"Thank you," Tasmin said.

She turned to Rosa.

"It'll be a hard journey, I know. I'm grateful to you for attempting it."

"I never took no journey till I was stolen," Rosa said. "That trip was hard enough."

"This one will be easier," Jim told her. "The weather will be easing, and I'll get you a better horse. That old sack of bones you're riding barely made it this far."

He talked for a bit, discussing the practicalities of the journey. Tasmin and Rosa listened with only half a mind, half an ear. Jim was thinking of guns and blankets, meat and bullets. The women were thinking of dead children, those they had brought into being, had suckled, had cleaned when they soiled, but had lost.

"I expect it will take four months," Jim concluded.

"I'll be in Saint Louis by then," Tasmin promised.

. . . they were still good shoulders, she considered.

"I think it pays to be particular about cocks," Buffum told them. "I've been lucky twice." She was pregnant again and glowing. Corporal Dominguin was evidently given little rest. Somehow Buffum had turned into a beauty; no one seeing her now would suppose she had ever been plain. Whether this change was a result of a particularity about cocks no one could say; but Buffum was rapidly becoming the beauty of the family. Tasmin, feeling old and dowdy, was too distracted to do much about herself, although, once they got to Galveston Island, where some adornments were available, Father Geoff urged a few purchases on her: a new hairbrush, scent, a frock. Still, when General Houston gave a ball for the Berrybenders as they passed through, Tasmin had as many young men petitioning her for dances as Buffum. Tasmin bared her shoulders; they were still good shoulders, she considered. She let herself be swept up in the dancing for an hour—it took her mind off other things.

General Houston, rather grumpy, somewhat dyspeptic, did not dance. Tasmin had hoped that someone would recover her father's body from the Alamo, but the hope was forlorn. The heaps of dead had been thrown into common graves. Vicky still teared up when Lord Berry-bender's name was mentioned, which was more and more seldom as they straggled on toward the port of Galveston and began the confusing business of attempting to decide which of them were going home to Europe and which merely to Saint Louis with Tasmin and Petal.

"George and Geoff have no choice," Tasmin said. "I need them until Jim brings me my boys."

The two men made no protest.

"After that you two can go anywhere you please, with my gratitude," Tasmin told them.

"I'll have to go somewhere where I can

sell my pictures," George told her. "And pronto, else I'll be bankrupt."

"Somehow bankruptcy suits you, George," Buffum joked. "I doubt any of us could stand you if you were rich."

Cook was the first member of the company to declare herself resolute for England. Tom Fitzpatrick's suit, in the end, had been firmly rejected.

"He's not young, he's not handsome, and he has no money at all," the ever-practical Cook informed them. "I can't see the point of it, miladies."

"I should have thought the point of it might be that he cares for you," Tasmin said, a little taken aback by Cook's firm refusal of the man who had loyally helped her across thousands of miles.

Mary and Piet also opted for Europe.

"I want my child to be born in a safer country," Mary told her sisters.

"You once were almost wholly demonic, Mary," Tasmin reminded her. "How odd that you should have become the most practical among us."

"We may come back," Piet suggested. "The arachnids attract me—spiders. I may just want to do a study."

Buffum refused to hear of England.

"Afraid of being disappointed by the cocks?" Tasmin joked.

Buffum merely chuckled, in her new, sultry way.

Vicky chose England.

"I suppose I had better go see if there is anything left in Northamptonshire," she said. "And I do need a new cello."

In the evenings Tasmin and Petal, sometimes accompanied by Elf, took long walks on the gray beach, looking at the gray sea. Petal and Elf busied themselves collecting shells.

"That sea looks *too* big," Petal declared. "Why don't we go back and find my Jim?"

"He's not just *your* Jim—I had a share in this too," her mother told her. "Besides, our Jim is hard to find."

"I still think this sea looks too big," Petal said.

Kate Berrybender was the last family member to choose Europe.

"It's my mathematics, you see," Kate explained. "Piet assures me I shall have much better tutors in Europe—he suggests perhaps Göttingen. I should like to advance my mathematics and I fear a lack of advanced tutors here."

But as the ship was loading Kate burst into tears.

"It's because I don't know if I shall ever see Mr. James Snow again," she sobbed.

"*We* will see him, and anyway he's not *yours*," Petal insisted.

"You ought to smack that impertinent brat," Kate advised.

. . . a frustrated trinity . . .

On the voyage to New Orleans both George and Geoff were desperately seasick. They could seldom drag themselves to the card table. Buffum, wilder and wilder, spent the voyage sequestered with Corporal Dominguin, now merely called Juan. Petal and Elf wandered the ship, fighting like cats and dogs. Petal persuaded a sailor to help her up into the rigging, where she clung to a rope. Tasmin shouted herself hoarse but Petal refused to descend. A team of sailors was finally dispatched to fetch her. One of the sailors was so exhausted by the effort that he fell into the sea.

Tasmin had begun to feel rather guilty about her shameless use of George Catlin and Father Geoffrin; and yet for her it was an intensely lonely time, her husband far away and with another woman, her sister occupied with a lover, her daughter opposing her every wish. George and Geoff were old and well-trusted companions. When they were well they were able to provoke at least a semblance of gaiety in her—a bit of the old, teasing Tasmin would return. Yet the cruel fact was that both men were in love with her and were not going to get what they wanted. She resolved to send them away when they reached Saint Louis, and yet they reached Saint Louis and she didn't send them away. They had been welded, through travel and travail, into a frustrated trinity from which none of the three could find the strength to leave. Except on her waspish days, Tasmin was kind to her old friends. They avoided all talk of romance except when the vibrant Buffum—who was actually having a romance—joined the discussion. The better Buffum looked, the more sour the three of them felt.

Once in Saint Louis, they settled into a large house, lent them by Captain Clark, and settled in to wait. Petal and Elf immediately stuck themselves in a chimney, finally emerging very black. Once off the water, George's and Geoff's health improved; there were card games again, and a semblance of levity. George made a great many sketches of scenes along the docks and the river-bank. Geoff and Tasmin shopped, buying things neither much wanted. Buffum paid a visit to the great Bent brothers warehouse, being run by two younger Bents—Buffum considered the warehouse so very disor-dered that she could hardly understand how the business continued to operate. Unop-posed by the younger Bents, she began to reorganize the inventory and standardize the accounts.

"She's become a regular American—practical," Tasmin said.

"I know, but don't criticize her," George replied. "She's the only healthy one among us. Geoff and I ought to leave—you ought to make us. You're not going to accept ei-ther of us, yet we can't stop wanting you."

"Can't you understand, this is a death-watch!" Tasmin said, flaring up. "I'm waiting for my dead boys. I only hoped for a little help from my friends. You're both free to go, if that's your attitude. In fact I wish you *would* go. Go! Go!"

But then they made it up.

"If only I were a better dancer," George sighed.

"Do you really think it matters that much—how well a man dances?" Tasmin asked.

"I suspect it does," George replied. "I rather fear it does."

67

In the full heat of summer . . .

In the full heat of summer, Jim came. He stepped off the boat with Rosa, Charles Bent, Greasy Lake, Kit Carson, and the drovers who had brought across a large shipment for the warehouse. Amid the stores, carefully protected, were three tiny bodies—they had brought Randy too. Rosa had purchased blankets from the Bents and had made each boy a tasteful shroud. In a pine coffin were the remains of Little Onion. Jim had felt it wrong to leave her. Charles Bent had marked the shrouds so that Tasmin might know which was which. Jim looked no less gaunt. Rosa was with child, a fact Tasmin noted but did not remark on. She had traveled that road with Jim herself: it was hard to deny comfort to the man, if you liked him.

Tasmin held tight to Kit for so long that it embarrassed him—she couldn't help it; she was too flooded with feeling to turn him loose.

"I did miss you, Kit," she said finally. "Are you a father yet?"

For a moment Kit himself looked sad.

"We had one but it was born too early—didn't live," he said, in a tone of some discouragement. It reminded her that in every life there were disappointments, some as acute as her own.

Greasy Lake was carrying what appeared to be a rolled-up buffalo skin, rather yellowish.

"Where's Mr. Lake going now?" she asked.

"To Cape Cod—hard to believe, ain't it?" Charles Bent told her. "Some Comanches killed that yellow buffalo he found. It's upset him a bunch. He thinks it's the End of the Indian peoples—I disagree. When we've killed *all* the buffalo—and we will—*then* it'll be the End of the Indian peoples."

"Why would he want to go to Cape Cod?" Buffum asked.

"Because he thinks that's where the sun is born, out of the ocean," Charles Bent told them. "He's going there to do some big-time praying."

Later, when he saw the huge improvements Buffum had made in his warehouse, he confessed himself much impressed.

"Do you think I could hire her?" he asked Jim.

"Buffum? I think she's rich already," Jim told him.

"That don't mean she couldn't be richer yet—and help me get richer too," Charlie told him. "She's better than Vrain with inventories, and Vrain's no slouch himself."

. . . the Missouri's shores were vague with summer heat.

The three boys were buried on a green hill, beside a little frame church. Little Onion was laid by Monty, her dearest. Captain William Clark read the Twenty-third Psalm, and his wife, Harriet, who had a beautiful voice, sang a bit of Handel. Charles Bent carefully took Tasmin's order for the headstones, making sure he had each name right. Tasmin stood by Jim, with Rosa on his other side. Buffum watched over Petal and Elf. George Catlin and Father Geoffrin were ashen. Their wait was over, but what next?

The funeral party then repaired to Captain Clark's house. Jim had scarcely spoken to Tasmin—he merely said hello. At the house he busied himself with the Captain's great map of the West, suggesting certain changes in the region of the Pecos River—things he had noticed on his recent travels. Tasmin was afraid he didn't mean to speak to her at all—not in punishment, but because talk was not his way. Helpful as Little Onion had been, months might pass with Jim scarcely addressing a word to her. Jim looked haunted still. The violence that had coursed through him when he was among the slavers must have seared something in him, as perhaps the long-ago lightning had when it flung him through the air.

Tasmin finally decided to corner him—after all, she merely wanted to thank him—nothing more.

"I do thank you so much for bringing them, Jimmy," she told him. "It's an immense comfort to me that our sons are together, in a nice place where we can both visit them."

"Do you mean to stay here, then?" he asked.

"Petal and I are going to England—we're going, but I don't know that we'll stay," she told him. "We may come back. Petal regards you as her own—and she's quite right. When we do come back I'll get word to you through the Bents—or Kit. I'm sure someone can find you."

"Charlie wants me to work with Vrain, up on the South Platte," Jim said. "I may do it—I like the cooler country."

"But you won't mind, if I send word that Petal's here, will you?"

"I won't mind," Jim said—it was the most she could get him to say.

She did, though, thank Rosa for the nice shrouds.

"I hope your child is healthy, when it comes," she added. She didn't want Rosa to think she held a mere frailty of the flesh against her.

"I hope—I don't want to bury no more little ones," Rosa said.

Tasmin began to drink straight brandy—a lot of it. She felt no certainty that she would ever see the man she regarded as her husband again. At some point Buffum came over, an excited look on her face.

"What's colored you up—not an impressive new cock, I hope?" Tasmin said.

"Hush, Tassie—no," Buffum told her. "Mr. Bent's just made us rather a grand offer—he thinks we should settle here and start a store. A very big store, with all the finest things from Europe."

"What, us aristocrats?" Tasmin asked, astonished. "Sell thimbles?"

"Oh no, much better than thimbles," Buffum announced. "The latest frocks from Paris—Geoff can help us pick them out. And furs and muffs and bonnets, and parasols and opera glasses and combs and jewels."

Tasmin, quite drunk by then, felt like laughing at the idea. But Buffum was very fired up by the idea, and Father Geoffrin was looking cheerful for the first time in weeks.

"Mr. Bent says Saint Louis is the coming town," Buffum went on. "He'll help us get the capital. He thinks the two of us would be excellent managers. And we'd call it Berrybender's—if this one works, he thinks we might even put one in Cincinnati."

"Why would Charlie Bent think I'm a good manager?" Tasmin wondered.

"Well, you did manage *us,* all the way west and back," Buffum pointed out. "Without your spirit none of us would have made it. Please consider it, at least. It would be so very boring just to go home and be a lady."

Tasmin thought that might be true. What *would* she do in England? Take lovers and quarrel with them? She had almost forgotten how it was to feel happy, as Buffum was happy now; and yet she had once considered herself perfectly happy, in the days before she met Jim Snow.

"It's nothing I would have expected, and yet I suppose we might run a store. At least I'd be near Monty and Petey and our Onion. I don't know that I'll be able to tolerate being across an ocean from where we put them today."

The next morning George Catlin caught a steamer. He was going to Washington to attempt to sell his Indian portfolio to the American nation. Tasmin saw him off. She held him as tightly as she had held Kit Carson the day he arrived.

"I know I've been hard on you, George," she told him. "I don't know why I have to be so hard—nor do I know why you tolerate me."

"Well, because I love you, dearie," George said. "Are you really going to London?"

"For a bit," Tasmin told him. "I want Petal to see it."

"If my pictures don't sell in Washington you may see me in Picadilly," George told her. "I've heard the English do buy pictures, and the bloodier the better."

Tasmin had expected Father Geoffrin to pester her, once his rival was finally gone; but she soon saw that Geoff had transferred his delicate attentions to the glowing Buffum. The two of them were engrossed in plans for Berrybender's, their store.

"You little deserter," Tasmin told him, the next time she caught him alone.

Father Geoffrin merely laughed.

"Oh, you've been so bitchy to me," he reminded her. "I'm not like humble George Catlin. I don't turn the other cheek."

"If you did turn it I'd slap it," Tasmin replied.

Later, they made up, but it was clear to Tasmin that the newly beautiful Buffum was in the ascendance where Geoff's attentions were concerned.

A week later, having loaded up a great load of goods from the Bent warehouse—all meticulously accounted for by Buffum—Charlie, Kit, Jim, and Rosa got ready for their journey up the river and across the plains.

Tasmin and Petal came down to the Missouri docks to see them off. While Petal did her best to charm her father out of going, Tasmin gave Kit another tight squeeze.

"I'm sick of good-byes—but I hope your next baby lives," she told him. "I've a notion you'd make a fine pa."

Kit choked up. Tasmin was so changed, sadder, yet kind to him. He could only mumble a good-bye.

Rosa gave Petal a little white cap made from rabbit skins, much like the one the young Hidatsa girl Coal, wife to Toussaint Charbonneau, had made for Monty when he had been an infant. Tasmin thanked Rosa again for the shrouds—then she suddenly ran out of words. She smiled, Rosa smiled, Tasmin turned away.

When the boat was ready to leave, Jim put Petal down. Tasmin felt desperate to say something—anything—since it seemed Jim wasn't going to make even the simplest farewell.

"I'll be sure to let the Bents know when we get back," she told him again.

"That'll be fine," Jim said. He stuck out

his hand—startled, Tasmin shook it. Behind
him Tasmin saw Rosa put a hand to her
mouth, shocked—perhaps even appalled.
This was a wife he was leaving! Was that
all?

It was all. Tasmin turned away—hurt,
confused, crushed. Jim Snow seemed to
her quite the oddest man she had ever
known—Rosa by now had probably realized
as much herself. Tasmin tried to buck up. It
was just his shyness, his deep unease with
females, she told herself. And yet she felt
not merely lonely: she felt negated, as she
had that day when Jim left to go kill the
slavers.

Soon the boat pulled away. West of them
the Missouri's shores were vague with summer heat. Jim Snow stood in the rear, with
Kit and Charlie Bent. Petal stared, silent.
Tasmin remembered going ashore at dusk
that first evening, to inspect the great dun
prairies. She remembered her ecstasy at the
first sunrise—that had been but a scant four
years ago. Then, she had been wholly innocent of the brutalities the distant vistas hid,
though only the next day the Osage tried to
kill her. And yet, for long, it had seemed a
grand adventure, rather than the death

march that was to bring her two sons to their new grave in Saint Louis. And not just her sons: Pomp Charbonneau, Little Onion, Fraulein Pfretzskaner, Old Gorska, Signor Claricia and Señor Yanez, Tim and Milly, their big Juppy, and all the others who had fallen to the implacable land.

Thinking of Jim and Rosa—she could still just glimpse Jim; Petal was hopelessly waving—Tasmin wondered if she could have displaced Rosa and kept Jim, had she cared to throw her whole self into the fight. She knew him; she had her wiles; she might have summoned all the ruthless brilliance of the Berrybenders, pitched everything into the effort. And yet, even assuming that she could still summon that pure force, what would it have accomplished? It was not the sad, kind Mexican woman who kept her husband from her: it was the merciless land, where Rosa was at home and she wasn't. She could never, it seemed to her, win Jim, her American, from this place that he fit and she didn't. Rosa could go with him, be useful in the ways that Little Onion had been useful. She could make him fires, cook his prairie meats, mend his buckskins, accept him if he wanted her, doctor little wounds.

Tasmin herself might still love the man—it was the land she couldn't love. Perhaps it was better, though it was terrible, that she lose the man with whom she had had much pleasure, pleasure that now seemed hard won. They had begun their lovemaking far out on the prairie, where the buffalo bulls in hundreds roared in their rut. Naked, those first few times, Tasmin had been convinced that she was now a child of nature—and there was the folly hidden under the glory: she was a daughter of privilege, English privilege, and Jim was a son of necessity— American necessity. Such a combination might thrill, but could it endure?

Petal had stopped waving.

"My arm got tired," she said.

"I shouldn't wonder."

"You made Jim go!" Petal accused.

"Not so—he made me go," Tasmin said.

"Will I ever see my Jim again, or is he gone'd forever?" Petal asked.

Tasmin picked her daughter up and looked at her sternly.

"You mustn't ask me that, my dear," she said. "It's rather too soon to know."

Petal cried; but later, for the next many months, she made good use of her mother's formulation. When anyone taxed her to explain some ambitious mischief, Petal would look them in the eye and say: "You mustn't ask me that, my dear. It's rather too soon to know."